VALSE TRISTE

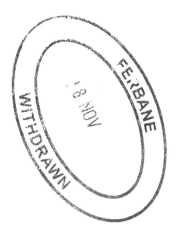

Also by Marcello Fois in English translation

The Advocate
Memory of the Abyss
Bloodlines
The Time in Between
Perfect Light

MARCELLO FOIS

VALSE TRISTE

Translated from the Italian by
Richard Dixon

MACLEHOSE PRESS

QUERCUS · LONDON

First published as *Del dirsi addio*
by Giulio Einaudi editore S.p.A., Turin, 2017
First published in Great Britain in 2021 by

MacLehose Press
An imprint of Quercus Publishing Ltd
Carmelite House
50 Victoria Embankment
London EC4Y 0DZ
An Hachette UK company

Co-funded by the
Creative Europe Programme
of the European Union

This publication has been funded with support from the European Commission.
This publication reflects the views only of the author, and the Commission cannot be held
responsible for any use which may be made of the information contained within.

ISBN (TPB) 978 0 85705 884 3
ISBN (e-book) 978 0 85705 886 7

Typeset by CC Book Production
Printed and bound in Great Britain by Clays Ltd, Elcograf S.p.A.

MIX
Paper from
responsible sources
FSC® C104740

*There are those who in expectation of paradise
create hell on earth:
this novel is dedicated to everyone else.*

. . . First of all

When they told Gaia her father was dead, she had been living for several days with the Ludovisis. The court had decided they were to be her new family.

It certainly couldn't be said that his death had nothing to do with her. He was her father after all, and the man who had harmed her brother Lilo.

Years later, when she was a grown woman, she would read somewhere that Oreste Bomoll had died claiming he was innocent. More accurately, the words "had died" should have read "had killed himself" – which might seem a linguistic subtlety but was, in every respect, the expression of something altogether different. At least in Gaia's eyes. Yet she knew perfectly well, however things had turned out, what she had seen. And when the police had questioned her, she had hidden nothing, just as her aunt – the one person who cared about her and Lilo – had told her to do.

* * *

It happened one autumn afternoon. The family to whom she had been entrusted lived far away from where she was born. From the windows of her new home she could see rocky cliffs and a strip of pure white sky. The Ludovisis were good people and had welcomed her with all possible affection, while she had responded only with a kind of passive inertia, just letting herself be comforted, fed, clothed, combed and everything else. In other words, she had let them do all that a family would do for their own children. So when they told her that afternoon that her father was dead, she received the news as though it was one more piece of unfinished business that had finally found its place: Lilo, her twin brother, had vanished; her aunt had gone; and now her father was dead.

Signora Ludovisi hadn't dared to give her a hug, though she felt a hug might have been fitting. And Gaia kept such a distance as to make any contact difficult.

But that evening, in the bedroom set aside just for her, she showed Nicolò, the Ludovisis' son, how people hugged.

* * *

"Your father died. Three months ago, while you were at the care centre," Signora Ludovisi explained, with a tinge of regret that she hadn't managed to find a less direct way of saying it.

* * *

A few minutes earlier they'd been talking about how the really cold weather was on its way, that it would snow, that they'd need to wrap up warm to go out and that the hot chocolate season would soon be here. And then, suddenly: "Gaia, there's something I ought to tell you," with a change of tone resembling those unexpected passages of clouds that turn a sunny morning into a smoke-grey afternoon. "Shall we sit down for a moment?" Signora Ludovisi suggested, moving ahead to the sofa and patting the place beside her. Gaia had come to join her, but instead of sitting where she had indicated, had taken the armchair in front. "Your father died. Three months ago, while you were at the care centre," Signora Ludovisi explained. "They wanted to wait until you had a foster family before telling you. Now you have us." She went to make a gesture as if to stroke her, but realised the child was too far away and the gesture would seem awkward, so she gave up.

Gaia looked at her, then looked around. She could hear Nicolò playing football with friends in the yard. She saw that the sliver of sky over the mountain ridges had turned cobalt blue. "That hot chocolate, I'd really like one now," she said.

Earth

I swear the earth shall surely be complete
   to him or her who shall be complete,
The earth remains jagged and broken only
   to him or her who remains jagged and broken.

WALT WHITMAN, *Leaves of Grass*

Several millennia ago Gaia was called Chthonia and lived underground. She was an albino and just as unmanageable as a troglodyte – as far as we can imagine one – who has never seen the light of day. It was Zeus who pulled her from the hole in which she lived. Why the god of gods had decided to do so remains a mystery. For she was no beauty. Instead she was as fat and white as one of those larvae that Australian aborigines find so tasty, half-blind with it and possessed of a terrible nature. But Zeus enjoyed challenges. And of all of them, this was by far the most difficult. First he had to find her, for she was hiding in the most inaccessible ravines or in deep tunnels, and then to try over and over again to get her out, thrusting his hand edgeways through the earth's crust as though through jelly, and stirring it about not knowing what or who he had caught hold of. It took some two hundred human years – ten minutes for the gods – and several failures before he managed it. Eventually, and after persistent attempts, Zeus felt Chthonia's soft body in his hand and, overjoyed, he was careful not to close his fist to avoid smothering her in the grip of his red-hot fingers.

Dragged from the depths, Chthonia looked about her. What she now saw she neither liked nor disliked. Inside the god's hand she had lost her whiteness and become dark and sullen. But she had probably always been sullen, even when living in the bowels of the earth, and, as it happened, Zeus didn't seem to find her dark looks too bad. But there was much to be done, so he would start off like Rex Harrison in "My

Fair Lady" when he makes the still unrefined Audrey Hepburn repeat and repeat "the rain in Spain falls mainly on the plain".

That dissolute god of gods had a certain passion for impossible tasks. He had made love in the form of a swan, in the form of a shower of gold, of a stallion, of a white bull and once, in order to seduce Alcmene, he had had to turn himself into her husband Amphitryon. He had an excellent track record of refusing to believe there was anything he couldn't do. A characteristic he has since passed on to billions of humans.

Once pulled from her earthly womb, however, Chthonia lost her whiteness and gained her sight. What she saw was a tangle of solid, liquid and gas. The celestial vault, as far as she was concerned, was not sufficiently reliable to reassure her, all the more since it exposed the terrestrial world to winds of every kind.

In that great hand of Zeus lay Jessica Lange in the clutches of King Kong, looking about her ever more suspiciously and certainly not resigned to her fate, for she was planning to return to safety as soon as she could, to where there were no winds and where the vaults were of rock, not air. To her safe haven where the animals were blind and the surface storms were no more than crystalline streams filtered by layers and layers of earth and rock. But she hadn't counted on the persistence of the one who had dragged her into the open. Nor had she counted on the charms, those positively subterranean charms, of the external world. First of all the smell, since it wasn't exactly fragrant where she came from down below. Though the cave was marvellously safe, it had a putrid smell of guano and salt, something which Chthonia realised only now that she sniffed the wondrously pleasing smells that came from the open sky. Today, with the wind in the right direction, she would have smelled the recycling centre on via Lungo Isarco Destro. And Zeus gave a satisfied nod that this creature, in which he had invested a few minutes of his time – centuries to a human – was proving remarkably gifted and quick to learn.

Immediately after the smell came the temperature which, long before it became a human obsession, gave a sense of being a part of things: the skin thickens through coldness, and grows thinner and perspires in the heat. In Zeus' grip, Chthonia had sweated and now, exposed to the air, she shivered and had goose pimples. In the depths from which she'd been snatched there was no hot and cold but just one single, constant and predictable temperature.

Next came the tears of salt water springing from the eyes. Chthonia didn't know what strange phenomenon made her lose that water, which seemed from the sea, nor did she know what to do when she felt it flowing down her cheeks. The Thunderer spoke to reassure her and named each thing: smell, temperature, tears. He looked the creature in the eye and told her that, like all animate and inanimate things on the surface, she too needed a name, and that name would be Gaia. Then, like the giant in "Jack and the Beanstalk", using his hand like an immense tipper truck, he carefully laid her on the ground and made her walk. And so, after the hard living rock she had always felt beneath her feet, she discovered the marvellous softness of meadows together with the softness of her earthly name so different from the harshness of her underground existence. Chthonia, now Gaia, looked around her, lost yet excited and, speaking now to Zeus for the first time, said she really couldn't understand how anyone could be so unhappy and happy in the same moment. It takes time but you'll understand, thought Zeus, who never spoke directly but communicated instead by thinking, pondering, musing and without opening his mouth, giving answers that everyone could hear just the same.

Exactly as was happening to Nicolò Ludovisi as he sat, silently, with his family – his wife Gaia and their son Michelangelo – at table seven in the Antica Trattoria Olimpo at Sanzeno.

* * *

"'A few thousand years' how many?" Gaia asked her son, more surprised than amused.

"Four or five," Michelangelo replied, after he had done a quick calculation. "If we reckon the Mycenaean civilisation can be dated to around 1600 BC . . ."

"But you're sure you're only eleven years old?" Gaia asked her son. "You do see what I mean?" she added, turning to Nicolò, who was sitting opposite. In her voice and expression, there was a mixture of sincerity and falsehood, as if, contrary to the impression she wanted to give, she was in fact pleased with that young genius. "I think you ought to be enjoying your childhood, that's all," she said, turning to her son. "Nicolò, you tell him too . . ."

But Nicolò seemed distracted by the ugly prints hanging on the wall behind Gaia. Picturing Zeus and his transformations they doubtless had something to do with the name of the restaurant: in the first there he is in the form of a galloping stallion trapping Dia; in the second he's a magnificent swan lusting after Leda; in the third a crowned bull carrying Europa on his back; in the fourth liquefied gold trickling down Danaë's thighs; while in the fifth a bearded man stands in front of a bed on which a semi-clad woman is lying and, positioned close by, is a herm that looks exactly the same as the standing man . . .

"Nicolò?" Gaia said. "Are you still with us?"

Nicolò nodded. "That one's impossible to understand," he said, pointing to the last of the five prints.

"That's Amphitryon," Michelangelo explained immediately, just as he would have done at school in defiance of his classmates, who hated him because he knew it all.

Some months before, at the start of the school year, Gaia had been called in by the teacher, who had suggested Asperger's. Gaia had always thought this, but felt she had to make people think otherwise.

"Ah," Nicolò said blankly.

"That's enough now," Gaia said after a while.

"Enough of what?" her husband asked, placing his hands flat down on the table as though he needed to make contact with something solid.

"You haven't said a word all evening." At this point her mask slipped, since, despite her relaxed conversation, it was clear she hadn't lost sight of him for one second. With what Nicolò called her third eye, through which she exercised her obsessive control over everything.

Nicolò wished he could have confessed to her all that had upset him that afternoon.

"Is it something to do with work?" Gaia insisted. Now at last she was being open with him. Nicolò shook his head. "So what is it?" And she waited with an odd expression on her lips, like when grown-ups blow kisses at children. "Words fail me," she said in defeat, after pausing in vain for some sign of life from her husband.

Some people think that words are omens. Instead they are keys that unlock the doors of darkened rooms. Of rooms kept locked for years, of rooms that have been forgotten. Perhaps it is the fate of men and women on this earth to live in houses with locked rooms concealing both hidden treasures and also, all too conveniently, unmentionable secrets.

This brief exchange left Michelangelo silent for a long while. Gaia noticed and gave him a look of surprise.

"Amphitryon," he said, as though stirred again by that gaze. "Zeus pretended to be Alcmene's husband, that's Amphitryon. So she's unfaithful to her husband without realising it."

Now, just for a few moments, Gaia felt things had returned to their natural order. "And what's that strange animal you see lower down there? she asked without any real interest, pointing to an area of the print close to the caption. Then, without waiting for an answer, she turned back to her husband: "For God's sake, what's wrong?" she insisted.

"It's the Teumessian fox," said Michelangelo. "An animal that's impossible to catch."

"Nicolò." There was now a promise in her disconsolate tone.

"Amphitryon thinks he can get Cephalus to catch it but in fact it's Zeus, who then pretends to be him – Amphitryon – and seduces his wife," Michelangelo said to himself.

"She probably didn't even notice the difference." This was the first comment of any kind that Nicolò had made on the subject.

Gaia puckered her face, as she did every time she wanted to give a quick rundown of what had happened so far . . .

* * *

The meal had been tense. Michelangelo had talked obsessively about everything until Nicolò, who was looking at some point of the room in front of him, had suddenly waved his hand, as if to strike him but without actually doing so. "You really can't keep quiet!" he had hissed in a tone far more frightening than any physical blow, at which Michelangelo had stopped still, staring with that typical wide-eyed look of highly imaginative children.

In other circumstances, Gaia might have reacted angrily to her husband's gesture towards their child, but not this time. Or rather, she seemed about to react but then held back, with the look of someone resigned once and for all to taking a different route and not ending up in the usual blind alley.

Nicolò sensed the abrupt change, though without understanding what it meant. The solemn silence in which they headed for the car park, once the bill was paid, gave him the illusion of having manoeuvred into a position of advantage.

So much so that, standing at the car, he felt confident enough to offer some prospect of continuing.

"We'll talk about it at home," he said.

Gaia looked sceptical. "I'll drive," she said, holding her hand out for the car keys.

* * *

In the car they limited themselves to feeding their mutual anxieties, stretching silences to breaking point or sullying them with any old remark.

They drove for some twenty minutes towards Bolzano without

speaking and with Michelangelo seemingly asleep in the middle of the back seat. "Will Baffo die?" he said, as if from nowhere. "The vet said he'll die."

"No-one's going to die! Cristina said nothing of the sort." Gaia used the vet's first name since they had been to junior school together. Then, at secondary school, their paths had separated.

Nicolò pulled a pack of cigarettes from his jacket pocket, took one out and put it in his mouth.

"You know you're not meant to smoke in the car. We agreed, didn't we?" Gaia said, as if the only way she could speak to her husband was by attacking him. These were moments when she found it hard to be civil. She leaned towards the windscreen, which was beginning to mist up, gripping the steering wheel as though it were him and to stop herself punching that bastard next to her. Bolzano was now less than ten kilometres away. "It was *you* who agreed," he snapped. "Anyway, I haven't lit up, have I?" And he looked at her as though everything between them depended on the fact that he could light his fucking cigarette at any moment he wished, or keep it in his mouth, unlit, like a promise, or a threat.

"You shit," she muttered, though not quite to herself, as he pretended to take a long draw on his unlit cigarette.

"Aren't I worth at least an answer?" One thing could be said about Gaia: she didn't give up easily.

"At home," he hissed, with an immediacy that unsettled the atmosphere.

"Are you two quarrelling?" Michelangelo asked, just as the argument seemed to have ended. He had learned that it was the heavy silences between his parents that were the real quarrel. "Shouldn't you get a divorce?" he asked.

Nicolò gave a shrug of irritation. "What do you know about such things? Weren't you asleep?" he said bluntly.

Gaia changed gear into the bend so that the SUV wouldn't lose speed. Driving helped her pretend she could ignore the tension thick enough to be cut with a knife. "No-one's getting a divorce here," she insisted, catching Michelangelo's eye in the rear-view mirror and adopting an inflated and reassuring tone. "You haven't fastened your seat belt," she observed without looking round.

"Got eyes in the back of your head, have you?" said Nicolò.

"That's right, didn't you know? I'm a mum with rear-view eyesight. Belt yourself, Michelangelo."

"What is 'belt yourself' supposed to mean?" asked Nicolò, without managing to look any more cheerful, however hard he tried.

"It's an expression," answered Michelangelo.

"Which doesn't exist," said Nicolò. Gaia kept her eyes fixed on the beam of the headlights in the darkness. "You're making expressions up again," he remarked with a hint of a smile.

His comment annoyed her, or rather it was that tone of his that annoyed her even more. She had known it for years, his way of putting other people down. That subtle way of highlighting what he thought were other people's faults. Once during an argument he had promised to list all those things that she did and shouldn't do and making up expressions was one of them. Yet Gaia continued to say that language is important, that words are important. And now, here she is, inventing expressions, and not even very effectively. "Make sure you've fastened your seat belt correctly," said Gaia in the end, enunciating each single word as though she were swallowing it. "I need to go," she added.

"You need to go where?" Nicolò asked.

"What sort of question is that?" Gaia could no longer hide a trace of anger – a remnant of her previous annoyance.

Nicolò sensed he had been wrong-footed, but it took him only a moment to recover: "And yours, what sort of question is that?"

"Calm yourself!" she retorted.

"Are you quarrelling now?" Michelangelo asked.

"Fuck!" Nicolò muttered.

"I heard that," his son declared. "You used a swear word."

"Clever," Nicolò sneered. If only the earth would open beneath us, he thought, closing his eyes. Open up right now and swallow us. And swallow this whole fucking place. "Don't you have your video game?" he asked instead.

"Mamma doesn't like me to use it in the car, and not at mealtimes either. I need to go too."

"We'll be home soon," Nicolò cut in abruptly.

"I didn't like your attitude in the restaurant, not one little bit," Gaia continued, pulling into a lay-by to make it clear she hadn't given up in any way.

"Gaia, you don't like anything that doesn't fit with your ideas," he said, provoking her without making it obvious: it was enough to roll the unlit cigarette between his lips. "What are you doing now?"

"I'm stopping. We both need to go." Gaia gripped the steering wheel even tighter until her knuckles turned white. "So you reckon lately I've never been right?"

"Mamma . . ." Michelangelo tried to intervene.

"What is it?" she shouted, exasperated.

"I need to go, a lot."

"All right." Gaia braked suddenly.

Without waiting for his son, Nicolò threw open the car door and got out. He went into the undergrowth and lit his cigarette as a matter of urgency. Then he heard a rustling noise as Michelangelo and Gaia headed in among the rhododendrons. In the moonless darkness that icy-cold and serrated landscape seemed fixed in a glassy equilibrium. Everyone was saying how there had been little snow so far but that plenty was on its way. You can tell it from the sky, they said, with its unmistakeable tone of dense grey. The headlamps left on nearby cast a cone of light over a pervious expanse, an asphalt strip of black tulle bordered with smoothed wedges of dwarf spruce trees. Nicolò set off back to the car thinking how he hadn't even needed to pretend: that this was the most important cigarette of the day.

Just at that moment the fox appeared.

Two to three metres away, as if it had materialised from that milky fog, just waiting there for him to notice it. He saw it as soon as he looked up from the cigarette that he had just stubbed out. The darkness echoed with the calls of night birds. He could recognise them one by one: scops owl, screech owl, snowy owl, tawny owl, eagle owl . . . And the gnashing jaws of deer rhythmically stripping bark from the trees . . . and the furtive footsteps of smugglers and refugees . . .

This is what the fox said. This is what it revealed.

And it revealed also a crevasse opening up suddenly out of nowhere as far as Nicolò's feet, so exact and real that he was forced to jump back so as not to fall in. The headlamps of the car flickered and went out; the light suddenly dropped; and from nowhere he heard the voice of Gaia calling . . .

"Leo?"

"I'm here."

"Here, where?" Sergio asked, stretching his neck over the edge of the bed.

"On the floor," the other replied. "My back," he mumbled.

Sergio joined him. "How many times have I told you to get it checked out?"

Leo closed his eyes. "It's going now. I need to stretch out like this. It's going, it's going . . ." he assured him with a wince.

"Turn over," Sergio said, holding him on one side.

"Ahh!" Leo groaned.

"Turn over, I said!" But without waiting for him to move, he pulled him over to lie stomach down, with his back exposed.

Ignoring Leo's groans he pressed his thumbs into the middle of his magnificently curved spine. "Why are you so fucking beautiful?" he asked as he massaged him firmly.

"You're hurting," Leo said, though without much conviction. The light skimmed over him with pictorial mastery, as happens to certain bodies particularly blessed by nature.

"Relax," Sergio ordered, but with the same identical lack of conviction. Leo let his head sink between his crossed arms. "Is that better?" Sergio asked, with the voice of one who knew what he was doing.

Between them, in fact, that tone served the particular purpose of endorsing their difference in age. Seven and a half years. This, for Sergio, was a sensitive subject, as it had now also become for Leo.

"There, that tone of voice," Leo said, with his face kept from the floor only by his forearms.

Sergio suddenly stopped and sat up. "What tone of voice?" he asked, immediately regretting having asked it.

"Yours. Leave it alone, I've more experience, move away, little boy . . . and so on," Leo joked, without shifting from his position of penitent novice. It was as if he were speaking from another world, for his words were directed straight into the floor, giving them a strange resonance.

"I wasn't using any particular tone," Sergio said, trying not to seem defensive. Leo's back was something close to perfection: precise, compact, designed at every point to enthuse the light. "Why the hell do you have to be so beautiful? You realise it's a problem?" The back in question sprang into restrained laughter. "Anyone could see that," Sergio insisted, massaging Leo's sides and hips once again. "Anyone," he continued, with a hint of rebuke tinged with passion. "But not you. With this back of yours, for example, you go about without giving it a second thought."

"I can't see any alternative," said Leo, and with a sigh he made it clear that Sergio was resolving his back problem most effectively.

"The solution would be not to love you at all," Sergio remarked.

Leo sprang up, kneeling with his back to him, almost banging Sergio's nose with the back of his head. "Don't say that, not even in fun," he replied to the wall in front of him. He was reluctant to turn round, not knowing what expression he might find if he chose to look him in the face. "Never again. Never again," he repeated, as though the idea expressed just once was not sufficiently clear. Then he stood up.

Sergio gripped his knees to prevent him from going any further. "Never again," he assured him. "Sorry."

"You know what I'm like! You know what I think, no?" Leo asked from above.

* * *

Sergio was well aware he was referring to an argument of a few years back. When both were still living in Bologna and they had only just met, one rainy evening, in the bar where Leo was working part-time. Sergio was drinking with a group of colleagues and Leo, on the other side of the bar, had done all he could to attract his attention. He had seen him too: how could he not have noticed that beautiful boy? The difference was that he would never have done anything to make it apparent. Those were times in which he could think and tell himself that being a man doesn't mean not noticing the beauty of another man when it's there to be seen. And in Leo's case it was. But they were also times when he wouldn't have admitted it even under torture. It was hidden, deep down. So he had remained firm in his resolve not to turn round to look at him, nor to reveal even the slightest interest.

He was talking with his colleagues either about work – he was Chief Inspector of the forensic unit in Bologna at that time – or about cunt. Whether married or single, they talked about "awesome" cunts, or "wooden" cunts. He didn't mind because it prevented him from feeling that sharp lump in his throat which stopped him breathing each time he was gripped by the thought that he preferred men. But not men in the generic sense of the word. His classical education spoke clearly to him, resurfacing in his thoughts at the wrong moments. Not *oi anthropoi* (οἱ ἄνθρωποι), but *oi andres* (οἱ ἄνδρες), the same difference as in Latin between *homines* and *viri*. Chief Inspector Striggio had plenty of reasons that evening for pretending he wanted to talk about cunt and not to notice the beautiful boy who worked part-time at the bar opposite the headquarters of the forensic unit. The first reason was that he had turned thirty just three days before; the second was that he had disappointed his father in everything; the third that just two hours later he had to meet his girlfriend; the fourth that he had no intention of succumbing to that terrible, wonderful sensation that stirred his groin each time the beautiful boy passed in front of him; and the fifth that he couldn't let himself be distracted because his colleagues were right now waiting for him to recount some sensational episode.

It was a day in the middle of autumn, one of those days that give the impression of early spring but instead harbour an underlying malice and suddenly grow dark and turn to wind and rain. So Sergio, more as a diversionary tactic than anything else, looked at the sky outside the window and said they had better go back to the office since one hell of a storm was brewing. A distant flash of lightning seemed to confirm what he had said and so he was spared the anecdote and could return to the office.

The storm hit an hour later. Sergio was returning home by car to get ready for his date, the rain pelting loudly against the bodywork and almost drowning out the sound of the car radio. Driving past the bar he saw him again: the beautiful boy pressed flat against the closed shutter, but with the rain catching him all the same. This wouldn't do, so he pulled up and, without getting out of the car, lowered the window and asked if he needed a lift. Leo didn't wait to be asked twice. He jumped in, soaked through, smelling of earth and rain, sweat and metal and breathing heavily like a climber conquering a mountain peak without oxygen. He was so magnificent, pure in his self-effacement, overwhelmed with emotion to the point of suffocation, and yet he had accepted the lift without the slightest hesitation. Sergio understood that in that beautiful boy, with that resolve to overcome his embarrassment, with that prospect of facing the abyss despite his trepidation, there was a desire that no-one before had ever revealed to him. And he fell in love, as happens to men – *homines* and *anthropoi*.

And so, to that rainy autumn gift, he could concede everything. Though it would take time before he felt ready to express it.

Leo got into the car. "Leo," he announced, as if it were more important to introduce himself and give his name than to close the door against the pouring rain. Sergio told him to get in without further words. Leo sat down and shut the door with sudden zeal. It seemed he had been running and yet he had been standing there getting soaked, flattened against the shutters of the bar. Sergio asked whether the name Leo was short for Leone. Leo broke into laughter that betrayed a flash of excitement, and answered no – Leo in his case stood for Leonardo. Sergio also gave a hint of a smile, as if to say he forgave his excessive excitement only because he'd had the good fortune to make him fall in love before he'd even realised it. Then he started up and, without even asking where he was to go, turned into via Cesare Battisti and, from there, the short stretch of Ugo Bassi that leads to via Marconi. At last, on passing the trade union headquarters, he asked where he should take him.

The rain had begun to ease and a few brave pedestrians darted from the porticoes to the other side of the road, though most waited under the bus shelter for the rain to stop. A strange gusting wind blew up and the light responded, for the sunset seemed to have been delayed for an inordinate length of time. "Bolognina," Leo spelled out his desired destination, as if all else were irrelevant. Then, clearing his throat, he told Sergio he shouldn't have mentioned the rain a few hours earlier at the bar. Speaking as though he had understood why the sexy policeman had wanted to distract his colleagues, he could well understand, he added, how tedious and one-track certain conversations can be, but reckoned that saying things can somehow make them come true. No-one in the world would have considered it acceptable to speak like that to a stranger who hadn't yet told him his name. Except for Sergio, to whom the reproach seemed entirely appropriate, especially now that he realised what an awkward situation the rain had put him into. Yet he had carried on driving and saying nothing, leaving the talking to the beautiful boy who was within kissing distance at every traffic light, within touching distance at every gear change, who spoke words that struck him as though they were alive. Once over the bridge by the station he had to turn right just before piazza dell'Unità.

* * *

"I know what you're like," Sergio admitted as he stood up. He put his hand on Leo's shoulder to make him turn round and to look into his eyes. Naked though he was, Leo never seemed defenceless. For some while he had been letting his beard grow, but without making him look any more adult as he had hoped. On the contrary, it made him look younger, like an adolescent wearing false whiskers for an end-of-year school play: a hairless fifteen-year-old acting the part of a bearded Risorgimento hero.

* * *

He stopped the car in front of a nineteenth-century apartment block surrounded by a strip of bare garden and they sat in silence, watching the rain ease on the other side of the windscreen, in a state of concentration, as though the very secret of existence were to be found beyond that speckled glass. Their silence occupied every space inside the car until it sucked away the air. Leo, with a deep breath, said he had to go and Sergio asked how old he was, since it was impossible to guess. A few hairs over his forearms confirmed that he was past puberty. Leo replied that he was twenty-two, then asked Sergio's name.

"Sergio. And four days ago I was thirty," he replied, before reflecting that the beautiful boy hadn't actually asked his age. The engine idled making a soft hum; spasmodic gusts of wind outside flapped the red and white tape that cordoned off a section of roadworks; white, black, grey, purple clouds sped like a herd of antelopes whose leader had raised a sudden alarm; their Adam's apples leapt each time they felt constrained to swallow the excess of saliva accumulating in their throats; and their hands were reduced to realising it was impossible, or inappropriate, to touch each other. Leo said he lived alone. He said it flatly, not even turning his head. Sergio tightened his lips as if to say that such information was to be taken for what it was. The other nodded to indicate it could be taken as an invitation, unsure whether he would understand and betraying his nervousness by compulsively drying the palm of his right hand on the taut cloth of his jeans above his knee. Sergio said he had to make a telephone call. Leo nodded once again, then added that there was no rush, that he lived on the second floor, the door on the right.

* * *

"This beard growth doesn't make you look any older," he said, stroking his face with both hands.

Leo gave that giggle he made each time he felt powerless to disagree with the man he loved. Looking at himself in him he saw a faithless mirror, or maybe one that was too faithful. It requires a great deal of conjecture to acknowledge your own reflected image. And if that image is reflected in the eyes of the man you love, that conjecture becomes quite arbitrary. The Leo that Leo could see in Sergio's eyes was inconsistent: a lean, well-formed young man with a sleek body lightly covered with tawny down, with a thick, crude, limp, circumcised member and that absurd beard that made him look like the disciple of a secret society. In short, all real and all false, and looking more like a herm on the Janiculum than a hipster. Or perhaps it proved the general rule that there's nothing that exists today that couldn't be found in ancient times: or that we can talk nonchalantly about originality only when we are sufficiently ignorant of the past. The young and the ignorant always tend towards enthusiasm: two different kinds of enthusiasm, of course, but enthusiasm all the same. And if he, Leo, always rushed hotfoot into his own time, perhaps it was because he didn't recognise his ignorance of the age from which it originated.

"Fine, eh?" asked Leo, still referring to his beard, stroking the hands that were stroking it. It was indeed fine, very dark and surprisingly full.

"You're always so enthusiastic," Sergio said. "The only thing I don't like is that it covers your lips."

"Yes, I need to clip it, shorten the top bit. I hadn't realised it bothered you so much." Leo raised his voice as Sergio was heading to the bathroom for a piss. A few moments later, in fact, he heard the toilet seat being lifted and the splash of urine. Absurd as it seemed, that splash of urine was more reassuring than he might have imagined. If he had to list those things he most loved about Sergio, it would have started there, from the manly splash he made as he was pissing. Or the strong, electric aroma of his sweat, the ginkgo leaf shape of the dark hairs of his chest or the rustic leanness of his ankles. All characteristics, he thought, that weren't limited to eminently physical qualities, but had to do with something else.

* * *

Having finished his telephone call, Sergio had to face the four flights of stairs that separated him from the right-hand door on the second floor. He had had to adopt a vague tone to explain he'd had some unexpected problems at work and couldn't be there in time for their appointment. That was all. He didn't overplay it, since that arouses a girlfriend's suspicions more than anything else and women prefer to think you're a shit rather than a two-timer, even if the two things are much the same in the end. So when Laura answered, Sergio spoke as you do to someone who understands the situation. They'd been over it plenty of times before: you know what job I do, you know what I'm like, you know I hate these things . . . He'd kept it short, settling on a few brief words, to which no further information was expected: "Problems at work, so our date is off . . . I'll call you again tomorrow." And she, who knew what his job was like, what he was like, and what those things he hated were, knew straight away that further questions were pointless. "So tomorrow, then," she said. And he replied: "OK, tomorrow." And she added "I love you," and he replied "Sure, sure: me too . . . tomorrow, then." Then he had hung up and sat there for a few more moments at the steering wheel, staring at the road in front, trying to summon all the energy he could find to drive off. Instead he got out, inhaled the surrounding ozone as though he needed to fill his lungs for a deep-diving competition, clicked on the automatic locking system, took another look at the unimpressive building and walked the two metres between him and the gate.

Reaching the second floor he found the door on the right ajar. He entered with his arm stretched out, as a blind man might have done. Inside it was dark and it took a few seconds before his eyes began to adjust. He closed the door by just leaning against it with both shoulders, careful to make some sound so that the person expecting him would know he had arrived, and walked down a long hallway in semi-darkness as far as the last room on the left. Leo was sitting on a bed with no headboard. He had taken off his wet clothes and let them fall inert onto the floor. A little earlier those clothes had seemed to breathe with him, and now they lay on the ground, a few paces from the door, formless and lifeless. Leo hadn't felt the need to put anything else on. And so, for the second time, Sergio looked on at the incarnation of an immensely secret desire, a desire so secret that it went beyond the barrier of impossibility. The first time had been many years before, one hot summer night when he was thirteen and one of his father's colleagues had come to stay and had slept in his room. And this was the second. This beautiful boy, luminous in the semi-darkness, with eyes that didn't look anywhere in particular, as though a surreal embodiment of Sergio's most repressed imagination and desire – that had been formless before but had now taken shape. He told him he didn't know – words so unconnected and uttered in the strangest voice as though by someone else, someone he had never seen. "I don't know," he said. Leo asked him exactly what it was he didn't know, and he answered that he didn't even know what it was he didn't know, at least not at that moment. And the boy asked what in particular was happening "at that moment". Then he stood up and held out the palms of his hand – "*but I in vain stretch out my palms to you*" – but only because he couldn't delay by another second his desire to touch him. And he touched him. Touched his flesh through his shirt, felt his skin pressed against the thin cloth. He began to unbutton it and Sergio let him continue: "*and let me share your quiet haven*".

* * *

"Do I have to take everything away?" Leo asked, coming into the bathroom. Sergio was in the shower and didn't answer. Leo took his toothbrush, putting it in one of those transparent bags used for air travel, together with several bottles of body cream, a beard lotion, mouthwash, scissors and nail clippers.

"It's just for a few days," Sergio said, smoothing back his wet hair. He tried to sound calm, like someone not wanting to worsen a situation that was already embarrassing.

"Yeah, sure," Leo agreed with an excessive hint of resentment. Sergio went up to him at the mirror. "We've talked about it, haven't we?" he ventured. "It's just for a few days," he repeated.

"Yes, you've already said that," Leo said, gathering up the last of his things.

"I'm not ashamed of you," Sergio said pre-emptively.

"Ah, then what exactly are you ashamed of?"

Sergio gazed into the mirror as though searching for an appropriate answer in his reflection. "Of myself, I think," he said after a pause.

"And therefore of me, don't you think?"

"You don't know my father," Sergio explained, without considering how ridiculous it was for a man of almost thirty-four to be saying such words.

"No, you're right, I don't." Leo wasn't going to give up. Yes, he was resigned to moving out of Sergio's apartment but didn't want to make it too easy for him.

"Leo . . ."

"It shouldn't be like this after four years, don't you think?" he asked, not expecting an answer.

Sergio answered all the same, but without managing to avoid that touch of self-pity that had sometimes produced good, if not excellent, results. "We're together, aren't we?"

"It would be more accurate to say that I'm with you, and you're there when you can: when your father's not around, when your colleagues aren't about and when you don't have to go back to Bologna . . ."

"Leo . . ."

"Yes, that's my name, you keep repeating it . . ."

"Leo, please . . ." Sergio began to plead. But no-one was listening, since the beautiful boy was taking some underwear from the bedside drawer, a box of condoms and tube of lubricant.

"I'd better take these too, no?" he asked.

Sergio shook his head: "Leo, his wife's only been dead two months! What can I do? I don't want us to part like this, please . . ."

"Please? Then please me," Leo replied, closing his bag. Meanwhile he had slipped on a pair of briefs and a T-shirt with the words "I HATE INDIFFERENCE".

* * *

It was a T-shirt Sergio had given him years before at a summer festival Leo had really wanted to go to in the south of Italy, and barely a week after he had finally talked to Laura.

They had arranged to meet for dinner. Laura looked as adorable as ever, sober and fragrant as attractive women of real beauty know how to be. She was radiant, intelligent – and intuitive. Once in the car, before fastening her seat belt, she kissed him, brushing his lips regardless of her fresh lipstick. He set off and drove five or six hundred metres in silence. Then, as if he had suddenly remembered something of extreme importance, he pulled up by the walls of the church in piazza del Baraccano, switched off the engine, gripped the steering wheel as if to steady himself and told her he had something to say.

It wasn't easy, as she had already understood before he could utter a word. She realised it was over between them, though she hadn't understood why. Laura was anxious to make it clear that it was all down to him, and he accepted this charge with alacrity. He agreed it was exactly so, that nothing, nothing was her fault, that theirs had been a wonderful experience, but he realised he just didn't love her. And she asked why and what she had done wrong. Without a shadow of doubt, she declared, there was another woman, something which he was able firmly to deny without lying. But don't people love each other, he said, for exactly the same reason that they stop loving each other? She replied that she didn't know and that it was strange he had only now suddenly realised it. Unless, of course, he had always been lying. If he had lied to anyone, he replied, it was to himself. And Laura looked at him with a certain irritation, for dealing with this man had become like trying to grapple a salmon out of water with her bare hands. The more she tried to grasp him and the meaning of those last few years, the more he wriggled free, slipping away. So in the end she said she had understood. She wanted to land on her feet. And he said sorry once again for disappointing all her expectations but then made the mistake of adding that he understood how she must feel. And she, who had been just about to leave the car, with one foot out, stepped back in, settled herself back in the passenger seat and shut the door again. Then she took a deep breath. He, with his manly understanding, had eventually managed to get rid of her, and now he had to suffer the consequences of that fatuous comment.

He knew what job she did, didn't he? Sergio nodded. He knew how she liked things to be done properly? Again he agreed. Everyone thinks history teachers serve no useful purpose. Sergio didn't know where this was leading, but Laura commanded silence, just as with some know-all pupil who had to be kept under constant control. He remembered, didn't he, that not long ago she had arranged to take her class on a study trip to Auschwitz and Birkenau? He remembered, didn't he, that she had invited him to go too? He nodded. Well, at a certain point during the trip, at Birkenau, they were taken to visit the camp latrines. Those latrines were just a single slab of marble with a row of holes, one after the other, thirty centimetres in diameter. The deportees, one per hole, had ten seconds to defecate and do all the rest, after which they had to get up and vacate their place for others in the queue. That was the time they had, whether sufficient or not. They couldn't clean themselves, were often forced to get up before they had finished and no exception was made even for menstruating women or people with diarrhoea. The height of human cruelty was concentrated on that pure white perforated marble, perhaps the only non-terrifying structure in the whole camp and outwardly respectful of bodily requirements. They claimed they understood the need to evacuate faeces and urine from the body, but that claim meant nothing. They claimed to be respecting something they weren't respecting at all. And that was worse than what was happening a few metres away, where the clear and incontrovertible rule was that the bodies and lives of prisoners were totally unimportant, not worthy of any respect or concern.

Did he now understand how she felt? Sergio remained completely mute. But she was a river in full flow and added that not only did he pretend to show a consideration towards her that he had never felt but now he was also claiming to understand things he had never understood.

Getting out of the car she said there was absolutely no point in continuing the evening over dinner or anywhere else, and that what had to be said had been said. Sergio made no reply. What he had heard seemed absurd and exaggerated, but, like a true soldier, he granted her the honours of war. And that ostentatious outburst. Yet for years he would think of the latrines at Birkenau as a metaphor for the horrific cruelty of certain apparent acts of kindness. Before driving off he waited until Laura had diminished to a speck and disappeared, swallowed up by the narrow streets of the city centre.

* * *

"It's not true that I don't care . . ." Leo said after a while, now fully dressed with a light quilted jacket over his slogan T-shirt.

"I know you care. I'll talk to him."

"I wish you could understand just how important it is."

As always, when everything seemed clear, Sergio began all over again, allowing that tell-tale furrow of consternation to form between his eyebrows. "At precisely what point of our conversation did you feel that

I hadn't understood just how important it is?" He balanced his words, making an effort not to sound resentful, although without success.

"Now you're angry," Leo said. "We'll talk about it some other time. If I've forgotten anything, you can always say you've had a colleague from out of town to stay."

"Fuck," Sergio replied. Such behaviour made him feel powerless. He felt a sudden urge to punch that presumptuous son of a bitch standing in front of him, but it just so happened he was very much in love with that same individual: "Don't make me do anything rash," he hissed under his breath. "When am I going to get a break?" he muttered again. "Where are you going?" he asked.

Leo enjoyed standing on the edge of the abyss. He knew all there was to know about Sergio. For example, that it could be dangerous not so much to put him in a corner as to end up in the same corner. After all, this was love, wasn't it? "Home," he replied. "My home."

"Every time you go out of that door, every time, I'm terrified I'll never see you again. I know I've asked too much, that I'm asking too much," Sergio said. "His wife died only two months ago: what can I do? You know how much it cost me to persuade him to come. I thought we'd agreed."

"What exactly do you want from me?" Leo asked, a little confused by the change of mood.

"Don't leave me like this."

"Like how?"

"Like this, as if we're not going to see each other again."

Leo realised that this moment of complete weakness made Sergio all the stronger. "How can you think such a thing?" he protested, feebly, like a tenor rehearsing his part while saving his breath. It was a limp, ineffectual protest.

"It's not you. It's me," Sergio said. "Tell me you understand, that you agree." He was on the verge of tears.

"Are you going to cry?" Leo asked, addressing an invisible entity between them. In four years he had never seen him cry.

"Anyway, you don't have to go tonight."

"Yes. Hey, you'll have more time to get everything ready."

Sergio's mobile began to buzz as if alive. He looked around to find it. Leo pointed to the half-empty bookcase behind him. He answered reluctantly, since at that hour the Commissariato never called him just to say goodnight. He stood there listening long enough for Leo to reach the door and open it. A blast of freezing air arrived from the landing, reminding Sergio that he was completely naked. "Twenty minutes and I'll be there," he said abruptly, addressing the nobody in the ether. He put his phone down and ran to kiss Leo before he vanished through the doorway.

"You'll catch cold," Leo said returning his kiss. "Go back inside and get dressed, you're shameless."

The Novacella district Commissariato headquarters was a notably recent building with a certain state-of-the-art pretension. Whoever designed it had fondly imagined that stripping its lines back to the bare minimum would give it that New York style that provincials like so much. That ugly suburban sprawl in a sterile Nordic guise allowed for integration as long as there was no evidence of integration. This was why things had been so radically altered, along supposedly rationalist lines, from the old piles in working-class districts.

The building in which the local Commissariato had its offices was no exception.

In the Novacella district the same anorexic buildings – mostly cubes and rectangular blocks plastered beige or iron grey, and with cornices, window frames and ledges in red brick – could function as both models for those migrants that history had delivered from the agony of what is paradoxically described as an emergency, and district headquarters for the border police.

In practical terms, its position was not ideal: very hot in summer, very cold in winter, so that for the first two years of occupation there had been a seasonal proliferation of fans or electric radiators and frequent drops in power with blackouts as a result.

* * *

Two months earlier, when his father's third wife Dina had died, Sergio had had to go down to Bologna. The ceremony was brief, not to say hasty, and less than forty minutes after the last goodbyes the corpse had been taken to the crematorium. That too was over pretty quickly. The final farewell reminded him of when, as a child, he used to sit in the pizzeria at the table nearest the oven, watching the pizza shovels moving in and out of the cave of embers. A kind of metal shovel had also accompanied the coffin and its contents into an incandescent tunnel, so white-hot that they were reduced to ashes in no time at all. A very cursory way of applying the biblical injunctions, he felt. He looked at his father, who didn't seem to be showing any particular emotion. His third wife was gone. Could she be called a stepmother? Who knows.

Next day they were leaving the cemetery with the urn – a brown plastic object shaped like a Canopic jar, chosen previously from a catalogue – filled with what remained of Dina and her coffin. Before leaving the building, Sergio had approached his father as if to seal that brief moment of intimacy with a handshake or even some hint of an embrace, but he had abruptly moved away, towards the coffee machine, and had begun nervously pressing a few buttons.

"You have to put the money in first," Sergio told him, offering the encouragement of an attentive care assistant, but Pietro didn't seem to understand, so that, after the umpteenth failed attempt, he started to bang the machine. "Let me do it," Sergio said, taking over. It was clear his father only knew how to express his awkwardness and grief through ineptitude. It was as if each time he needed to react with strength, he discovered just how weak he was. Expressing his feelings was one of the very few things Pietro couldn't do. The coffee was terrible, but it had served its purpose of fending off any kind of intimacy. So they headed back to the car. Pietro placed the urn in the middle of the back seat, as though he wanted to keep an eye on it during the journey, and Sergio took the wheel.

"The point is that you were on the right track," Pietro said.

"The right track for where?" Sergio asked, conscious of the risk he was running.

"For getting nowhere," his father said. "Fathers pretend they want their children to get somewhere, but what they really want is for them to be happy," he added. Sergio wasn't sure whether this was a compliment. So, instead of replying, he concentrated on moving into the right lane. "When you were a boy they all said you were a little genius. Then you got it into your head to show me how it's done."

"Ah, is that what I did?" A bicycle signalled right, cutting across his path.

"Yes, you had a whole wonderful and happy pointless life ahead of you, full of those nice things you loved, which brought tears to your mother's eyes: painters, art . . . And then nothing . . ."

At the road junction into the city centre, Sergio had to slow down for traffic. "One thing doesn't rule out the other," he said.

"Oh it does, because in order to prove something to me you've chosen a job which makes you cynical and which destroys all beauty. Is this how you want to end up?" his father asked, pointing a finger at himself.

Imprisoned inside was a nagging pain he was searching for a way to avoid. "It would be no bad idea to get all this off your chest," Sergio said simply. "Why not use me? Drag up what I could have done and didn't do? Or our supposed rivalry? Go ahead. That's what I'm here for." Being forced to brake at the red light gave his words a certain finality.

"Don't you see?" his father said. "That's just what I wanted to say: what the hell is someone like you doing in the police?"

"I like it."

"You like it? And do you like going to the dentist?"

"What do you mean? No, of course I don't like going to the dentist . . ."

"Ah, you see?"

"What's that got to do with it? It's not the same thing at all . . . that's absurd . . ."

"That's exactly the point: you've lost your enthusiasm for the absurd. When you were young and happy, all you ever did was absurd things."

"Such as?"

"When you were nine and did that project about some old artist no-one had heard of, and your teacher got you to read it out in front of the class . . . You were happy, really happy . . ."

"And what was so absurd about that? I was a kid and it wasn't a project but a pretend diary of the artist and, in actual fact, he wasn't someone no-one had heard of: his name was Leon Battista Alberti . . . and I was thirteen."

"So you do remember . . ."

"Yes, of course . . ."

"It's turned green."

Sergio drove off, careful not to pull away too fast and with no wish to continue this conversation about his childhood. "Certainly, not much goes on in Bolzano, but I can't complain: it's nice enough, lovely surroundings. Just yesterday we caught a Tunisian red-handed stealing bicycles outside the station," he said, trying to stress the irony. "But at least there are no slums. The streets are well kept, pleasant for everyone, so you don't notice any difference."

"It's true that the ethnic groups change, but the *neo-realismo* remains," said Pietro Striggio with a touch of bitterness. Sergio agreed – those who pretend the past is gone forever don't have the faintest understanding of history. That was what his father meant in those few casual words. "And don't imagine it's a good sign just because you don't see what's going on: your silent neighbourhoods are full of people who pay lip-service to an integration they know nothing about and meantime they are making bombs on the internet."

"That's not true, these communities are totally peaceful and well-integrated," Sergio protested. He was prepared to make allowance for his father's ill-humour, especially after taking his last wife to the crematorium, but was not going to allow him to get away with ideas that were frankly reactionary – and provocative – just for the sake of it.

"That's what they said about the districts of Brussels too. They were planning their attacks in houses belonging to the city council. That's how democracies end up: funding those who destroy them."

"And how do dictatorships end up?" Sergio asked, more to avoid admitting defeat than out of any real interest in the conversation. He couldn't remember how long it had been that he had felt absolutely no interest in his father's world-view.

Sometime later he recounted every detail of the conversation to Leo, who commented that for someone with so little interest in his father he seemed unusually anxious to discover what his view was about their relationship. And he had felt in some way touched by the frankness with which Leo could expose his weaknesses.

Nevertheless, in the car with his father, just a few hours after the cremation of his third wife, Sergio had cleared his throat to announce he had something important to tell him.

"You understand the game they're playing? They pretend to keep to your rules and then they shaft you, with all due respect," continued the old man, with his unspeakable extremism. "Once they've reduced whole districts to souks or favelas, or whatever the hell you want to call them, then at least you know who you're dealing with. Did you want to tell me something?" he asked eventually, demonstrating that his peripheral hearing was still working as it should.

"Well, Dina," Sergio asked. "Should I regard her as another step-mother, or does the status of the stepson come to an end after the second wife?"

His father paused and looked at him as though weighing up whether it was worth answering. And he decided it was not. "I hope at least you have your own parking space in that dump you've had yourself sent to?" he asked instead.

* * *

He did, and was just reaching it in that very moment. He checked his watch: it was just after 11.20. Leo would be home by now and boiling his Alessi kettle, the one Sergio had given him, to make himself a tisane with ginger and green tea. The first-floor lights at the Commissariato were on, the illuminated sign at the entrance blinking oddly, like eyes flickering. Sergio parked tidily in the area reserved for police vehicles, in a space with its own sign, COMMISSARIO, switched off the engine and sent a text to Leo before getting out. He waited for his reply, which arrived immediately, less reassuring than he had hoped but a reply all the same, though affectionately non-committal. I'LL TELL HIM WHEN HE ARRIVES, he had written. OK WE'LL SEE, was Leo's reply. That was it.

Entering the building he was struck by a clammy warmth, like a single breath in endless circulation.

"Open some windows, there's no air in here!" he told the security guard, who a moment before had been watching the closed-circuit monitor as though it were a Champions League final, and had jumped up as he arrived, almost to attention. "Trevisan, you ought to be in the Carabinierie," he joked. "At ease, at ease," he continued. "Who do we have on duty?"

"Chief Inspector Menetti, Assistant Inspector Fanti, junior officers Caputo and Steltzer and yours truly, simple officer Trevisan, Commissario."

"A lot of people," Striggio commented, as he headed towards his office at the far end of the corridor, where he was joined by Elisabetta Menetti: "Sorry I've called you out at this hour, but we've had a report from a motorist, someone on his way to Sanzeno. You know the road for San Romedio?" she asked without waiting for a reply. "It seems he came across a couple at the Bolzano turn who claimed they'd lost their son in the car."

"Lost?"

Chief inspector Menetti fingered her ponytail and checked what she had written on the tablet that was always with her. "From the car: a second earlier he was on the back seat and a second later he had gone. They had stopped a moment to answer a call of nature."

"Oh, I see. I thought you were saying the child disappeared while the car was still moving. Does this good Samaritan have a name?"

"He's a priest," said Menetti, taking another look at her tablet. "Don Giuseppe, a parish priest . . ."

"That's lucky," the Commissario said. "The only ones who give their names in cases like this are priests and military personnel . . . all the rest hang up as soon as they're asked for details."

"Anyway, according to this don Giuseppe, it seems the child's parents have no intention of leaving the scene where they've lost the boy, since they reckon he'll find the road again once it gets light. It might be an idea to go and take a look. Was I right to call you?"

"Let's go," Sergio agreed. "Can we get the entrance sign fixed? It's like one of those on a massage parlour."

Menetti smiled. "We sent a request form off to the Questura a couple of weeks ago."

They were still smiling as they reached the car park. "Let's take mine," Menetti said, "the heating isn't working in the patrol car . . . Or rather it works too well – we had to go round today with the windows down."

"We'll take mine," Striggio said, heading towards his parking space.

Don Giuseppe saw the headlights of the vehicle in which Commissario Striggio and Chief Inspector Menetti were travelling a few curves before the turning into the lay-by where he and the Ludovisis' SUV were parked. He stood in the middle of the road waving his arms as though slowing them down to warn them of a landslide or bridge collapse. Sergio stopped a few metres away, and don Giuseppe ran up to the car window.

"Are you the police?" he asked, since the car didn't look like a police vehicle.

"Commissario Striggio," Sergio announced, "and Chief Inspector Menetti," indicating Elisabetta, who leaned across so that he could see her.

Outside was the dry scent of the mountains in winter, thick with the breath of vegetation caught in the midst of slumber – heather and oak – and also of the fur of restless animals worn down by hunger. As a child, Sergio had been frightened of dogs and, to be honest, he still regarded them with a certain suspicion. "Are there wolves in these parts?" he asked abruptly.

With the tips of his fingers, don Giuseppe made a sign of the cross the size of a postage stamp over his lips. "Indeed," he answered, "but they don't go round eating children . . ."

"That's not what I meant," protested the Commissario, who yet had no intention of explaining what flight of olfactory fancy had produced his question. He saw Menetti busy with her tablet.

"The signal's not so good around here," she said. "I wanted to get some idea of the area from Google Maps."

Meanwhile Gaia Ludovisi had emerged from the darkness. Her hair was ruffled and she was hot, despite the temperature being several degrees below zero. "It's the police," don Giuseppe said. "I took the liberty of calling them."

The woman shook her head, as if annoyed that someone was interfering with her concentration. Then she turned back again to the undergrowth and began shouting at the top of her voice: "Michelangelo! Darling! Mamma's here!"

Further away in the darkness the dim light of a cigarette could be seen. It was Nicolò Ludovisi finishing his packet. He was sitting on a campion-covered rock and looked up as Striggio approached to see who it was though, with no apparent interest.

"Commissario Striggio. What exactly happened?"

Nicolò Ludovisi winced as if some smoke had got into his eyes. "Everything went dark. Everything," he said in a voice almost completely expressionless. "I thought he was with Gaia and she thought he was with me." His leg began visibly to tremble. "You know the feeling of losing control?" he asked. Striggio didn't exactly know, but nevertheless said he did. "First there was the fox. Then the ground opened up. Then it all went out."

"All what?" Striggio asked.

"The car, the headlights, every light, every noise: everything!"

"And how long did this darkness last?"

Nicolò Ludovisi said he didn't know. The only thing for certain was that, when everything was back to normal, Michelangelo had gone, vanished . . .

Gaia started calling again. Nicolò put his hands over his ears and screwed up his eyes.

"Every moment counts," Sergio insisted. "How long since it happened?"

Nicolò Ludovisi relaxed a bit. "Of course," he repeated to himself.

"Every moment counts." Then he seemed to make a tremendous effort: "Two hours?" he asked. Striggio spread his arms in disbelief. "We were at the restaurant . . ."

He was in shock, which made him slide continually between deep depression and unprompted laughter – and now he was chuckling to himself. As Sergio became used to the dark, he was able to gather some more information about the man's face. Nicolò Ludovisi was an alpha male, as Sergio could see from the force with which he showed his fragility.

The first man with whom he had fallen in love, without ever openly admitting it, was a colleague of his father from Calabria who wept each time he heard certain Neapolitan songs which he, not yet thirteen, loathed. And yet those tears, rather than demeaning him in Sergio's eyes, made him even more irresistible. Ludovisi, in short, with his straightforward confusion, with his upright attitude even in despair and with that incipient baldness, now reminded him of his first secret love.

"We'll find him," Sergio promised, caught by a sudden wave of affection and human solidarity. "As soon as it gets light we'll send out search parties. He can't have gone far . . ."

Nicolò Ludovisi gave a slight smile. "Do you have a cigarette?" he asked.

The Commissario shook his head. "I've stopped," he said.

Nicolò Ludovisi looked at him with the ungrudging pride of one who thinks that giving up smoking is an honourable gesture so long as it's done by others. "A good thing," he said. "A good thing indeed. I haven't even tried."

A silence of another kind had spread all around, as if someone was about to cry out at any moment. Not far away, Menetti was talking to don Giuseppe. The priest was moving his hands jerkily as though he were finding it more and more difficult to answer the Chief Inspector's questions.

Striggio headed across to the parked SUV. He could hear the sound of Gaia Ludovisi wandering aimlessly in the dark. She had stopped calling out but couldn't stay still. "Is this your car?" the Commissario asked. Nicolò Ludovisi raised his eyebrows as if he were having to answer and ask questions at the same time. "Do you mind if I take a look?" Striggio asked.

Ludovisi paused for a second too long before agreeing, but then gave his consent.

"I'm allowed to do so only if you agree," the Commissario explained.

Ludovisi nervously repeated his consent.

Sergio Striggio switched on the torch of his phone and approached the vehicle, lighting up the interior. There was nothing on the back seat to suggest any violent removal of the boy from the car. Striggio sometimes surprised himself when he realised how easy it was to start seeing things through the eyes of a policeman. The car seemed clean, the boot in spotless condition.

"Has anything unusual happened this evening? Did you have the feeling, I don't know, that anyone was following you? You'd been out to eat?"

"Yes, at the Antica Trattoria Olimpo."

"Yes," Striggio repeated, waiting for Ludovisi to continue.

"Everything normal, I'd say. Perhaps . . ."

"Perhaps . . .?" the Commissario encouraged him.

"Some tension," the other said. "It happens, doesn't it? Gaia and I, it's a period when we're arguing," he said.

"Arguing about what?"

Now that Ludovisi seemed more relaxed he struck a statuesque pose, seeming even broader, as though he were expanding. He was one of those men who control their poise from above, who peer at themselves in shop windows to pull in their stomach muscles. He shrugged. "About those things that couples usually argue about, I suppose. Gaia has her own way of doing things. And Michelangelo isn't easy."

"For example?" asked Striggio, taking advantage of their sudden intimacy.

"I'm a vet," he said. It seemed an incongruous detail. "Our cat's ill, but she took it to a colleague of mine who went to school with her. You wanted an example? Well that's an example."

The man's face revealed a dangerous candour. "I see," said Striggio as if to seal a true complicity. "So," he added in passing, "this is the vehicle you use for work?"

Ludovisi said yes, and even raised a smile.

Menetti joined them and turned to Striggio, who gave her a nod. "The story doesn't fit," she said as soon as they were alone. "The priest says he heard shouting as he was returning along the road for San Romedio and stopped. But not even he could work out precisely what had happened. So he decided to call us. I've tried talking to the woman, but you've seen her . . . I'd say she needs immediate medical assistance."

"I agree," Striggio said. "First thing is to call an ambulance. It could be some kind of joint delirium from substance abuse."

Menetti nodded vigorously as if to say that was the only real solution to the conundrum.

Procuratore Susini, the chief prosecutor, prided himself on not being deceived by appearances, and this despite the shade of a colour unknown to nature with which he dyed his hair. He kept it long, thinning and back-combed. Its amber colour could turn to a shade of pink or salmon according to how recently it had been dyed. That particular morning it was candy pink, and he flicked it lightly as Striggio entered his office and was invited to sit down. What they had to say was quite simple and wouldn't take more than ten minutes: missing boy, parents inadequate, accident. Full stop. The Procuratore expected an indication of total agreement, but it was clear from Striggio's expression that he considered the theory flawed.

The Commissario tried instead to explain that the circumstances of the disappearance were far less straightforward than might be thought. Firstly an entire dog unit had failed next morning to find even the slightest trace of the boy and secondly there was no evidence to show the boy had escaped of his own free will. Susini this time pointed his finger at the Commissario as if to disagree on that point. The boy had clearly run away from home, as every brat of his age does.

"Not me," said Striggio.

The Procuratore pursed his lips in a childish pout. "Not me?" he asked.

Striggio responded with the same expression. "I never ran away from home," he repeated. "And you, sir?"

The Procuratore looked at him as if to reassure himself that Striggio had actually asked the question. "No," he said at last. "Of course not!" as if to make it clear that his was certainly not a family from which any child would have wished to run away.

Striggio put on a smile of encouragement. "Far fewer children run away than stay at home. Michelangelo Ludovisi is an unusual boy, with a suggestion of Asperger's. Do you see what I'm getting at?" The Procuratore pretended he had. "He's a boy who displays a marked intellectual independence: decidedly more intelligent than his average classmate. But from a practical point of view he's far worse equipped than others."

The Procuratore brightened up: "So an accident is the most likely explanation."

"If there were some trace of blood, some cliff from which he might have fallen, a corpse . . . In that case we could develop the theory of an accident or murder, but we have nothing."

The Procuratore, now with a certain anxiety, could see where Striggio was leading. "Abduction?" he asked.

Striggio scratched his nose before answering. "Abduction leaves no trace of blood, needs no cliffs, leaves no corpses, at least not at the scene."

* * *

Menetti joined him at the Commissariato: "We're working on the assumption of child abduction, correct?"

Striggio smiled: "I'm not exactly sure what we're working on."

"You had a look at the father's car?"

"He's a control freak. He does a 'dirty' job but the car's in perfect order. How did you get on with the priest?"

"He was driving past some twenty minutes after the event. He knows the Ludovisis by sight."

"Conclusions?"

"He was the only one who thought it necessary to call the police."

"Exactly. Why not the parents?"

Menetti brightened up. "Theory number one?" she asked.

"Joint delirium: difficult child, mother exhausted and father at the end of his tether."

Menetti shook her head. "Unpremeditated then. An argument, one tantrum too many during the car ride ... the boy could be anywhere between the trattoria and the lay-by. It won't take much to find out. Theory number two?"

"Ongoing separation: one or other of them has the child kidnapped. But I admit it's far-fetched."

"It is," Menetti agreed. "And her?" Striggio understood immediately that "her" meant Gaia Ludovisi. "I reckon you're one of those who's not much geared to the idea of mother killers. Like most men."

She was quite right, Striggio thought. For he rejected the idea that the mother might somehow be behind Michelangelo's disappearance – which said a lot about his view of the world.

"So you're in favour of a guilty father but not the mother. Striggio, I thought you were out of the ordinary, but you're average after all." She gave out a laugh.

The Commissario didn't laugh, not because he felt insulted but because he was trying to work out when his colleague had decided he was out of the ordinary. "Out of the ordinary?" he asked after a while, without seeming to expect an answer.

"In three years, you're the only one in this place who hasn't, at his own risk and peril, tried to pinch my bum," she said.

"That doesn't mean I haven't thought of it," Striggio said.

"But it suggests you're more cautious. And caution is a virtue quite out of the ordinary in a man."

"You mean in a male."

"It's not the same thing."

"No, I suppose it's not ..."

"It's not like saying woman and female. Between man and male there's a vast difference: you for example are a man, but certainly not male.

"As a girl I hated dolls but liked guns" – A statement which seemed quite enough to demonstrate the extent of her gender awareness.

"For me, quite the opposite," he said, but in a manner too ambiguously provocative. "And I still like dolls," he added, trying to gauge how far Menetti was capable of sensing where truth ended and falsehood began.

"Are you trying it on with me, at last?" she said, arranging her hair unselfconsciously.

"No," he said, but in such a way that sounded like a yes. Menetti shook her head. "Something to drink?" she asked.

"Not this evening: I have someone to see, and my father to collect from the station."

1468

On the dialogue with Giovanni Rucellai about the new frontage to the Basilica of Santa Maria Novella in Florence

* * *

I see it this way: for me, without Ancient there is no Modern. So once again I sit and explain to Rucellai that the frontage of Santa Maria Novella, as he wants it, is impossible to construct. He wants niches and statues and a design that tells of Prudence and Charity, which he says are the qualities of his family. But for almost a hundred years someone has had it in mind to finish the church before us. As for Prudence, Rucellai knows much about it and I joke that with Cosimo's return from exile, things have gone better for him than they might have done considering his kinship with the Strozzis and his wife Jacopa belonging to that family. In short, the Medici come back and all their rivals pack their trunks and send instructions to open up their country houses far from Florence. But not Rucellai. On the contrary, he tells me that sooner or later he intends to complete the frontage of Santa Maria Novella as an offering to the Madonna for having inspired him with Prudence. And how he would like it he has already made clear: all whorls and curlicues. He comes with several sketches and asks me what I think. And I think that in those designs there is surface without substance, and the love of things unfiltered by reason. He proposes to raise the frontage to conceal the pitch of the roof, which is in truth most unsightly . . . And he says he has in mind the cathedral of Ferrara, which I know well, as justification for the hotchpotch of niches into which he would place old-fashioned sculptures of the arts, seasons and pilgrims. He, Rucellai, sees only the representation of the Ancient, not its geometry and almost never its harmony. In Trajan's Column he sees sculpted bas-reliefs, whereas I see the incredible use of space. The sculptor faced the problem of having too much to tell and too little space to do it, so he invented a parchment that encircles the column. I see that spiral harmony. Giovanni does not. He is like the farmer who learns which season to sow seed by looking at the Cathedral facade. So I tell him to leave it to me if he truly wishes to honour his vow. No niches and no statues but the idea of niches and statues, if he understands me. For modern man, like all succeeding generations, has the privilege of conserving the ancient as well in the architectural experience. Giovanni looks at me and still does not understand: being modern, I tell him, means having the ability to see what the others do not.

"When your father-in-law Strozzi and Albrizzi came to ask you to support the banishment of Cosimo de' Medici, what did you reply?"

Giovanni looked at me. "I said no, that it was unwise, that if they hadn't killed him then he was not dead; and if he wasn't dead then he was still dangerous."

"Well, and if I had come and said you were wrong and that it was unmanly not to side with the families of Florence?"

"I would have told you to stick to your own job and leave politics and business to me."

And as soon as he had said it, he saw what I had been getting at and slapped me on the back. "Bloody artist . . . No niches, then?"

"No niches."

* * *

Leo looked up from the sheet of paper. Sergio had been waiting with a certain trepidation for him to finish. They had had sex without even undressing. Sergio had then got up and gone to his jacket on the back of the chair in the kitchen and taken from the pocket an exercise book covered with kaleidoscopic patterns of ochre and green and yellow and red. Without saying a word, he handed Leo the exercise book, who took it without comment, opened it and had to fight back the tears at the sight of that neat and orderly handwriting that filled the page. Sergio went back to sit on the sofa beside him and they remained like that in silence, one reading and the other waiting for him to finish. "Did you really write all this?" Leo asked with a smile, trying to soften his surprise, which might otherwise have seemed offensive.

"Yes," Sergio said with a shrug.

"At the age of nine?"

"No, that's what my father says. I was twelve or thirteen."

Leo went as if to wipe sweat from his brow in an eloquent gesture. "Ah, that's OK then. Thirteen."

"I think I was in love. One of my father's colleagues."

"Sergio, but do you realise?" Leo said, in a way that Sergio almost mistook for annoyance.

"I'd thought no more about it. I wanted to write a novel, a sort of diary of Leon Battista Alberti. Look, it seemed quite crazy to me that a genius of that calibre should find himself having to put up the facade of a building constructed by others."

Leo started laughing. "A kind of make-up artist for churches."

"Kind of," agreed Sergio. "But then I left it."

"Why?"

"How do I know? As I said, I was confused . . . I was convinced at that time that my father's colleague was a 1.618 . . ."

"A what?"

"A 1.618: the golden ratio, absolute beauty. He was tall, hairy, one of those who kept saying things like 'I'm so full of spunk, how can I help it if I like fucking?' I was only thirteen . . ."

"And you wrote these things down."

"One summer evening this colleague of my father's came to sleep at our house because some building works were going on in the living quarters at the Commissariato. So he slept in my room. My parents had put up a folding bed there, not much higher than a yoga mat. That was the first time I'd been within touching distance of the object of my desire and I couldn't sleep a wink all night. Then there was you."

Leo stretched out to hug him. "Where have you been hiding that little boy for all these years?" he asked.

Hidden away. In effect, that was how it was. He didn't know exactly when, but at some specific moment he had decided to play safe. And most probably it was the very moment that male began undressing in front of him, twenty years before, and stood there in nothing but his underpants and said things like: "Between men there's no need to stand on ceremony." Or "What's the matter, embarrassed?" and then he listened to music on his headphones, mangling the words of some Neapolitan love song – it was "*Era de maggio*" – and crying like a child. It was clear: young Sergio didn't have a chance.

"I'm happy you've let me read it," Leo whispered in his ear.

"I should have done long ago," Sergio said. "But if my father wasn't so obsessed about making me look a fool I would never have thought of it," he lied.

Instead he was obsessed with not appearing to be as he was. Or rather, as he thought he was. Leo's question about where he had hidden the little boy who was besotted with that hairy ogre, the little boy who wanted to write novels, had penetrated to the heart of the matter. And Sergio didn't have an answer. He could have tried saying that some adults aren't up to their given task; and that children sometimes hide from themselves so as to live up to the expectations of those who ought instead to teach them to express themselves freely. But in his case it wouldn't have been true: his mother had adored him to the point of hanging on his every word. It was she who had kept the composition that Leo had just read, while his father was such a cynic that he didn't want to fall into the trap of becoming a role model for his son. So the decision to vanish didn't come from the fear of disappointing the people he loved and who loved him. It came from the realisation that his desire only meant suffering. And so, on that night with his father's colleague half-naked in the summer heat, snoring lightly beside him, his legs splayed, his arms crossed above his head and the thick fleece of hair on his chest rising and sinking with the steady breath of his deep sleep, he could have decided either to get up and touch him or to vanish. To hide away in an inaccessible corner. To be swallowed up by the earth. Buried alive inside his own disappearance. Everyone thought his gift was to know more than some people know in their whole lives.

While still in middle school – he hadn't yet decided to vanish – he had asked his father whether he knew that Kafka's main purpose for visiting Paris in spring 1912 was to go to the Louvre to see the empty space left by the "Mona Lisa", stolen the year before. The news didn't surprise his father at all. In fact he turned to his wife – at that time still the first wife – and asked whether it might be a good idea to start locking the boy's bedroom. It was years before Sergio understood what he meant. Who knows whether his father had really thought the moment had come to start being afraid of him.

"You look worried," Leo said, handing him a steaming cup. "Is it to do with your father's arrival? It'll all be fine," he assured him.

"Yes, but not just that. There's the business of the missing boy . . ."

"The Ludovisi boy."

"You know him?"

"Yes, yes . . . He's in the class of one of my fellow teachers. A strange child."

"In what way?"

"Well, Sara Heller, my colleague, has often described him as highly gifted: language skills above average, interests well beyond the average. Quite advanced for his age, though I don't know him myself . . ."

"And the father?"

"Nicolò Ludovisi, you mean?"

"Yes, the father . . ."

"Why do you ask?"

"Perhaps you've seen him at school . . ."

"Don't know, maybe. I can't say I have. I know he worked at the Animal Health Institute as some kind of lab technician."

"As a vet, I'd say . . . and quite good-looking . . . What does the teacher say?"

"Sergio, how do I know? Michelangelo Ludovisi's not in my class!"

"What are you getting cross for?"

"Me? I don't know. Because you're interrogating me . . ."

"Interrogating?"

"All these questions."

"Hmm," Sergio frowned but with no indication of disapproval. "We've sent out search teams but found nothing. The husband and wife blame each other. Susini has called us in to see whether a more aggressive approach might be better."

"Aggressive?"

"Well, nothing in this whole business makes sense. At one point we even thought the Ludovisis had invented a child that didn't exist."

"He exists, that's for sure."

"Yes, of course, I was going too far."

Sergio took a long sip of his tisane and closed his eyes.

"You'll be late," Leo said after a while.

"Yes, yes . . . I'll be off in ten minutes . . ." And he burst out laughing.

They were listening to Björk's "All Is Full of Love". And soon it would be getting dark, though without that suddenness with which night usually fell in that part of the world. January was on its way out, "off to rest for eleven months", as his mother used to say when he was little. In fact his most distinct memory of her was the nursery rhyme describing the year as a business of twelve workers: January was the most industrious, February the laziest, March the strangest . . .

"Why are you laughing?"

"Nothing." Sergio shook his head. Leo kept looking at him, knowing that he would soon stop. In the meantime Björk ended her song in a kind of cosmic embrace. After a pause he said. "His name was Massimo and he called himself Max." Then, seeing that Leo was still looking at him, he continued: "That colleague of my father. And in the morning he had an incredible erection."

"A sign that your sleepless night hadn't gone to waste . . ."

Sergio almost choked on his last mouthful of tea and had to leap up to avoid staining his shirt. They laughed. All was full of love, full of love.

In his mouth he felt the sour taste of waiting. He had waited for people on that platform so many times, yet now, with the sun dropping behind the mountains, the rails, the station, all seemed totally unfamiliar.

January had been warmer than usual, but winter was now relentlessly making itself known, in all its freezing rigidity every time the sun set, as just now when the train was due.

A season that he liked, for he couldn't stand the heat of summer, which seemed increasingly torrid and increasingly endless, even though it always finished up by sending him into a boundless melancholy. And this winter, he thought, now also had the face of his father who was about to arrive.

He looked up to the electronic indicator board to check the train was on time. It was. After all, he thought, there was no way it could be late if it was carrying his father.

There was a family group on the platform of the large, half-deserted station: husband, wife, adolescent daughter with headphones, standing silently with eyes fixed on the same indicator board. They seemed to be waiting just like him, waiting for Pietro Striggio to get off the train. He watched them from the corner of his eye. They seemed ordinary people but over the course of his career he had learned not to consider anyone in the world as ordinary. In that detestable twilight hour of transition, neither dark nor light, humanity held its breath as its heart began to pump out of control and its throat felt a harsh, acrid taste of anticipation. The air turned deep amber, as happens when it is time to recognise that a day is coming to an end.

He had begged his father to take the earlier train, wanting at all costs to avoid that little death in every sunset. He saw nothing good in anything that comes to an end. He had asked the old man to take the train in the early afternoon so as to be pointing his nose up at that electronic indicator board, which was fixed too high, in broad daylight and not in that dismal twilight. But his father was someone not easily persuaded. His arrival had cost weeks of negotiation, even though at home the day after Dina's funeral and cremation, with the urn in pride of place on the dining-room table, he had promised he would come and spend long periods of time with him.

Now he was keeping his promise, though not without protest and petty arguments to counter Sergio's repeated requests by referring to his age and health, which he said was poor. His son, he said, was young and energetic, and it would be easier for him to make the journey. Sergio had replied a thousand times that it wasn't so easy with a job like his to take a train south, whereas someone in retirement has all the time in the world. And yet he realised, just as he was setting out his theory, that the truth was otherwise and that, in reality, you have all the time in the world only when that time is coming to an end.

And so it was that in the delayed column, beside the train number, the message 10 MINUTES now appeared. Instinctively he looked towards the family a few steps away, attempting a gesture of solidarity for the non-arrival, then moved towards the track, where the smell of iron and wood predominated, and took a deep breath. That particular feeling of melancholy had an acrid taste of wind and stone. It also had a colour, a particular shade of dark orange, like the sliver of amber that traps the primordial insect, and with it a sound, vibrant and distinct, a bourdon of solid air that slid downwards, penetrating the mountain clefts. Oh, that feeling had a distinctive texture to the touch, like running a hand over the cold surface of a polished marble slab. As a child he used to think that ice and marble were identical and wondered for what magical reason the surface of the table on which he and his family ate each day didn't melt away, liquefied by the hot dishes laid upon it. He had had to learn with time that things apparently similar are in reality completely different.

Like a world sinking into anarchy, the ten-minute delay became fifteen and then twenty. Now even the immobile father of the holy family nearby gave a gesture between annoyance and amazement. The mother nodded at something he hadn't said, and even the adolescent daughter lifted her headphones and made momentary contact with the surrounding reality.

There, he said to himself, the triumph of Time and Disillusion: his father who hadn't arrived, the first delay he had encountered at that perfect mountain railway station; and the day that was dying, flapping its wings before him. Any certainty could melt away in a trice. It was like that extra pinch of salt that ruins the meal or the anxiety of going back to rest after having suffered the wearying affront of the unexpected.

A station manager no longer in the flush of youth came up to the family and to him to warn them that the train had been held up a few kilometres away. A collision with a stag as it was crossing the line. A young male, impatient, improvident, that had leapt across just as the train was emerging from a tunnel. And now it lay dying with its porcelain legs shattered between the tracks. The manager looked at her watch and then at the indicator board and announced it would be at least another fifteen minutes before the track was cleared.

It was the last train of the day. Like the last show when people still went to watch films at the cinema. A general emptiness, a reminder of approaching stasis, defining the vague substance that marked transition from day to night. The neon lamps turned the station surroundings yellow as a shield against the reality that obliterated everything else. Before him there was nothing but obscurity broken by distant clusters of lights, like jewels set in the deceptive nothingness of total darkness. The girl with the headphones had found a seat that looked comfortable but wasn't, and had sprawled across it with that pliant nonchalance that only adolescents have.

Just as he was trying to forget the memory of himself as a child being constantly told off for the way he dressed, for how he was sitting or how he combed his hair, his phone rang. It was Menetti, to tell him what he already knew: stag, train held up, etc. He got rid of her with his usual no-nonsense haste and then regretted it. Menetti, after all, was an extraordinary colleague, even if she had never understood that he couldn't abide kindness and courtesy, though afterwards he would appreciate it. And so that telephone call, which had interrupted his concentration, was inopportune in his view, however thoughtful and considerate it might have been, and Menetti accepted his brisk goodbye.

* * *

By the time a pre-recorded voice announced the arrival of the fast train from Verona, the delayed column had risen to forty-five minutes.

First to leave the train was a lad not yet twenty for whom the family had been waiting. Father and mother ran to greet him; his sister got up slowly to join them. They hugged, talked excitedly, for their boy had escaped the horror of a train accident, which could have cost who knows how many lives. At last the sister joined them and welcomed her brother with calculated coolness, as if her age prevented any mawkish affection. He gave her a kiss, and she let herself be hugged.

Two or three people got out, evidently confused, as though not quite sure they had arrived where they were meant to: victims of the deception of stations at night, which all seem stubbornly the same, for if you don't see those blue signs with white lettering then each stop looks like every other.

A tall man got out and walked as though every step he took was the subject of intense study.

Other youngsters followed with rucksacks and hiking boots.

Then nothing. Sergio leaned back to look at the narrow tail of the train, seemingly about to set off again, but only pulsating before settling comfortably to sleep. He moved towards the door of the carriage in front of him just as all the interior lights went out. In his mind he began to list all the possibilities: that his father had fallen asleep and was somewhere inside the train; or had been overanxious and had got off at a previous stop; or, worse still, hadn't known which train to take from Verona.

Just then a voice from behind made him jump: "Sergio."

Striggio turned round in a flash: "Papà," he said with the relief of someone who had to stop devising and discounting theories.

"Hey," said Pietro, as if to say yes, it really was his father.

"Where did you get to?" Sergio asked, bending down to take the handle of the small wheelie bag his father was pulling behind him. "Is this all you have?" he added without waiting for an answer to his first question and understanding only too well the message his father wanted to convey with that meagre quantity of baggage.

While it couldn't be said they much resembled each other, a closer look revealed many features, traits and attitudes in common. The same shape of shoulders and neck, and Pietro still had the same mop of hair as his son, though it was turning grey, and shaped to the same point over the forehead. Other than that, Sergio looked more like his mother, who had been a beautiful woman, taller and more elegant than her husband, making him seem inadequate to anyone who saw them out walking, always arm in arm.

"What else did I need to bring? After all I'm not going to be here for long," the old man said.

Sergio Striggio sniffed as he headed off towards the car. "You're catching a cold, hadn't you noticed?" his father asked.

"We talked about it, I seem to remember."

"Talked about what?" Striggio senior looked surprised, but with markedly theatrical excess.

"You know what," the other said, opening the car with the automatic button on his key. "The fact that it makes no sense you living alone at the other end of the world."

"Ah," the old man said. "Did we talk about that?"

"Yes, we did. And you told me you'd think about it."

"Indeed, I have thought about it."

"Yes, yes, sure, of course you have . . . Aren't you getting in?" Sergio asked, leaning across the passenger seat to open the door for his father.

Pietro got in and settled into the seat if it were an armchair. "Nice car, this. Comfortable," he said, as though talking to himself.

Bolzano flowed past outside like liquid. They remained silent for several minutes. "You make it sound too easy," Pietro said suddenly, just as a traffic light was turning from amber to red.

Sergio Striggio shrugged his shoulders, though he had understood perfectly well.

"Do you think it's easy to leave everything and move somewhere else, as you say . . ."

"But to leave what everything?" The question was asked too forcefully.

"Everything: the house, the neighbourhood, friends . . . At my age these things are important." Sergio searched in vain for an appropriate way to answer his father. "It's green," he said before he could reply.

Sergio Striggio pressed hard on the accelerator, and the car moved off as though sucked along by a strong magnetic force. "What neighbourhood, what friends?" he said when he could hear the engine was turning normally again. "I reckon it's five years that you haven't been out of the house. So far as I know, you've never been a great socialiser."

His father slowly nodded in agreement. "All the same, it's still my home and I'm too old to change anything . . ."

The car turned into a side road, like the entrance to a world apart. They were soon in a hillside district of low apartment blocks surrounded by small gardens. Sergio braked, positioning the bonnet of the car in front of a gate, at which he pointed a small remote control. The gate began to slide open, disappearing into the boundary wall like a blade vanishing into the mouth of a sword swallower. He drove slowly into a neat courtyard and manoeuvred into his allotted parking space. With the engine off, the car interior seemed to reverberate with unspoken words. They sat for a while without speaking. "It's nice here," Pietro said, breaking the silence.

Sergio nodded, it certainly was nice. Everything was nice there, almost too nice. He undid his seat belt and they got out of the car. An astonishing star-filled sky hung above them with that nonchalance that only wonders can produce. The night was bright, despite the light from the moon being shielded by the looming mountains. He could smell imminent rain, a sign rather than a certainty.

Sergio took the bag from the boot and headed towards the entrance of a small apartment block. The old man followed.

The apartment was spacious and tidy. The large sitting room looked too empty, giving the impression of being more or less unused; the orderly kitchen was airy and stark. "I had the woman come to clean this morning," Sergio said in apparent justification.

"Perfect, perfect . . ." his father announced.

"Your room is here."

The old man followed him into a surprisingly large room, with a double bed and very large wardrobe.

"And that's your bathroom," Sergio added, indicating a closed door in the wall opposite the bed.

Pietro gave a smile of approval. "It has everything, even a TV," he said with a certain irony, while being careful not to sound sarcastic. A table and armchair stood at a window looking out over a wooded slope. "Really perfect . . ." the old man said again.

"Are you hungry? I thought you'd be too tired to go out for dinner, so I've had something prepared. It just needs warming up: chicken alla diavola and a glass of good wine, OK?"

"I'll eat anything," Pietro replied. "Chicken alla diavola is perfect." He repeated that adjective as though, despite careful thought, he hadn't managed to find one better.

Dinner passed almost in silence, broken only by a few polite words on the excellence of the food.

Towards the end, Sergio started talking in general terms about what he called "the case of the missing boy". His father asked whether they had investigated all possibilities, for example, that both parents might have decided to get rid of the child. Which to Sergio seemed a very appropriate theory coming from the man sitting in front of him. He replied, though, that if they'd done such a thing, then they had done it not just well but extremely well, since they had never contradicted each other, and there was absolutely nothing to suggest such a plan.

"Some children are a real problem," Pietro suggested.

"As you know all too well?" Sergio said darkly.

"Not at all. Why would I?" It was clear they were playing their usual game of trying to outsmart the other. "By the way," Pietro said after a moment, "your grandmother sends her love . . ."

"Ah," Sergio said, "Grandma, how is she?"

Pietro stopped chewing, swallowed and wiped his lips. "Well, she's trying hard to prove those right who say she'll bury us all. And she will, of course."

"And Aunt Amalia?"

"Your Aunt Amalia does what she can, tries to get her to smoke less, to eat less fried food and to water down her wine . . . She too sends her love." Sergio nodded, as though it was an effort to keep the conversation calm. "You should go and see them, you know your grandmother thinks the world of you."

This time Sergio knew how to reply. "Grandma thinks the world only of herself," he said. "You don't live as long as that without a megadose of selfishness."

And Pietro was forced to admit his son was right. He knew exactly what he meant by "a megadose of selfishness".

Sergio's mother's last months had been terrible, and they'd had to arrange to take turns to sit up with her at night in the hospital. Pietro, Sergio, who was little more than a child, and Aunt Amalia took it in turns at the dying woman's bedside. But not Grandma: she couldn't stay anywhere where they wouldn't let her smoke.

"I'll see if I can get to visit her next time," Sergio lied. "There's a semifreddo in the fridge."

Pietro shook his head. "I'm full," he said. "But I'd love a coffee if you have one." They tried to look relaxed but couldn't hold back that sense of embarrassment that overwhelmed them each time they were alone and feigning some kind of intimacy. "So then?" Pietro asked, after a pause, as he stood behind his son watching him drop the capsule into the coffee machine. "All's well with your well-integrated Pakistanis?"

Sergio waited for the machine to stop squirting the coffee into the cup he had centred under the spout. "I don't feel like taking you up on that conversation, not tonight," he said, giving him the cup. "Sugar?"

Pietro was forced to consider how far they had grown apart. "No thanks," he said. "You've never had a great opinion of me," he continued after he had downed the whole contents of the cup in a single mouthful and carefully wiped his lips and chin with the napkin. His words were direct and distinct and arguably totally inappropriate. Yet they had clearly been the result of deep reflection.

Sergio sized him up: "What exactly are we talking about now?" he asked, trying to appear surprised, though deep down he wasn't. It was the usual unfinished exchange between him and the man in front.

"About us," his father cut in before he could say more. "About this attitude of yours, ever since you were a child," he added, to make it clear that what might seem wrong in what he was saying was in fact appropriate.

"Look, really . . ." the other said, curling his lips into a kind of grimace intended as a smile.

"Don't worry, it wasn't a criticism. Just so you know that I've noticed. You know, by playing dumb so much, perhaps you've convinced yourself it's me that's dumb."

"And you've come all this way to tell me that?"

The old man fell silent and seemed to focus on some particular point of the room behind his son. He slowly nodded his head. "Now that you've made me think about it," he said, "yes: I'd say that's precisely what I've 'come all this way' for."

"To tell me you're not dumb? I've never thought that," Sergio said in a tone of voice meant to bring the conversation to an end. "What about that semifreddo?"

Pietro was still staring at that precise nothingness over his son's shoulder. Then, speaking with serene precision at that nothingness, he said: "I'm dying."

The truth was he couldn't respond. Instead he leapt up and began clearing the dishes, glasses and cutlery from the table as though nothing had happened, or as if he had decided to leave the scene only after he had tidied everything up. He really had no idea what to say. And so he adopted that state of busy indifference assumed by butlers on witnessing the reprehensible goings-on of their masters. He went into the kitchen with the dirty dishes and cutlery and glasses balanced on top, and dropped them into the bowl. Then he ran to the window to see whether, beyond the dense darkness given off from the wall of woodland, there was any sign of life, any possibility of salvation or any prospect that things might turn out right.

"No need to be frightened," his father murmured from the doorway.

But Sergio still couldn't or wouldn't talk. He was familiar with that speechlessness, that kind of aphasia that seized him. Deep down, it was anger. In a certain sense it was spite: "Damn, damn you," that aphasia hissed. "You've come to ruin my life. Go on then, die . . ." With his forehead against the coldness of the windowpane, he almost wanted to pass through it with his whole head. There was a comfort in that icy contact and there was a hint of ultramarine blue at that very point where the mountains evaporated into the sky. It required from him a stubbornness of mind to recognise that sky and mountain weren't all one, for in that very moment of rejection each thing seemed indistinguishably fused with everything else. As if he were peering at reality with eyes half-shut. Yet within that stupor of reason, inside that warm nest in which his reasonableness was sheltering, there was still a glimmer of that capacity for discrimination that had always been his ruin. And so that tinge of sky beyond the windows and, further on, beyond the wooded slope, beyond the black texture of the mountain and the darkness of the gorge that had swallowed up the day, made him shed a few tears.

"For me it's alright," his father murmured behind him. Sergio opened his eyes with such force that he feared he would faint, but it was just a passing moment. He told himself not to cry, and managed not to, as if he'd held back a sneeze. There outside, in the pitch-blackness, he began to see the glimmering lights of life proceeding on its course. "What have I taught you?" Pietro asked abruptly from behind.

"What?" Sergio asked in reply, as if hidden in that question, posed with such indifference, was yet another attempt by his father to snatch away all consolation. Not many years before, in the same calm voice, he had announced that his mother had come to the end of the line. "That nothing is for free," he answered at last. "That nothing is for free."

"Exactly," Pietro agreed. "You see, it explains everything . . . I mean, all of this: how you look at me, how you talk to me . . ."

"Ah, and how do I look at you?" Sergio asked, so stubbornly intent on controlling himself that he feared he would suffocate.

His father moved a few steps into the kitchen, gripped the back of a chair and moved closer so he could sit down. "Do you know how I fell in love with your mother?" he asked the silence.

* * *

And so, in the impending half-light, he began to tell the story he had preserved like a bottle of good wine kept in the cellar for a special occasion. The situation called for a matter-of-fact tone.

Sergio kept his eyes firmly fixed on all the shades of darkness on display outside the kitchen window. They were Flemish drapes, variations of non-colour, satins, damasks and velvets that changed texture according to the light they managed to absorb, sponges soaking up every quality of light.

The old man hesitated. He had no idea how many times he had tried to find an adequate form of words, an appropriate beginning for what he was about to tell.

He began by describing *where*, a garage converted into a private rendezvous – a club, as it was then called. It was the late 1970s, and the walls of the room, five by four, were plastered with egg boxes as sound-proofing, to make sure the blast of all that diabolical music could not be heard outside. It was here he spent his afternoons after school, mangling the words of Procol Harum's "A Whiter Shade of Pale", which, though more than ten years old by then, was still an essential piece for cementing the first feelings of love or for ending affairs that just a few hours before had seemed everlasting.

A homemade spacecraft.

Pietro had spent the whole of his adolescence there . . .

And so he was swallowed by the darkness. Eaten alive. When the tired sun disappeared behind the sharp set of mountain teeth, the jaws closed. And it was darkness.

The thaw – so soon? – had made the clearing resonate with a continuous lapping of streams and trickling water. Winter, taking its leave even though it was still only the end of January, dripped from the branches and oozed from the rocks. And a myriad of expectations were there ready to emerge and take form all around, when, instead of that greenness streaked by drifts of snow still unmelted in the shade, there would be a single, uniform expanse of daisies in flower. And when that solitary trickle would be replaced by the busy hum of pollinating insects.

To don Giuseppe or Emilio Frari, as he used to be called long ago before becoming a priest, all this still seemed incredibly surprising, as if that daily cycle of death and regeneration was not yet sufficiently repetitive to be taken for granted. He had always thought like this in relation to everything. And so when people start taking something for granted, when they stop being surprised, when they stop being children or being on the alert, then it means they have reached that stage of life when one thing is much the same as another. He instead adhered to the parable of the wise virgin who keeps her lamp well charged to lighten the doorway. Pondering this and other matters, he left the A22 to Trento and began to negotiate the series of bends which, led to Sanzeno and, from there, to the Sanctuary of San Romedio.

That was the place, well known to everyone, from which shuttle buses would soon drive pilgrims as well as tourists – the two, don Giuseppe thought, were often confused – to admire the cluster of buildings, five churches linked by a stairway, and to pray to the patron saint. Now that this incomprehensible thaw was making the narrow roads, which twisted like the wires of headphones, passable again, the car park below the sanctuary could be reached even in a small car with poor acceleration such as his. There he was, driving as though nothing were amiss, keeping the doors of anxiety well shut. For there was no reason to fear the worst, since what he feared might have happened could not have happened. Certainly, everything under the sun, and more often under the moon, had come to pass. Certainly mankind, as the bishop had said in his homily just a few weeks before, was whirling in a kind of boiling cauldron, incapable of stopping to think. He, however, wanted to stop to think things through, to put the possible before the impossible and the expressible before the inexpressible, and in that way not to feel concerned.

Then, without knowing it, he slowed down, taking his foot off the accelerator, and felt the car continuing to climb but as though the wheels had partially sunk into a muddy ford. Outside, the landscape was dazzling under the raking caress of the disappearing sun. The branches of larches whistled, shaken by a light wind that skimmed the tops. Some late visitors who had taken their children to the bear enclosure were coming towards him driving with that act of faith needed when negotiating narrow stretches.

Don Giuseppe steered across to the right, taking up the last available inch of road. The car approaching from the opposite direction did the same to the left and they slid past each other, almost touching. Then he was alone for the whole uphill stretch, where the road seemed to cut straight through the vegetation, with the military order of the orchards giving way to the disorder of pine and spruce trees . . . before returning to meadows. That same innocuous grassy mantle which, scholars say, contributed towards the extinction of the dinosaurs. He was calm, taking the bends with care, as though he had someone with him who suffered from car sickness. But he was alone and unnaturally calm. Which made him fear the worst. For he, don Giuseppe, knew himself only too well and how his synapses worked. He knew exactly what his mind was telling him, whether his whole body was in a state of agitation or stuck in a kind of blank fixity. And right now he felt calm precisely because he didn't want to give in to panic. Only a few hours before, just as he was closing the doors of his church, a woman he knew well had appeared and asked to confess. The confession had lasted less than five minutes. She hadn't even waited for absolution but had vanished before he could do anything or give any kind of response.

"Can it happen again?" was all he had asked.

But there was no reply since she was no longer there.

He had leaned out and, from the corner of his eye, saw her leaving through the church door.

What had been revealed to him was terrible.

And so he had driven off towards San Romedio. For even in moments of surest certainty there is always a gnawing doubt: one that was working its way into him as he drove his car through the dense woods.

"What has she done to him! What has she done to him!" he kept repeating to himself as the city lay behind, waiting for him. It would still be there, in the same place, on his return.

Listening now as he muttered to himself, he remembered how as a child he had tried to give a name to the many things he couldn't explain. Those were strange times, filled with expectations followed by disappointments, with everything appearing as though simply known: the setting sun, the frosty globe, the supple leaf, the shimmering sky, the tremulous line of the horizon, the song of water ... Everything, everything suddenly proved wondrous. Rationally miraculous, like something about which we know everything without realising it. That was the essence of his vocation. The reason for his anxiety, but also the source of every consolation. Being born into the world had not been meaningless if the ordinary could be judged as extraordinary, if everything could be seen as a miracle, the unexplainable explainable, the unaccountable accountable and the illogical logical.

For this reason, all of a sudden – was it now day? – he felt completely calm and looked at himself as if the man at the steering wheel was a complete stranger who could be looked upon with indifference as one of those people who were not made for thinking but only for devouring every second of existence. Evil had now revealed itself in its imperturbable obtuseness. And he made those words "What has she done to him!" seem like some form of weak barrier against the flood of plain facts.

No-one could know better than he how what had been revealed in the confessional could fall within the category of the thinkable. It was a confession with no possibility of correction and with no consolation. It would make anyone shudder, thought don Giuseppe as he looked at himself in the rear-view mirror. And indeed he could see himself shuddering.

Meanwhile the inextricable tangle of woodland had finally opened out and the upland meadows were ringed by the very last light of the dying day.

Once he had spotted the place, he switched on his indicator and pulled across to the left, even though there had been no-one to signal to. He stopped and got out of the car. The sky had turned purple, ready to plunge into absolute darkness, and the grass had lost its lustre, changing into the grey coat of an old wolf. He walked a few paces before turning to look up at the sanctuary. The top of the slender bell tower reproduced in miniature the immense pyramidal roof of the fifth church, the highest point of all. He took another few steps forward, wading ankle-deep into the tall grass, then turned once more. The celestial sphere was now pitch-black except where the sun had skimmed the mountain tops, and soon the stars would appear. He had to walk as far as the point where only the tips of the roofs could be seen. A few steps further on and he was back among the dwarf pines and mountain rhododendrons. There, vaguely, he began to sense the vibration. He walked on for a few minutes among the twisted shrubs and finally reached the clearing. Nothing more than a corridor two and a half metres wide and three long, completely bare, and at its centre a heap of dry leaves, which the thaw had polished and made waxy.

He was surprised to be panting by the time he got there, so much so that he had to bend double, flexing his knees, to catch his breath. Now, from the persistent noise of the undergrowth, the vibration grew ever stronger. Following it, he stepped forward to a pile of dead leaves and soil and, kneeling, stretched his arms out towards it. A kestrel screeched overhead as if to warn him that there could be no turning back from what he was about to do. But don Giuseppe ignored it. The vibration persisted. It was enough to brush away the surface layer of leaves and soil to free the child's face. It seemed still to be breathing and about to reproach him. The body was unblemished, for the intense cold had not permitted any corruption. But now, with winter receding, animals would be coming to feast.

"Michelangelo," don Giuseppe murmured, trying to unbury him like an Antigone in reverse. "Michelangelo."

The child had an obsidian gaze, as though he had tried to cut a hole in the layer of earth and leaves that covered him. He had presumably been rearranged in the pose of a recumbent effigy with hands on either side. The vibration came from his right hand. It came from a mobile phone, dry and in perfect working order. Don Giuseppe slipped it out, encountering no resistance, and pressed the green button.

"You took your time, Emilio, I was about to hang up."

"Why?" was all that the priest asked, refusing to consider the absurdity of the situation in which he found himself.

"You know why," came the answer. "You know very well." Don Giuseppe shook his head as if that person could see him. "Oh yes," the voice continued, as though his interlocutor could actually see him. "And now what do you want to do?" he asked.

The priest dropped the phone, almost as though it were scorching hot. Night was drawing in around him. Pitch darkness fell before he had realised it. The corpse of Michelangelo Ludovisi could surely see him from beyond that darkness, which was the protraction of the nothingness into which he had been exiled at the age of eleven. The shrubs nearby began to rustle, for creatures real or supposed were assembling in that night of awakenings, sensing the anxiety of humans and attracted to them as by a refreshing stream.

Don Giuseppe stood up, unable to think of any possible solution however much he wracked his brain. Maybe the best thing was to return to the car and find help. But then: how could he explain?

The phone on the ground started vibrating once more. Don Giuseppe closed his eyes, deceiving himself for an instant that it was all a nightmare in the literal sense of the word. And yet it wasn't. It was happening. It had happened. He felt the phone vibrating at his feet and stamped on it with the heel of his shoe until it fell silent. He pressed the outside pocket of his jacket to find his cigarette lighter, taking just enough time to think he had never managed to break that accursed smoking habit. In that total darkness the flame produced the effect of a torch inside a cave. Michelangelo Ludovisi's gaze now glimmered as if caught by a fever of reflections. Then the lever grew too hot and he had to release it. The flame went out and he was swallowed by the darkness.

His eyes sprang open, exhausted by the absolute truth of his dream. He had gripped the steering wheel so hard that he had hurt his hands. Gaia mumbled something from the place next to him in the double bed. Don Giuseppe sat up with a jolt. He looked at Gaia, then at the luminous face of the alarm clock on the bedside table. We've fallen asleep, he thought, but didn't yet say it. Gaia didn't seem at all worried.

"We've fallen asleep," don Giuseppe said. His throat felt tight.

Gaia looked at him with a smile. She was dishevelled and naked. He too was naked, but with a body fatally handsome, marmoreal. He pressed his flat stomach, as if trying to recognise himself, but couldn't. His eyes sprang open.

He sat up, sliding his legs out of the bed, and noticed his erection. For some time it had been difficult to fight it. He looked around in the simple solitude of the modest room. The other side of the double bed was undisturbed. The cold darkness of a sudden awakening in the very middle of the night. He looked at the time on the face of the digital clock, a present from his parishioners years before: how could it still be two o'clock? He felt hot, perhaps he'd been woken by the central heating set too high. He removed his pyjama top, leaving his T-shirt, his advancing years revealed by his body's flabbiness. As if from thirty onwards its fibres, muscles and epidermis had given up the fight. Right in front of him, on the other hand, Nicolò Ludovisi seemed untouched by time – fit and nervous and waiting for don Giuseppe to notice him.

"How did you get in?" the priest asked, noticing how the temperature outside the blankets was beginning to drop.

Ludovisi didn't reply but instead inflated his chest and tightened his fists. "You cannot," was all he said, making those abrupt words, while not uttered as a threat, seem dangerous.

"Cannot what?" murmured the priest, to play for time more than anything else. Then he let out an uncontrolled laugh, for the funny thing was that he knew perfectly well *what* he couldn't do.

His eyes sprang open.

Fire

If you fled, the Earth would be unthankful; the animals, enemies to each other; the sun, baleful fire.

UGO FOSCOLO, *The Last Letters of Jacopo Ortis*

Vulcan has no father. He is a fiery divinity, though not bad-tempered. His fire burns with measure. He is often regarded as the Roman version of the Greek Hephaestus, but this is arbitrary and a form of, so to speak, academic prejudice. Conventions, of course, often simplify matters, but sometimes they can make them more complicated; and the conventional idea that Vulcan is the son and headstrong child of Jupiter and Juno complicates rather than simplifies. For Jupiter is not only not the father of Vulcan but, some say, might even be his son. Paternity has the characteristic of working its way into the endless game of general rules. And while maternity is beyond doubt, paternity is taken on trust, and even with a certain presumption of mistrust. This is the meaning of the words *mater certa*, around which whole cultures have formed their substance. Yet the uncertainty about fathers has made them more worthy of their task. *Pater autem incertus* is a blunt way of putting it, for sure, but children, without even knowing it, spend a great deal of time facing up to this suspicion. Every father is three fires in one: the fire of welcome, the fire of sacrifice and the fire of revenge. Children look upon their fathers in precisely these three forms: as welcoming companions to their mothers, as smoky and fleeting, and as unrelenting and punitive. Very rarely all three are seen together during the course of a lifetime. Some children grow up too quickly, and some fathers never grow up. Some expectations are so different that communication becomes impossible, while some complicities remain right up until children stop being children at the graveyard watching their fathers being buried. Finally, there are terrible, solemn declarations of war, honed over time, that provide no hope of reconciliation. Nor any feelings of guilt.

Not long after, during one of their discussions that always see-sawed between Graeco-Roman wrestling and how to prepare steak tartare with a knife, Pietro complained that his son kept bringing up what he dismissively called the sense of History but which too often turned out to be no more than a tiresome accumulation of facts and the illusion of being able to control uncontrollable events.

"I wasted my money on you," he said. "Still this business of History as life's teacher . . ."

"You didn't have any money," Sergio interrupted, recalling his father's past. "It was Mamma who had the wealth."

But Pietro Striggio wasn't one to let himself be put down by a well-aimed retort. On the contrary, he attributed his son's wit to himself. "Always harking back to History! You know, your teacher at junior school thought he was paying you a compliment when he told us that each time he asked you a question it seemed as though you wanted to make History yourself. A History all of your own."

"Perhaps if you didn't continually pretend a world exists between the literal version of things and the things themselves, you might imagine it too."

"Sorry, imagination no. Imagination is for children, when you're a parent you stop imagining. There, I've said it."

"You've said what?"

"'When you're a parent'. Just like saying 'This house is not a hotel'. I swore never to say it. And yet, you see? I've just said it."

"Hmm, this makes you suddenly like everyone else – and it's not such a bad feeling. Yet without that tinsel of History, I couldn't begin to understand where I come from."

"But is it really so useful? History, you say: your grandparents hugged each other to the *Cumparsita* tango, your mother and I to Procul Harum, and what do you hug your girlfriend to?"

"Recently? Björk or Sam Smith, I'd say."

"Ah, and they're famous?"

"Very famous, I'd say."

"Do you always have to say 'I'd say'?"

"I don't know, do I always say it?"

"Yes, always."

"Do you fancy a pizza tonight?"

"I'm happy with anything, you know I eat anything."

"I thought you'd have to follow some special diet."

"Nonsense: I've got a tumour in the brain, not the stomach."

Pizzeria Vulcano had pretensions of elegance. The pink Formica finish was vaguely reminiscent of Procuratore Susini's hair dye, and the chairs were heavy, as though the owners wanted to be sure that none of their customers could shift them about or walk off with them. Sergio, as usual, chose a table from which he could see the wood oven. Here, he had told his father, they did the best pizza in Bolzano. Striggio senior had ordered a simple pizza Margherita. "Because," he declared, "a Margherita tells you everything." It was clear he was pretending to heed his son on the question of excellence. And it was clear that he would make the most of it.

"Anyway, to talk about a pizza being the best in Bolzano is a bit of a mystery," he reflected, casting a clinical eye over the steaming plate a waiter had placed before him. Sergio, who had ordered a pizza with capers and anchovies, made a first cross-shaped cut. Vulcan's titans meanwhile, white with flour, worked busily at the mouth of the oven. "It would be like saying in Campania: you'll eat the best canederli in Posillipo," Pietro mused, and began slicing up his pizza.

"It would be a remarkable step forward in our relationship if you could manage to spend just half an hour without saying anything directly or indirectly racist," Sergio said with just the right dose of nonchalance.

Pietro Striggio remained silent at first, as though there were no need even to take note of his son's sermon on political correctness. Then he set to work on his Margherita. "Let's taste the best pizza in Bolzano," he said, before placing it in his mouth.

"You could have ordered canederli, of course!" Sergio snapped.

"You were so enthusiastic about the pizza," Pietro replied with an air of pure innocence. "Racist?" he asked blankly after a while.

"Racist," Sergio confirmed. "You've always had this way of making whatever you say seem racist. I think it's the way you say it."

"Ah," said the other. "Like saying that Negroes, sorry, blacks, have rhythm in the blood?" he asked, amused. Meanwhile he took another slice.

"Very funny."

"Humour, my boy, has never been your strong point . . ." he said with his mouth full.

"I spent a large part of my childhood trying to cope with yours."

"Oh yes? So you're saying you wouldn't have entered me for the father of the year competition? That was obvious. But there was no chance of getting you to laugh."

"Whereas it was very easy to get me to cry."

"You played the sissy. It was your mother, I'd say."

"Perhaps I actually was a sissy."

Pietro paused for a long while, staring at his son. Then he returned to his meal. Sergio waited for some response that didn't come.

"You enjoyed winding me up, you always cheered the team playing against the one I was supporting. And you kept on saying 'Now they'll score, yes they're going to score'. And the more wound-up I got, the more you kept on."

Pietro had now finished his pizza. "It was a way of keeping you under pressure," he said as he filled his glass, as if that explanation were quite enough. "You were a conceited little boy and you enjoyed making people feel inferior." He took a drink.

Sergio let his knife and fork drop on his plate. "Are you serious? Are you really telling me this crap, that I liked making people feel inferior?"

"You spent your time harbouring grudges," Pietro jibed. "I pointed it out to you, and hoped you'd have enough guts to answer back!" Sergio couldn't believe this was really his father talking like this. And his incredulity produced a heavy pause into which Pietro dropped: "Yes – I used to wind you up, but the result wasn't so bad, I reckon . . ."

"If you wanted to produce someone your opposite, then I have to agree, it wasn't."

Pietro pursed his lips as though he were about to smile, but didn't. "You're letting the best pizza in Bolzano go cold," he said.

Somehow he had managed to relieve the tension. "Fuck it," Sergio muttered, pushing his plate away and clearing a space to rest his arms on the table.

Pietro took the plate and put it on top of his empty one. "If you don't want to finish it . . ." he said. Sergio made a gesture as if to say go ahead. "How are your inquiries going?" he asked. Whether or not he was really interested in the reply was unclear. "They say this treatment blunts your appetite, but in my case they've either got the wrong treatment or the wrong illness."

"We have a suspicion about the father," Sergio replied coolly.

"Any particular reason? From experience, or just a hunch?"

"I don't know. A hunch, I'd say."

"And the evidence?"

"None. Just a feeling: he seems distant, a control freak, something of an obsessive. I'd say emotionally lacking."

"Well," Pietro said, finishing what remained of Sergio's pizza. "That might easily be a description of you, don't you think? Though not emotionally lacking – each time you saw a stray animal you wanted to bring it home."

"Yes, OK," Sergio said. "Are you saying I'm distant and obsessive?"

"I'm saying that being a father doesn't automatically make you guilty. The fact that you have something against me shouldn't influence your point of view."

"I've got nothing against you. And, actually, I know my job . . ."

"Which, incidentally, is a job I'm familiar with."

Now they were arguing over their level of competence. Like when

Sergio was eight or nine and Pietro had found himself having to admit that he would never have finished a crossword without his help. Sergio knew the names of rivers he'd never heard of, or the names of places like Brabant or Taipei, or he knew that Magyar meant Hungarian and that the Dacians were ancient Romanians, or the names of kings nicknamed 'the Short' or 'the Fair'.

"Pepin and Philip." Sergio's voice seemed to return to what it had been as a child.

"That's right, those jerks Pepin and Philip . . . those two," said Pietro, who had begun to feel his vision blurring slightly.

"There's something I have to tell you, or rather, I want to tell you," Sergio muttered, looking down.

"You mean you don't have to?"

"I mean it's something I have to say, that I've decided to tell you," Sergio continued, concentrating too much on his confession to notice what was happening in front of him.

"Something to say that regards you?" Pietro asked, fumbling for a glass of water.

Sergio kept his eyes fixed on the area of table where his plate had been. "There's a person . . ." he began. But he couldn't continue.

Pietro fell backwards in an uncontrollable spasm. Sergio jumped up to reach him. He had fallen on his back, overturning the heavy chair, with his legs in the air, like the monument of a legislator seated on his bench, toppled during a revolution . . . Before he closed his eyes he had enough time to notice the horrendous cavern effect of plaster stalactites on the ceiling, and the mouth of the oven gaping open as if to accept human sacrifices. To Sergio it seemed there was something powerfully heroic about this man who had just collapsed. Defenceless, though not passive, he was still not someone you could take advantage of. A woman who had been eating a few tables away came up: "I'm a doctor," she said. "Give him some room. Call an ambulance." Then she bent over Pietro's body, pressed two fingers to his jugular and checked that it wasn't his heart. A few minutes later the blare of a siren could be heard in the distance, and the car park of Pizzeria Vulcano was lit by the flashing lights of an ambulance.

* * *

(NO GOOD . . . I DIDN'T GET TO TELL HIM

☹

HE'S ILL

☹ ☹

WE'RE HERE AT THE HOSPITAL

SHALL I COME?

NO, I'LL COME TO YOU IF IT'S NOT TOO LATE

OK, HOW ARE YOU?

OK, HE'S BEEN HERE AN HOUR . . .

ILY

☺

SOMEONE'S HERE, THEN I'LL TELL YOU . . .

OK, SEE YOU LATER)

* * *

A short, skinny female doctor had come to find him in the waiting room of the intensive care unit. Now that they were standing in front of each other, Sergio realised how short she was and had to tilt his head to look her in the eyes. Her name was printed on the label attached with a metal clip on her right breast pocket: DR. M. DERIU, ONCOLOGIST.

She fixed him with two deep-black eyes. "Striggio?" she asked. Sergio nodded. "The prognosis is not good," she said, though from Sergio's face she must have realised this was no revelation. "Glioblastoma multiforme, pretty extensive," she added.

Sergio thought how the first difficult words he pronounced when he wasn't yet two years old were "satellite-dish". Then there was the time, at the age of four, when he was totally besotted with the word "obsolete". He used it constantly, correctly and incorrectly: these trousers are obsolete, that film is obsolete, and so forth. "How long?" he said, struggling for words, the same as any relative of any terminally ill patient anywhere in the world.

"Difficult to say for sure," the doctor replied, knowing from experience that this is always the first question: how much time? "Not long, I'm afraid – excuse the bluntness, but I think it's the best way, especially as you need to be prepared."

"Be prepared?" Sergio repeated, playing the part of the idiot he had always detested in all the hospital dramas he had watched sprawled across the sofa with Leo. Every series of "Grey's Anatomy" of the last few years was distilled into those words and that blunt question. Perhaps hospital waiting rooms limit any capacity to appear linguistically equipped.

"We need to proceed with pain-control therapy. It will affect his sleep: narcolepsy or total insomnia: echolalia or pornolalia . . ."

"Yes, yes, of course." Sergio wondered why the hell it mattered to him that the doctor thought him worthy of her esoteric language. She was like the Sybil who looks into Oedipus' eyes and says what cannot be said. Did he want to give her the impression that he regarded her terrible predictions as merely the expression of a well-established repertory? Like a tragedy he had witnessed a thousand times as a spectator and which, thanks to those specific words – glioblastoma, pornolalia – was kept at a substantial distance from life.

The doctor could see he was scared. "In forty-eight hours we'll have him temporarily back in shape. But for now he has to rest."

"Can I see him?" he asked.

"Of course. Follow me."

Sergio's mobile began to buzz. If the doctor had heard it she gave no sign, apart from quickening her pace a little in the direction of a darkened corridor. The mobile buzzed again, and Sergio ignored it again. At last they arrived at a small lobby with three identical doors. The elfin doctor pointed to the right door before heading off towards the common area for doctors and paramedics.

Pietro was the only patient in a three-bed room. He seemed to have completely recovered.

"I don't like this illness. Rather than sending me gaga, it makes me sharper, more brainy," he said without waiting for Sergio to get close enough to the bed. "You know how I realised something was wrong?" he continued. Sergio looked about: the room was the quintessence of the impersonal. "About a year back, I was doing the crossword and managed without any hesitation to get the answer to seven across, four letters: springs from the mountains of Karwendel. Isar, I say to myself."

Sergio had decided at last to position himself, neither standing nor sitting, resting his buttocks against the window ledge overlooking the hospital car park. "It was stored in your memory," he said. "That's a fairly common clue, you also find it as: river of the Tyrol, or: flows through Freising . . . who knows how many times you'll have seen it?"

"Lots of times, of course," Pietro agreed. He was talking with such clarity that Sergio realised his voice had been slightly slurred until then. "And not once did it come to mind. That was how I was: someone who couldn't remember the shitty river Isar. And now? You know, I've decided to stop this treatment – it's better to die. I don't want to carry on living with all this lucidity," he said, as though the decision to die would automatically put things right.

Sergio breathed in more than was necessary. His mobile began to vibrate once again. "Papà, the question here is not so much living longer, but dying better," he said in the gentlest way he could find.

Pietro sniffed to drive away a tear that was welling inside. "I'd like to be able to die without having to rummage about, even just occasionally, in my memory files. There's so much stuff that I really don't want to find again. You ought to know: you had the habit of holding on to everything, but you had great difficulty finding anything in that chaos of yours."

"It wasn't chaos," Sergio protested, getting back on his feet. "I had a theory that things must naturally find their own place."

"You thought that if you left a pair of socks under the bed then, in time, they would find their 'natural place' inside the washing machine.

And you used to say that if they didn't do so then clearly they weren't yet aware of being sufficiently dirty. Well then, I can tell you officially now that there wasn't a single time when that decision was made *motu proprio*: it was always your mother who dealt with it."

They laughed.

"Socks have a limited capacity for self-analysis, this we know . . ." Sergio mumbled, attempting to contain himself.

"Like certain adolescents I have known: we had to draw mental maps to point you to the shower. Your mother used to say it was the hormones, but I'm sure it was more simply underpants stained with piss and skid-marks, bad breath from a toothbrush allergy and armpits in which mussels could have been farmed . . ."

"It was a cry for help . . ."

"Help for us, every time you came near, you mean?" They laughed again. And it was as if there had been a sudden alignment of planets, a rare conjunction. The room had become the galaxy in which phenomena were being witnessed that only occurred at intervals of centuries. Pietro started coughing. "In the pizzeria you mentioned a person," he said. "Will you introduce her to me?"

It was the only really perfect moment that Sergio could identify in his whole relationship with his father. The only moment in which he felt equal: neither superior or inferior. The awareness of imminent death, a presumption of course, since we are all dying, had finally shown that they belonged to the same species. There was no doubt about it, that beast the tiny dark-eyed female doctor had called "glioblastoma multiforme" already had in its name all the characteristics of something elusive, unpredictable. In all probability it would attack the visual and olfactory organs, reducing the body to a doubly blind mass – unable to see and with no chance to hone the ability of any other sense. In practical terms it was a beast that took everything for itself. Sergio's phone buzzed again. Pietro closed his eyes. The surrounding silence was the result of a feverish activity: rustlings, chirpings and pulsations. Although inside, the silence was the unmistakeable silence of the open countryside.

And civilisation was none other than a reproduction *in vitro* of what already existed. Now, in that precise moment of solidarity and affection, the cardio-respiratory machines, electrical switches, automatic shutters, photoelectric sliding doors, the squeaking wheels of doctors' trolleys, the physiological flow of the tubes of intravenous liquids, the microscopic tug of the butterfly needle entering the vein and the drip of the dispenser . . . all this imitated the sound of skylarks, grass snakes, wild boar, wolves, a breeze through branches, deer drinking water . . .

"Why don't you answer?" Pietro asked.

"It's nothing," he said. "Official business."

"Then you should answer," his father added. "I have to rest, you go home."

* * *

Alone in the car in the half-empty hospital car park, he took a look at his phone. Leo had called and left several messages with a meticulous care that was out of character, as if aware that something extraordinary was going on not far away. He had the sixth sense of those who become insecure when something happens to their lover. Leo, he thought, would never have asked him to change one tiny part of himself. He had known Sergio restless so became suspicious when he seemed calm. He had known him reticent so became frightened when he felt he was being completely open. He had known him apparently indifferent and expected him to keep that appearance intact. That call of his and the banal messages, such as HOW'S IT GOING? or THEN YOU'LL COME HERE? or I'LL WAIT UP FOR YOU, were none other than a plea not to let himself be taken in by change. I READ SIGISMONDO MALATESTA ran the last message – the one that had caused his father to react.

The night was spread out over everything. A difficult night, with nothing to inspire poetry. Sergio dialled a number.

"Yes?" came a surprised voice.

"Have I woken you?"

"No."

"It's not too late, is it? You know, I've lost track of time."

"I lost my sense of time just after my twenty-fifth birthday. What's going on?"

"That beer?"

"What beer?"

"The one you keep offering me. It would go down nicely now."

Elisabetta Menetti snorted as if she didn't know whether to put the phone down or burst out laughing. "Cocky bastard," she said.

"It's been a tough evening," he explained, "and I have the feeling that things ought to be done without too much thought."

"And when do you men ever think before doing things?"

"When you say 'men' what do you mean?"

"I mean like you."

"Ah, and those like me, what are they like?"

"Blackmailers? Childish? Mummy's boys? Two-faced? Take your pick."

"I'll take them all."

"There, exactly what I meant."

"The beer?"

"You're in Bolzano, Striggio. And it's almost one in the morning. You really think anywhere has stayed open just for you? I've some beer in the fridge."

Striggio hung up and started the engine. His phone buzzed again.

1453

On the dialogue with Sigismondo Malatesta about the refurbishment of the church of San Francesco in Rimini

* * *

The commission was to refurbish the old church of San Francesco and make it into a cathedral worthy of Sigismondo Pandolfo Malatesta, defender of the faith and lord of Rimini. At the time he was vicar of His Holiness the Pope, who summoned him to arms without fail whenever an enemy appeared. He led the troops of the Serenissima against the Ambrosian Republic and against Francesco Sforza. He routed the Ottoman infidels. He drove Alfonso V of Aragon from Tuscany on behalf of Florence and to the lasting detriment of the Sienese, making two deadly enemies for himself in one stroke. He always slept with his weapons, they said, and they also said he was so busy fighting elsewhere that he neglected the war looming in his own territory with his sworn enemy and neighbour Federigo da Montefeltro. So he set about fortifying his state with the construction of fortresses in Rimini, Verucchio, Gradara, Mondaino, Montefiore, San Leo, Montebello and Santarcangelo – all places where the name *Malatestiano* would survive longer than the family itself.

Like his enemy, he commissioned Piero della Francesca to portray him in profile so that the difference would be clear: flowing hair against arid bristles; and a sharp, pensive profile against the coarse and craggy features of the other.

The church of San Francesco was where Sigismondo used to pray and ask for blessing. He knew he had too many enemies but felt sure that God was at his side and had placed his immense hand upon his breast to instil courage. And so, for himself and for his church, he thought of a protective suit of armour – a great, new, dazzling cathedral to enclose the old one. Which served him as a reminder that not all that is new need necessarily destroy the old; and what is new often looks newer inasmuch as it embraces and clothes the old. Just like the armour that permanently covered his body or the pleasing idea of a casket that preserved sanctity within. The new church would be of white marble, designed and blended with rounded arches and surmounted by a colossal dome – like Mother Church embracing her favourite son. But men's fortunes change, and the past is often the lens through which the future is shaped. Three events followed one another: Sigismondo was excluded from the signing of the Peace of Lodi at the insistence of the King of Aragon, who had not forgotten the insult of Piombino; Enea Silvio Piccolomini, from Siena, was elected to the papal throne with the name Pius II; and Federigo da Montefeltro was elected papal vicar. Works on the new cathedral were moving slowly, and it was in this moment that Sigismondo arrived on site:

"Messere Alberti," he says to me, "you have dedicated this cloak to me, have you not?" I nodded yes, of course. "Well then," he continued. "This caparison has to be changed. You may notice that I no longer wear the papal insignia, which the Sienese vicar of St Peter has now handed to my enemy Montefeltro . . . I therefore order that this building be the true and final robe in which I dress myself, and I order that instead of a cathedral it will be known as a temple – my home – with no crosses or saints but only shrines to myself and those who have loved me and are thus worthy of sharing this my resting place. Finish it, Messere, finish it for your glory and for mine."

"But with respect, I must remind Your Lordship that, without the promised funds, the works cannot proceed . . ."

Sigismondo smiled.

"And so be it, leave it unfinished then, forever . . . Messere, forever . . . So they can say that even what I left half-finished on this earth was more splendid than many of the works that others have completed."

And that was the last time I saw him.

The digital alarm clock said three twenty-five. Sergio tried to slip out of the bed without waking Menetti.

"What are you doing, creeping off with your shoes in your hand?" she said just to show that, even if she seemed asleep, she wasn't.

Sergio should have told her it was very late, but said more simply: "It was a mistake." Now that he didn't have to worry about waking the Chief Inspector, he began to dress in haste.

"I suppose so," she said. "But it was a nice mistake."

"Listen . . ." he began, pausing just as he was about to put on a sock. Then he changed his mind. "Forget it . . ." he said. And stopped.

Elisabetta Menetti sat up in bed and fumbled for her cigarettes and the lighter on the bedside table. "We're not engaged and I won't be forcing you into a shotgun wedding," she joked after the first drag. "About the condom, you needn't worry. I've checked my app: I'm not ovulating."

Sergio was working out to himself how far the situation he had got into could be considered finished once he was out of there. As a child he had always thought that what has ended no longer exists. Tomorrow it will no longer be there, he told himself, for mistakes are events that self-destruct when they end. They were mistakes just as long as they were happening, which is why they could be called mistakes. But everything correct stayed boringly in place and, what is worse, had consequences. As if to say it was impossible to leave them behind. For some people it was exactly the other way around: the mistakes remain, but nothing else does. Or in other words, a person can be virtuous their whole life, but one single mistake wipes out that whole drawn-out virtue. "That's good news," he said quietly. "Weddings and children cost a hell of a lot. And anyway, I'm gay."

Menetti let out an expletive. "Whoever would have guessed," she said.

"In the office no-one knows, it's not something I care to talk about."

Menetti tossed her head as if to shake off an insect. "Fine," she said. "But before you rush off, what about the Ludovisis?" It was strange how, despite being completely naked, magnificently dishevelled and half-asleep, she managed to move from intimate questions to matters of work.

Sergio gave a slight smile: "We'll put a man onto Nicolò's heels," he said, putting on his coat.

"Fanti? For a couple of days?"

"Approved." Their exchange had almost blotted out his whole mistake. All it needed was for Menetti to get dressed again and nothing, nothing had happened: no kisses, no sex. No unrequested but much appreciated macho performance. No breasts, nipples and cunt. Zero absolute. "Something simple: where he goes, what he does, who he meets . . . Tell Fanti it's not an investigation, it's just . . . to clear up a doubt or two," he said as he went to the door.

"On the TV they're talking of nothing else . . ."

"Yes," the Commissario acknowledged, though not because he had seen it: he didn't have television. But he imagined it, since two of the calls he hadn't answered in the hospital were from Procuratore Susini. "I'm off," he muttered. He had the same feeling as when, as an adolescent, he left his bedroom pleading for some form of invisibility to escape his father's comments about his clothing or his hair: "What have you got on?", "What's that on your head?" . . . Now he really did want to become invisible, he would have liked to cancel the last two hours and be able to return home in a lighter mood. "There's something else," he stammered. Menetti stared at him, she had dropped the sheet, leaving her breasts bare. "It's nothing to do with work," he explained.

"You'll think it stupid, but I'd like you to come to dinner with me and my father."

"As a friend or a fiancée?" she asked with too evident sarcasm.

"Forget it, it's not a good idea . . ."

"If it's important to you," she said. "I don't have to answer to anyone."

"He's convinced that I, well, you get what I mean? He's very keen to meet my girlfriend. He doesn't have much time left. They've said he doesn't have much longer to go," he repeated.

"I'm really sorry. Alright, just let me know when . . ." She was looking for a chemise to put on, and found it.

"I will . . . he'll be in hospital for a while . . . I'm going . . . Thanks . . ." He wished he could have walked along breathing easily and with a hint of a smile, with a warm feeling and arms relaxed, with a spring in his step and a gleam in his eye, wearing fresh clothes and with a sea breeze to ruffle them.

But he couldn't.

* * *

When he arrived at the apartment he realised Leo was still awake. He went into his room. He was sitting on the bed with his laptop on his thighs like an Egyptian scribe, eyes fully focused on the luminous screen and earphones in. He was wearing a comic printed T-shirt: a mug of beer and a slogan: EDUCATION IS IMPORTANT / BUT COLD BEER IS IMPORTANTER, and a pair of old saggy boxer shorts. Sergio stroked his shoulder to draw his attention. Leo took a little too long to look up, a sign that he had seen him come in but was pretending he hadn't. All the same, he mimed a greeting.

Sergio sat on the bed without saying a word. He thought of that afternoon in March three years before, when Leo had told him he had just been assigned to a primary school in Bolzano and he, having just completed an exam for promotion, had replied that there might be an opening for a job as a commissario in those parts. And they had planned a future together even though it seemed impossible that fate would smile on them.

And yet it had.

The move from Bologna to Bolzano had been simpler than expected. And it had been easy to let it happen. A period of such happiness that seemed undeserved. He had been taught not to trust moments that are too happy since they only serve to make us feel how unhappy the rest of the time can be. But Leo was not an idea, he was a dream in flesh and blood – his very own dream at that. The problem was that Leo understood everything about him, even what no-one else understood.

"In hospital till now?" Leo asked without removing the headphones, an indication that he was listening to nothing or what he was listening to wasn't so important.

Sergio took forever to answer. Leo continued to stare at the screen of his laptop. He was watching the recording of Depeche Mode at San Siro. They had been to the concert together. It could be regarded as the first thing they had officially done as a couple. Which said it all. Proof of Leo's extraordinary capacity to grasp situations. "It was a mistake," Sergio said. It seemed he didn't know how to say anything else.

"Leave the house keys on the shelf when you go," was all Leo said in reply, as if he was telling him there was no more milk or the light bulb in the hallway had to be changed.

"Leo . . ."

"I don't want to argue, I don't want to shout. I need to be alone. And you need to be as well." His voice was so calm that Sergio understood just how frightened he ought to be.

"No, listen . . ." he began, but without the confidence of someone who knew what he wanted to say next. He was struggling: he knew he couldn't lie, but hated being forced to tell the truth.

Leo concentrated even more on his video and began to mouth a few words of "Personal Jesus", the Depeche Mode song he was listening to.

"Don't do this," Sergio begged. It was difficult to know what was worth saving from this disaster . . .

"What do you reckon I should do?" Was this a raft in the middle of the ocean? Was Leo throwing him a rope to grasp hold of?

"You should allow me to make mistakes," Sergio said. He had understood, ever since those times when he had feared his father's glowering look, that surrendering totally defenceless to your enemy determines to what extent he is worthy of love. "I have spent most of my life doing the right things."

Leo finally turned to look at him. His eyes couldn't conceal surprise: the surprise of finding him like this. So much in pain and so beautiful. He had never been one of those attracted by the aura of pain, but maybe it was just that he had never truly seen it before that moment. He was about to smile, but held back. He was about to touch him, but didn't. He was about to forgive him, but cleared his throat. "What's wrong with doing *the right things*?" he asked.

Neither of them moved, as though in a display devised by one of those window-dressers who astonish the customers of large department stores over the festive season. There was an extraneous warmth, a shred of depression, a clarity that made them seem the subjects of a late and undiscovered picture by Hopper. What would have happened if that moment had been nothing more than a pose? How much pain could have been spared if only there had been that realism between them that makes couples into moving, even flowing, bodies. But there was the trite romanticism of dissected passion. And the tacky sentimentalism of vows. Of *forever*, of *everlasting*, of *till death do us part*. All devices that favour passion, but make people weak. Totally vulnerable, when it comes to mistakes.

"But you never know if they are right for you," Sergio declared, almost calmly. There could no longer be any doubt, now, that they had drawn swords.

"Ah, and this I presume is true if someone is alone." Leo had used the word "presume" as an exaggerated form of courtesy. Once again he was gaining ground while pretending to yield.

"What do you mean?" Sergio asked, not just playing for time.

"I mean that someone cannot say he loves a person and at the same time ask to be allowed to make mistakes." Clear, simple, straightforward.

Sergio thought that this time he wouldn't manage it. He considered every remaining possibility. He calculated the exact number of hours and minutes that separated him from the end. The rope that Leo had thrown seemed too slippery to grasp. "No?" he answered, as if he were trying to work out just how merciless he was prepared to be.

"No," Leo retorted. He gave him enough time for a reply, but it didn't come. So he continued: "We're not just friends, me and you. You're the man I love, and I'm the one you say you love . . ."

"I don't just say it!" Raising his voice was an option, or the admission of an insurmountable difficulty. "It was a mistake," he repeated. He would have gone on saying it forever, for this was what it was. An error, a miscalculation. A return to that desire for self-destruction he had learned to control when his mother had taken ill and had died, and everyone seemed more worried about those who remained than about the woman who was dying. She had lost weight and had become the shadow of herself, so that, in his father's absence, even he, who was still a boy, could carry her in his arms when she needed to get to the bathroom. He would have preferred to disappear, to burrow down inside himself, but an invisible hand stopped him and pulled him out, exposing him to a pain so fierce that it caused him to laugh. Now here he was trying again. Here he was giving in. Without even the justification of youth.

"Of course it was a mistake. But saying that doesn't cancel it out. You see, Sergio, there's a syntactic error at the base of it all." Leo now really sounded like the teacher he was. "That past tense changes everything. A conditional would have been better. Something hypothetical, my love. I could have granted you that. Something such as: 'it would be a mistake'. Is that clear?"

It was all too clear. Sergio had never imagined that lucidity and love could coexist in the same company. On the contrary, he had thought – wrongly – that they were like water and oil. He knew the blindness of love, its indomitability, stubbornness, rashness, obstinacy, atrocity.

Anything else was a gift, a holiday. To be loved with serenity seemed such an immense step to take for the one experiencing it. And now, with a monster spreading through Pietro's brain from the right membrane to the cerebellum, he felt he had to go back into that underground labyrinth where he used to seek refuge before Leo pulled him out. "He's dying. He has a brain tumour, it's terminal," he told him.

"I'm sorry," Leo said, "but that doesn't change things."

"I understand . . ."

"No, you don't understand. But if we end it here then perhaps I won't keep dwelling on it, and I won't end up thinking not only that it doesn't change things but actually instead makes them worse."

And he fell silent.

"I've let you down," Sergio said, standing up.

"Don't even try it!" Leo snapped. Sergio looked at him as though he really had no idea what had prompted that flash of anger. "I know what you're doing," he continued, trying to regulate his breathing. "You pull back until you make me seem like a shit. You grovel until you make me say stop." It was all clear. But it was equally clear that just by saying it, it became a reality. If Sergio had had any courage, it would have been the perfect moment to take him tightly in his arms, even though Leo would have pretended to want to move away at all costs. And it would have been the moment to confess what he had in mind – that stupid farce in which he was going to introduce a fake girlfriend to his dying father so the old man could die happily. But then he would have had to explain why he hadn't managed to correct his father when he had asked "Will you introduce her?" Just a moment earlier he had been about to tell him everything, and then a second later had slipped up on that personal pronoun. All blue-pencil errors: past tense instead of a conditional; *her* instead of *him*. All this he could have done. But he didn't. He did precisely nothing and instead fell silent, as he always did when confronted with a situation he couldn't resolve.

"You make things worse because you're not even doing it for yourself," Leo said coldly, just as Sergio was hoping he might be out of danger.

"So you tell me what I want to do, and why, and who for." He had adopted an authoritarian attitude which, at the Commissariato, had sometimes worked miracles.

"Don't be ridiculous," Leo retorted, thwarting his attempt. "I'm beginning to get tired."

It wasn't clear whether he was starting to feel tired at that particular moment or tired of the whole set up. Sergio had always hated those kinds of phrases that relate to a particular moment but reverberate through everything else. When his mother found a lump on her breast the doctor said: "There are cases and cases," which meant they were sailing on the waters of probability: benign/malignant, initial/terminal, metastases/no metastases; but that empty formula offered no explanation of the case in question. Like his father, who was always saying: "One of these days I'll put an end to it," without ever specifying what he wanted to put an end to: whether it was something to do with himself or the person he was talking to. And Sergio likewise. Yes, he too, who had let that *her* slip past, forcing him to inhabit the world of untruth. He, Sergio, knew something of the complexities of language and was capable of understanding them even when unspoken. In Leo's case, words were accompanied by sighs, looks and peculiar gestures – all signals that he had learned over time, in the minutiae of intimacy, to intercept. But not now. For Leo had closed up like a clam.

"Tired of us, you mean?" And the question hurtled straight as a dart towards the centre of the target.

"Tired," Leo repeated simply, for had he continued he would have ended up forgiving him. "It's gone five," he said. "I have to be at school in less than three hours."

"Yes, of course, I'm going," Sergio replied. "I'll leave the keys?" he asked, softening the question mark so that it seemed neither a statement nor a question. And he searched his pockets to check whether the keys in question were there. They were. "Shall we talk about it tomorrow?" he asked, without even stopping to notice how much pathos accompanied that question.

"Leave the keys," Leo replied closing his laptop.

"I don't know where I put them," he lied, and was caught by an uncontrollable fit of tears. So violent that he didn't manage even to cover his face. So exposed that he sought no consolation. Tears unrestrained, held back for years, forever.

Leo gazed at him in a whirl of thought. He adored even that feeling of weakness that Sergio's absence generated. That holding of breath that suffocated him when he didn't answer his messages or his calls. He adored every droplet of that absolute and marvellous anger that he felt at that moment. He adored having to forgive him. He held out his hand, and Sergio ran to take it because this was the only *person* he was referring to when he pronounced the word *person*. He was the raft, the rope. Everything.

* * *

When he opened his eyes, Leo had gone. His comic T-shirt lay lifeless on the rumpled bed, and his odour of ripe orange was everywhere. He went to the bathroom, took a shower in the still tepid cubicle. He washed himself with *his* bath foam and dried himself with *his* bathrobe. He would have put on his very skin, if he could have done. He loved him infinitely, for he had to seek his forgiveness even for the simplicity with which he had been forgiven.

Outside it had begun to snow. Silent, muffled by the sealed double-glazed window, an aeroplane streaked past. That milk-white sky, that infinite expanse, was a sheet on which every extraordinary being could have been drawn. Are we worthy of the sky? he wondered incongruously. Before we deserve the sky we have to deserve wings. How is it that such magnificent creatures, perfect in everything, do not have them? That's the reason they invented dragons, hippogriffs, aeroplanes. And angels too. Even Superman. Who, now he thought about it, was perhaps the very first man in his life. It was enough for him or Clark Kent to put on a pair of glasses for everyone to think they were someone else. Which explained how disfiguring glasses were once thought to be. And yet they demonstrated that Superman knew how to be a superhero and at the same time coped perfectly well with the problems of wearing glasses. But Sergio was no super-hero – not even close. He had worn glasses until he was seventeen because, they said, he was too young for contact lenses.

Right now his right lens was hurting, probably because he had been crying, and he could no longer feel the left one because he had been asleep – or rather had passed out – without removing them. An exhausting sleep that made him prone to sentimentality and lengthy contemplation.

Now for example – wrapped in Leo's bathrobe, with his bare feet firmly planted on the ground, square in front of the window that sealed and insulated the room as though a spaceship or the cabin of a great transoceanic aircraft, with all that expanse of compact sky – he was overtaken by events and incapable of doing anything more than making spontaneous associations. Sky, aeroplanes, dragons, hippogriffs, angels, and his first real erotic emotion on film: Superman, Christopher Reeve, who tears off his shirt while still wearing his glasses.

His mobile buzzed:

ALL OK?

YOU ARE MY ANGEL, YOU KNOW?

BECAUSE I LET YOU SLEEP?

FOR EVERYTHING . . .

DON'T OVERDO IT ☺

Gaia Ludovisi took some time before deciding to answer. Commissario Striggio was about to knock again and had raised his fist to do so when the door opened, as if in surrender. Appearing in the gap between the door and its frame she looked more annoyed than surprised. An expression that Sergio had learned to recognise. "Have we woken you?" he asked as mildly as he could, and with no hint of surprise, even though it was late afternoon. Elisabetta Menetti, standing behind, looked over the Commissario's shoulder so that Gaia could see her.

"What is it?" she asked, trying to straighten her hair, thinking it might be in a mess. Gaia Ludovisi was strangely beautiful. She was one of those women whose beauty becomes apparent only after a few moments; and she had a way of carrying herself that was deceptive at first sight, easily mistaken for sloppiness, but which, after a while, expressed a kind of classic sobriety. Her hair, despite what she might have felt, was tidy and gathered into a short ponytail.

"We'd like to have a look at your son's bedroom." From among the various options, Striggio had gone for the direct approach. He felt the woman was trying hard not to fall to pieces. "There might be some clues that will help us find him." And he felt pleased he had made it sound as if the most likely possibility was finding Michelangelo Ludovisi alive.

"What do you mean by find him?" Gaia asked, having obviously construed Striggio's words differently.

Sergio drew back slightly. "I mean: to find him and bring him back home," he said, though he knew he hadn't sounded entirely convincing.

"You remember Chief Inspector Menetti?" he said, moving to one side so that she could see her properly. Gaia remained silent. "So, may we come in?" the Commissario asked.

"Michelangelo's room, yes . . ." Gaia said, more to herself than to them. "What are you hoping to find there?"

"Nothing in particular, and everything." Striggio now seemed resigned to conducting the whole conversation on the landing.

"It would be better if we came in," Chief Inspector Menetti suggested.

Gaia Ludovisi moved to one side and opened the door wider. Sergio and Elisabetta entered what turned out to be a much larger apartment than the building had seemed to suggest. A lobby, large enough to include a wall containing a built-in cupboard with eight doors and a shelf in contemporary style, led to a living room of some twenty-five square metres – Sergio had a habit of measuring spaces by eye – furnished soberly, though expensively, and with a taste that made it seem unlived in. In fact it seemed the most impersonal space he had seen in recent years, and Menetti thought the same: "I've seen show-rooms more welcoming than this," she muttered as they followed Gaia Ludovisi along the hallway / photo gallery that led to the bedroom area and Michelangelo's room.

* * *

Inside, it was dark. So dark that Commissario Striggio ended up bumping into a swivel armchair placed in a strange position between the door and the foot of the bed. Gaia drew back the curtains, letting in the light of the snowy day outside. Sergio had the clear impression of knowing everything about that space, despite never having been there before. It could easily have been a room in a smart B&B, sufficiently impersonal to be filled each time by the personalities of the next people – a kind of artificial blackboard to be marked with a special erasable pen and a container to be emptied as soon as the last paying guests had left.

Menetti watched him carefully. She had learned that the Commissario's expression counted as much as what he said, and sometimes more.

"Here we are," said Gaia, showing them the room in the manner of an estate agent. Then she sighed as if she found it hard to hold back the tears. "Don't touch anything or, if you do, put it back in its place," she begged. "Michelangelo doesn't like his things being touched."

"Your son doesn't have a computer?" asked Menetti who was struck by its remarkable absence.

"No," Gaia replied, without noticing the inspector's surprise. "He's not really interested in such things."

"And at school?" asked Menetti, who couldn't imagine a human being without a search engine available for every doubt. "They use it at school, they teach it, don't they?" she asked, turning to Striggio.

The Commissario hadn't heard a word. That room disturbed him. It had the peculiar atmosphere of certain Scandinavian films.

* * *

Some time back, he and Leo had watched a Bergman film from the early Sixties. It was about an actress facing a deep identity crisis, who was incapable of loving her son. A memorable film because in the first two minutes, during the title sequence, there appeared a momentary shot of a large erect penis. They had watched it online on Leo's seventeen-inch laptop, seated, as though ready for a church service.

"I have a particular theory about how to watch Bergman. 'Persona' is not child's play. First of all, you have to be very much in love," he said as he expounded his theory in apparent seriousness. "It has to be a Sunday afternoon with a thick layer of snow on the window ledge outside. And you need to have had good sex until at least lunchtime."

It was snowing, it was Sunday afternoon and they'd had sex. They laughed.

"Sounds like something fairly heavy. What happens if I fall asleep?"

"Simple. I'll wake you up."

"Yeah, simple enough."

"That sweater's too thick. For good old Ingmar there's a very strict dress code: light clothing. Heating at maximum and light clothing . . ."

"I'll have to wrap myself around you then: I'm feeling quite cold even with this on."

And Leo smiled. Then the film began, the controversial momentary shot had appeared and they had tried three times to press the pause button to freeze the image but had failed and given up.

* * *

"Commissario?" Menetti called him, as if she were frightened of some unguarded reaction.

Striggio shrugged his shoulders. He gave another look around the room. Gaia Ludovisi was exactly where she had been before he had lost himself in his thoughts. "How was his birth?" he asked point-blank.

Gaia, who had her arms folded across her breasts, seemed to tighten them further. "I can't see in what way . . ." she began, before having to accept that, if the Commissario had asked such an odd question, there must have been a reason. "Simple," she answered. As if she couldn't find a more appropriate word. "An unplanned pregnancy, but fine. A simple birth," she repeated.

"Good," the Commissario said. "It's a remarkably empty room," he commented.

"Yes," Gaia said.

Menetti took her iPad from her bag. "Can I film?" she asked.

Gaia looked at her in bewilderment. "Film?" She thought it a most unusual procedure. "I don't know," she said.

Striggio gestured to the inspector to put the tablet away. "It's not necessary. Not for now at least," he said. "Books?" he asked.

"I don't know," she repeated, as if she had only noticed the absence at that moment. "Recently Michelangelo was giving his things away."

Giving his things away, Menetti wrote down in a very conventional notebook she produced from her pocket.

Striggio nodded to encourage the woman to continue. "What do you mean by 'recently'?"

Gaia finally unfolded her arms and took a half-step forward. "I mean the last three, four months . . . In December he even got rid of his encyclopaedia. Nothing valuable, an old encyclopaedia that I had used at his age . . . But he was attached to it, he liked reading it. We were really surprised when he gave it away."

"But got rid of it to who?" Menetti interrupted.

Gaia Ludovisi looked at her, eyes fixed, opened her arms wider and eventually replied: "A Christmas bookstall, I suppose. He also took a set of clothes almost new. Nicolò told him off."

"A generous lad," Striggio commented. The woman gave him a grateful glance.

* * *

Sergio's first encyclopaedia had been in twenty volumes. His father, urged by his mother, had bought it in instalments and it had pride of place in the dining room. He could remember perfectly the weight of each of those volumes and their mutually incompatible contents.

In Volume II (Anac–Ato) the anaconda was no threat to the antelope. In Volume XVI (Pelm–Rhus) the persimmon and rhubarb were perennial and contiguous plants, but outside that volume they wouldn't so happily coexist.

In Volume XIX (Seru–Turch) he had found some famous ancestors: Alessandro Striggio, for example, the sixteenth-century composer from Mantua, not to be confused with his son, also Alessandro, who had written the libretto for Monteverdi's "Orfeo".

Just how much these men of the same surname counted in the world he was constructing in his impassioned mind is very hard to say. He himself couldn't explain the calmness he felt from the fact that what there was to know was stored there within his reach. Or rather, he could explain it all too well, but adolescence allows no respite. Children soon learn – though not from encyclopaedias – that the curse of childhood is to know more than can be put into words.

* * *

"I know you, Michelangelo Ludovisi," Striggio mouthed to himself. He had learned to understand in silence, like a Cassandra aware of the scandal of her own making. And nothing, nothing now seemed more akin to that silence than the room in which he found himself.

"Was Michelangelo worried about anything? Did he have problems at school?" Menetti asked. Striggio was jolted back from his thoughts.

Gaia replied as if it had been he who had asked the question and, looking him in the eyes, said: "Children like Michelangelo always have some problems at school."

Exactly, Striggio thought. "Curriculum too slow for him," he said.

Gaia agreed. "Between September and December we were called in four times. Not to complain but to suggest we consider the possibility of sending him to a special school." Gaia began crying helplessly, with a stream of tears running down her cheeks. She sniffed them back. "All those people outside are ready to bet we've killed our child."

* * *

She was referring to a small group of journalists who had set up camp in front of the building since morning. On their arrival, Sergio Striggio and Menetti had had to weave through them to get inside. The question was always the same: "Commissario, at what point are we in the investigations?" And Striggio, evasive: "We don't have enough details yet."

* * *

"They're just doing their job," the Commissario said. "Besides, with so little going on around here . . ." he added, regretting it a moment later when he saw Gaia's reaction.

"Do you think he's been kidnapped?"

The question was left hanging. This time Menetti exercised her prerogative as a subordinate to remain silent. "That's one possibility," Striggio said calmly. "I'd like to ask you something that might seem strange, but please trust me," he said, after a moment. "Has there been any friction recently between Michelangelo and his father?"

Gaia stared at him. "What do you mean?" she asked.

"At Michelangelo's age, the relationship with the father is important, that's all." Striggio softened his voice to a murmur. Gaia looked for somewhere to sit down. She went to the swivel armchair. "I don't know." These words were her mantra. "Nicolò works very hard and Michelangelo isn't an easy boy." Striggio waited in the protracted silence, warning Menetti with a quick gesture not to open her mouth. "On the day of Epiphany," Gaia Ludovisi finally continued, "Nicolò was cut up because he found that Michelangelo had given away his new boots. There was no way he could get him to say who he'd given them to. They were expensive, and Nicolò hates money being wasted. He has always been a good father. We have always loved that boy, how can they say the things they're saying on TV?" she sobbed. The silence was heavy enough that they could hear the snow building up outside. "He doesn't know how to react appropriately," she continued, fearing she had cast her husband in a bad light. "He's a stubborn man and gives the impression of always being angry . . ." She stopped and looked at them to make sure her words had hit the mark.

"I'd like to spend ten minutes alone in here, will you let me?" Striggio asked with what remained of his earlier soft voice.

Gaia Ludovisi jumped up and looked questioningly at Menetti, who gave her a reassuring look as if it were she who was the mistress of the house, and moved towards the door.

* * *

Alone in the room, Striggio closed his eyes. "Where are you?" he murmured. He gently stroked the leaf-green mass-produced bedspread that covered the single mattress on which Michelangelo had slept. It was so small, that bed. "Where are you?"

He was drawn to an area of wall, otherwise unmarked, which showed signs of holes, as if nails or drawing pins had been pulled out. At the right distance those holes appeared for what they were: evidence of something that had been hung, and was no longer there. Two small holes for each wall, above the headboard, in the wall by the door and the wall in front, which was almost entirely filled by a large window.

Striggio took out his mobile and wrote: "Check the plans of the house." If the sun rose in the direction of the window wall, the bed must be on the north wall and the door on the west wall. And the last wall, where the desk and the small two-door wardrobe were, was the south. For someone like Michelangelo, who read encyclopaedias and studied taxonomy, it would have been very important to calculate his exact position. As it had once been for Striggio, who had even worked out the exact latitude and longitude of his bedroom.

Those holes in the wall disturbed him. Rather than an empty room, it seemed like an emptied room. He quietly checked under the bed, searching for something that Michelangelo might have hidden between the springs and the mattress. But found nothing.

The rug was remarkably clean, the floor too. So were the curtains, of a pale apricot colour. A crescent-shaped pendant light hung from the centre of the room. A remnant from the recent past. In that room one could recognise the limbic essence of areas of transformation: childhood had been eradicated, but adolescence hadn't yet had time to impose any new character. Inside the wardrobe there were barely three changes of clothing: trousers, shirts, sweatshirts, pullovers and two quilted jackets – one of which was clearly too childish. Striggio felt the pockets and found a Nintendo cartridge.

The whiteness outside, passing through the windows and penetrating the walls, cast a strangely unsaturated light. Or rather, not a light but the precise expression of the suspension that had long reigned there. Like the tone of a Dutch painting, like the reflection of the greenness of the surrounding forests that shunned the white veil covering it. Such was that light, irksome and ingratiating, of no use in establishing fixed points and ultimately innocuous.

Those holes in the wall made him uneasy, reminding him of the iconostasis that had been part of his own childhood, adolescence and youth. Each hole corresponded with a picture that was no longer there, each picture existed in an exact sequence and each sequence had a meaning. Green, red, yellow, blue.

* * *

Gaia Ludovisi emerged from behind the door. "He's always been over-emotional. And he's sometimes convinced of things that don't exist." Sergio Striggio jumped to his feet. "I wouldn't want you to misinterpret what I've said about my husband," she added. She was tense.

"I've never been prone to misinterpretation, at least not in my work," he said, thinking at first that Gaia was talking about her husband and not her son.

That reply, which ought to have reassured her, made her even more tense. "Will you be going round asking questions?" she asked.

"Yes, of course. It's our job to go round asking questions." She stared at him with a touch of hostility. "And there are a lot of questions we still haven't asked," he added, unmoved by her expression.

"Who would have called the police after getting rid of their own child?" Gaia asked with the straightforwardness of having fully understood what hadn't yet been said. "Because that's what you're thinking, isn't it? That we got rid of Michelangelo ourselves," she said preemptively without raising her voice. She was making an observation, setting out a variable whose implication she had grasped only at that very moment.

"I'm not interested in drawing conclusions. What you have just suggested is a possibility, especially considering that it wasn't you who called the police . . ." The woman was about to say something but Striggio held up his hand to stop her. "You shouldn't talk to me. Very soon you'll be called with your husband before the investigating magistrate."

"That doesn't worry me," Gaia Ludovisi retorted. And she wanted to say that the idea the Commissario might regard her as a murderer didn't worry her either. "Bring my little boy home," she said, without pleading. She turned to go back to the kitchen.

"One more thing . . ." the Commissario added. "What used to hang on the walls?"

She made no immediate reply, but had to think for a few seconds. "Things hard to understand, belonging to Michelangelo: colours, symbols, reproductions of paintings, I think," she said, hesitating. "At some point he took everything down. When he began giving things away . . ."

Elisabetta Menetti appeared at that moment: "Fanti has just arrived at the Commissariato," she said.

"Good. We've finished here for now."

Reaching the vicinity of Laives he left the valley, and the lines of the orchards slipped away behind him. As the road gradually climbed on entering the chestnut woods, the light turned grey-green. He couldn't fail to notice it, even then, and to ponder. As if its purpose had changed: just below he had been exhilarated by the intricacy of vegetation along the riverbanks: the fragility of the flimsy alders, the pliability of the willows, the elegance of the black and white poplars. But now, on reaching the higher ground, a shadowy vagueness had blurred everything: whether tree, rock or blade of grass; whether bramble, bush or moss. It was like passing from a Vermeer to a Rothko, from Delft to the Houston chapel. The air became gradually purer. He had to close the window. He pressed the button and the window began to rise with that same humming sound as the savage hornets whose hive he'd had to destroy the summer before at San Giacomo with help from the fire brigade. The woods of oak and hornbeam indicated that he had climbed six to seven hundred metres. He accelerated until he reached the flowering ash and nettle trees interspersed with terebinth and, on seeing them, repeated their names involuntarily to himself. Next came the Schneider meadows, expanses of alfalfa and pastures dotted with larch. This was where he wanted to get to. Where he would find the signal. Where a beam of sunlight re-established the supremacy of the Flemish over the expatriate Russian Jews and formed a luminous disk among the vegetation that seemed to mark the end of a vast spotlight. He stopped, got out of the car and went to open the spacious boot. The creature's body lay bleeding on a large green tarpaulin that protected the SUV from any mess. Beyond the flat meadow, the basalt rocks formed a series of broad terraces before the wooded slope of spruce, thick as the bristles of a brush. He grabbed the shovel and walked to the spot. He began digging. A horned viper slithered between his feet. He jumped back, watched it slide away and carried on digging. When the hole was sufficiently deep he returned to the car and began to slide out the corpse holding two corners of the tarpaulin. The corpse turned out to be more resistant than passive, seemingly unwilling to leave. He gave it a tug. The inert creature fell to the ground with a heavy thud. Now he had to drag it towards the pit. The hem of his blue shirt caught in a bush. He pulled it free and continued on.

He arranged the corpse in the bottom of the hole and began to refill it with earth, shovelful after shovelful. His phone slipped out of the thin pocket of his shirt, but he would only realise this a few hours later. From his childhood he had had to learn how terrible it was to be unable to go back in time. "From the day of our birth we can only go forward, until it's all over" was what his grandparents used to say, or was it perhaps his cynical old great-aunt? He knelt down, placing his hand on the surface of the still-damp ground which had now completely hidden the hole. Externally the only sign of its existence was a darker, rectangular patch of ground. He searched for some dry leaves to scatter on top. It was an intimate burial: his creature's last home. He hurriedly brushed the dust and mud from his trousers. He banged the shovel to remove the last soil and carried it back to the car, slipping a bag over it and tying adhesive tape around the handle before returning it to the boot. Back in the car, he started up and reversed, then headed back down to the valley. It would soon be dark.

* * *

"A deer," Fanti announced. "Nicolò Ludovisi buried a deer," he repeated. He was someone who never appeared quite convinced of what he was saying, even when making simple statements such as this. Striggio stretched his legs under his desk, on which everything was piled. Elisabetta Menetti tidied her hair in an idle gesture that might easily be described as a tic. "Otherwise, nothing in particular: left home at seven-thirty, first two hours in the office, then by car from place to place . . . that guy doesn't half get around."

"For lunch?" Striggio asked.

"A bar at San Giacomo. He had . . ."

"Doesn't matter . . . he didn't go home for lunch," Striggio summed up, turning to Menetti. "What do you reckon about her?" he asked, ignoring Fanti.

"I would say pills: tranquillisers or sleeping tablets, take your pick."

"So one of them sleeps, and the other doesn't go home," Striggio noted.

"They're locals, valley people, so don't expect too much drama," Menetti said.

"Of course, but I'd still expect a minimum of collaboration."

"They are collaborating," the Chief Inspector said. "She allowed us into the house. Then she left you alone in his room, didn't she?"

"I reckon that's the absolute minimum when you think her son's gone missing, no?" Striggio replied.

Fanti had been listening and tried to attract their attention by raising his hand, like a schoolboy. "There's something else," he said. He rummaged in his pocket and took out a mobile phone sealed in a plastic bag. "It was half-buried where he had been digging. I wasn't sure what to do, so I took it."

"You think he dropped it?" Menetti asked.

"Did you see it fall from one of his pockets?" Striggio asked.

Fanti shook his head.

"So, technically it could belong to anyone."

"Technically," Menetti confirmed.

"It's a pretty cheap device," Fanti pointed out.

"Let's check whether it has a password and then we'll see what's inside. Who's on duty in Communications? But first send it off to Forensics for prints and the rest." Fanti sprang to his feet and was about to leave. Striggio called him back. "Oh, Fanti. Top priority."

When Inspector Fanti was out of the door, Menetti could relax. "Top priority?" she asked with a smile. "With all the work they have in Communications it'll certainly be a relief to be dealing with something 'top priority'."

Striggio didn't answer but set about tidying the chaos on his desk. A sudden, heavy silence fell. Elisabetta Menetti stood up. "A beer and then home?" she asked. "I mean, each to their own." Striggio looked her in the eye. "OK, forget it," she said, to break the silence, which had seemed more embarrassing than an outright refusal.

* * *

In the hospital-hive everything was buzzing. That particular hum filled every space with invisible, murmuring presences. Sergio Striggio paced the corridor towards his father's room with a sense of relief that he could spend the night with Leo. The prospect put him into an unexpectedly good mood.

Pietro was stretched out on the bedcover like those people who refuse to accept they are in bed but claim they are there in that helpless position only temporarily.

"In over thirty years of work I was off sick for about only three weeks in total," he said before his son was barely through the doorway.

"Aren't you cold?"

Pietro Striggio sighed. "You're really not interested in what I'm saying, are you?"

"You mean the fact that you were never at home?" Sergio joked.

"You've come here to argue?" There was a strong note of resentment in Pietro's voice. "Always with that know-all expression, passing judgement on your neighbour!"

Their conversation was clearly taking a turn for the worse. The doctor had warned that there might be sudden mood swings. The therapy was taking its course. For the moment it was holding the symptoms in check but as the illness progressed he would be unpredictably irritable or docile. Yet the truth behind his father's direct attack had caught him by surprise. And he had to some extent fallen for it.

"You come here and ask me if I'm cold," Pietro melodramatically declared to a vast crowd gathered before him. "I've been out on patrol in conditions that would have killed you in ten minutes, you little bugger," he hissed, looking him in the face.

They remained there eyeing each other for an indefinite time, like two super-heroes deciding whose laser sight is stronger. Until Pietro looked at him as if seeing him for the first time. "Sergio, my boy, have you been here long?"

Sergio waited to understand at what exact point he had passed from one parallel universe to the other before answering. "I've just arrived." Outside, there was utter darkness, as if they had built this human hospital deep in a well, outside the norms of high-rise apartment blocks. "You see what's happening?" Sergio mused aloud. "This place is fine in daytime, but at night it makes me anxious, it seems engulfed by total nothingness. When mother was sick, it was quite the opposite. The place was terrible during the day, but at night, on the fourteenth floor, you could see the stars."

Pietro Striggio broke into a smile. "Your mother was the only one," he said. "There were the others, of course, but what could I do?"

Sergio attempted a smile of reassurance. "Nothing, you could do nothing."

"That's right." Rather than looking for further confirmation, Pietro wanted to reassure himself. "I knew about you. I'd understood even before your mother did," he murmured after a while.

Sergio gasped, as if caught halfway through some supreme exertion and unable to fill his lungs. "Ah," was all he could say. "And you were probably aware of it even before I was."

He had wanted it to be taken as an observation along the lines that fathers know through experience what sons believe they alone are going through, but it sounded sarcastic. "Probably. Let's call it intuition," Pietro said. "There are loads of things that suddenly become crystal clear . . ."

"Like understanding, when people say 'Don't look a gift horse in the mouth', that a gift horse isn't the name of a breed?"

Pietro began to chuckle: "Good God, Sergio, that's exactly what I meant."

"And poker, for years I wondered silently who was poking whom. Instead of which . . ." He now laughed till tears came to his eyes.

Pietro gazed at him tenderly. "Those things always sent you crazy. Always, since you were a boy: you liked words, and you liked the ideas inside the words."

Sergio stopped laughing. The remark had saddened him because it meant that, in some obscure way, his father had always been keeping an eye on him. "I always thought you didn't think much of me," he admitted.

"And I always thought that after the death of your mother there was no place for me," his father replied. "Her only pain was in losing you. And I was stupid enough to think that you were responsible for it. But let's forget that, shall we? See what this bloody illness is doing? It sets things straight."

Sergio turned with his back to the door. He looked at his father as if what he had just said had arrived with a few moments' delay. "I realised that, you know . . . that you thought I was to blame."

"Confession on confession: it wasn't just an intuition . . . Just now, when I said I knew about you . . ."

"Oh no?" Sergio began to feel nervous.

"No . . . But let's leave it. I'm tired . . ."

"No, let's not leave it . . . What did you do? Did you look at my computer?"

"I've been a policeman all my life, for fuck's sake!" Pietro said. "And when I was a policemen it wasn't all a bed of roses . . ."

"Of course, not to mention your colleagues who ended up in handcuffs for armed robbery. That terrible December of 1994 . . . You've told me that story *ad nauseam* . . ."

"There we go again, back to the sarcasm . . . you've always got by that way."

"That way, how?"

"With that bloody look on your face of 'Why should I care what you say?' . . . when I was in the police, I used to eat little shits like you for breakfast. Oh yes: no-one looked on us kindly and, just for the record, neither could I stand the sight of the Bologna police back then in that bloody awful December of 1994."

"And that gave you the right to spy on me? To break into my computer?"

"To spy on you? Break in? You had the most predictable password in the world . . . GIANBATTISTAALBERTI . . ."

"Oh for fuck's sake: LEONBATTISTAALBERTI!"

"Well anyway, I must have got it right . . . And you know what?"

"No, what?" Sergio's voice veered towards a falsetto.

"Now you're angry, even if you try to make out you don't care . . ."

"Know-all, bloody little shit," he repeated, summarising what his father had been trying to say to him. Pietro stared at him as if to encourage him to continue. "Is this your conclusion after delving into the secrets of my computer?"

"If they're proved right, how could they be secrets?"

"So what did you do, sit down on the riverbank and wait for me to start putting on my lipstick and nail varnish?"

"It's this fucking illness . . . that's what it is . . ."

"Which illness are you referring to?" Sergio asked, and this time he wanted the sarcasm to be clear.

"Sergio, I'm tired . . ." Pietro seemed to give up. The machines around him suddenly seemed to hum with growing intensity.

"Yes, of course. I'm going."

"How are your investigations going?" he asked as if nothing had happened.

"They're going nowhere," Sergio retorted.

* * *

From the Lorenz Böhler Hospital, Sergio could get to Leo's house either by taxi or by walking along via Lorenz Böhler into a sprawling suburb, returning to the centre along what was the main road, which was flanked by greenhouses as far as the roundabout where via Castel Firmiano joined viale Druso. He then turned into via Resia, where the city proper began. Bolzano might seem like a surprising corner of the world: what they called a city was nothing more than a portion of tamed countryside, and what they called countryside was a portion of virtual city. There was everything, but there seemed to be nothing. For him, coming from Bologna, this was an extreme outcome, the extreme result of an austere vision of the universe. Each time he decided to go on foot, he was convinced he had ended up in the middle of a film set, so stopped being surprised about the lack of activity in that kind of immense shopping outlet that constituted the outskirts. He quickly walked the two kilometres that separated him from the first built-up areas. He left the district of the writers and musicians – Grazia Deledda, Maria Montessori, Gustav Mahler, Giacomo Puccini – and carried on, completely alone, along via Resia. After the Passaggio della Memoria, continuing towards the river Isarco, he was just a few hundred metres away from via Ortles and then via Similaun, where Leo lived.

Only when he was standing in front of the house did he realise why he had decided to go all that way on foot. A couple of cyclists passed close behind his back making him jump. Their presence, so unexpected, had caused him a kind of irritation – that of someone who had got used to the idea of living in surroundings uninhabited by human beings. And his uneasiness caused him to look back over those choices he had recently made. Deep down, what was he other than someone who pretended to follow his natural inclinations but who was hiding them instead? He too was a kind of virtual city, as if no passion were expected to dwell inside that body made for passion. It was the same with Bolzano, he thought: to be an ideal city, a place has to reject the notion that it is inhabited by people of this earth. Two weeks ago he had arrested a boy for being drunk and disorderly, a few days ago a woman for stealing from a pastry shop. Events of little importance or relevance, and yet the local newspapers had announced the arrival of bleak times: a place where some particularly rash adolescent had got himself arrested for making a noise and an old woman had eaten a zelten and tried to make off without paying. Not even the Christmas spirit had made the shopkeeper any more generous. The woman had been stopped and reported. Then, of course, there was the disappearance of Michelangelo Ludovisi. How can a child of eleven go missing? He can't. Of course not. This, according to the local papers, was the event that had put Bolzano on the list of cities that are "no longer safe". The local TV stations were filled with testimonies by those who remembered when no-one felt they had to lock their front doors. That was before youngsters got drunk, before people stole from pastry shops and before children went missing.

He rang. The door clicked and opened inwards, slightly ajar. No voice on the intercom had asked who he was.

Standing at the window, whose glass had gradually darkened as the minutes passed, don Giuseppe had watched the day draw to a close with the controlled manner of a mother of bygone times who fixes her eye on the train on which her firstborn son is going off to war. The priest's house was a meagre space and cold, even with the radiators turned up. The surroundings were cold, abounding in ugly pottery, ugly flimsy furniture and ugly, damask reproduction sofas. High up, in that same sky where saints, angels and blessed souls ought to dwell, a flashing light signalled the presence of a plane. From up there, don Giuseppe thought, the city must seem just a swarming, luminous, twinkling blob, like the Christmas lights of the year before one had pulled out of their box and laid in a tangle on the floor to check they were still working. He moved from the window as soon as the flashing light had vanished among the black clouds, went across to a small table on which there was an old stereo system and put on the LP record he had always had, belonging to his mother, whom he had never known. On it was Sibelius' "Valse Triste", played by a Canadian military orchestra in a special edition which had come as a free gift with a new colour TV purchased in instalments. It was a record with a selection of immortal pieces by Scandinavian composers: "Echoes of Ossian" by Niels Gade, "Morning Mood" from "Peer Gynt" by Edvard Grieg, "Maskarade" by Carl Nielsen, as well as "Valse Triste" by Jean Sibelius. Since childhood, this last piece had been the one he liked most. The needle on the turntable must have known it well and seemed perfectly familiar with the groove that held it. Music, don Giuseppe thought, floats along the vinyl grooves like water along river beds. The Valse began, as usual, rather tediously, with its pizzicato strings, almost out of duty or, worse, obligation. He had always thought Sibelius was one of those artists who don't need to know things in order to know them. And he was convinced, having listened to it so often, that this piece had inspired Dumont's music for "Non, je ne regrette rien" and also Gershwin's "Rhapsody in Blue". The piece continued solemnly and sadly, revealing how timeless geniuses could express themselves so prophetically. You might think on listening to it that Sibelius was familiar with the world as seen from the window of a modern aircraft, like the one that had just vanished into the darkness. In some way, and while yet having no direct experience of it, he had foreseen into what frothing wasteland the world is transformed when seen from up there.

But isn't that what artists do? he wondered.

His housekeeper, an athletic woman nearing seventy, appeared behind him. "I'll go now, I'm rather tired," she announced with that blunt but affectionate tone of intimacy grown over time.

"Of course."

"Supper's being kept warm in the oven."

Don Giuseppe nodded his head without looking round. The Valse faded out. Over the years it had grown shorter, he thought. The woman waited for the piece to end and for the needle to rub against the label at the centre of the disc. "It would be better to take something to get to sleep," she said without sounding as though she was pleading.

"The point is not that I don't sleep. So far as sleeping, I sleep," he said.

"So what is the point?" she asked, as if it were one of her prime duties to keep the conversation going.

Don Giuseppe turned towards the stereo to put the arm back on its rest. "The point is that for some time I've been getting up feeling more tired than when I went to bed."

"Days with no food, nights with no rest – it's madness," she recited.

"Yes, yes," the priest admitted. "See you tomorrow."

"Until tomorrow then," the woman said. She said goodbye as though she would have preferred to stay. "Shall I make you a camomile?" she asked.

"No, no. You go. I can manage."

"Oh yes," the housekeeper said doubtfully. "The cups are on the draining rack over the sink. I'll be off early tomorrow to go shopping, for toilet paper and bread. Anything else?"

Don Giuseppe restarted the music. The woman left, shaking her head.

The pizzicato began sluggishly, first the cellos, then the violins and, before it had reached the end, night had fallen outside the window. He pretended he still had to wait another moment, standing there just letting himself be filled with notes. As a child he had suffered from depression and this, they said, was clearest each time his body persuaded itself that doing nothing was his only course of action. He was under a spell, they said. And this before he had been channelled spellbound into the service of God. Because everything was so exact and perfect that stopping to think about it was annihilating. His own personal passion was precisely the kind of obsessive impotence that would have pleased an anchorite. Yet it was rarely granted to him since, despite often convincing himself otherwise, his calling to the priesthood had saved his life, rescuing him from his slothful and pitiless tendencies. It was his secret, his true curse, his objective: love, for him, meant having to care for his fellow beings. And having to do so despite the repugnance he felt for all fellow beings and his incapacity to empathise with all the human weaknesses he was told about each day. The Valse proceeded by itself, becoming lost in that nothingness from which everything comes and to which everything returns. The body of his breath was like an elastic depth that sent back all that he tried to swallow.

Take that confession, which had deprived him of his sleep. The revelation that had caused his nightmares and brought him back to himself. And now, disturbed by that clarity of thought, he felt a movement behind him, little more than a rustle. He had just enough time to turn round and see a silhouette against the light: "Michelangelo," he murmured, for he was absolutely certain he recognised him, even if he wasn't completely sure he was real.

* * *

The four flights of steps separating him from the entrance to Leo's apartment were lit by a diffuse glow from streetlamps shaped like flying saucers along the road. The stairwell was a cylinder of glass blocks perpetually lit even on the darkest nights. Sergio pushed open the door. In the kitchen he could hear that pointlessly emphatic or pathetic tone of voice adopted by every TV news bulletin. They were broadcasting a story about a woman mayor who had won a landslide victory thanks to a populist protest vote and was now proving unfit for office. Or rather, the opposition parties were accusing her of being unfit, while her own supporters, despite all their previous vows of transparency, were defending her to the hilt.

"I can't understand them," Sergio said.

"Huh, it was a real let-down," Leo agreed.

"Do you allow anyone in without asking who they are?"

"Yes. It's my secret fantasy, you know, to be raped by two strangers who break into the house . . ."

"Really, I had no idea." Sergio smiled. On the television they were shouting slogans in support of the woman mayor: "We're with her," they were saying. "She's honest! Those who say she's not are being funded by the communists!"

"Communists?" Sergio blurted out, truly amazed. "You have to defend yourself with complexity. I mean, by loving your own ideas so much that you can lay them open to questions." Leo was setting the table and stopped to look at Sergio, expecting him to continue. "I think it's like when you're in love: if you can't imagine hating, it means you're not yet sufficiently in love."

"You can't go round dropping bombs like that . . ." Leo smiled. "There's some rice salad."

"Pre-prepared?" Sergio asked, even though he knew the answer.

Leo didn't answer but removed the plastic film from the polystyrene container and tipped a portion into the dish. "And anyway, if the question of hating is true, it means I love you a lot."

"Excellent, that's just what you want when you get back home: ready-bought rice salad and a smart-alec boyfriend. I'll go wash my hands." He uttered the word "boyfriend" like a vegan utters the word "meat": for in both cases no alternative words have quite the same effect.

He got up to go to the bathroom and realised he hadn't yet given Leo a kiss. So he bent across and kissed him, happy to feel the tickle of his bristles. "When I start saying 'I will love you forever' it will mean I'm on the point of leaving," he murmured. After a few minutes, when he returned, he found Leo exactly where, and how, he had left him, with the vacant gaze of someone who had used the momentary pause to let their thoughts roam. The TV news announced the forthcoming constitutional referendum, which would determine how long the current government would last.

"They realise they're fighting a dangerous battle," Leo remarked, as if waking from a daydream.

"They'll fall, though," Sergio prophesied as he tackled the rice salad. "If it's a Yes vote, then they'll win by the smallest of margins but will have still lost half the country. They'll hang on for a while and then fall."

"Alright and then? I see a void."

"A void can be filled," said Sergio with his mouth full.

"Hmm, to make the most of these few moments before the fall wouldn't be a bad thing, but I reckon we won't get even that – people won't vote and we'll end up with the Seven Moons Movement."

"Why, aren't we already making the most of things?" Sergio protested, pouring himself some water. The rice salad was sticking in his throat. "We're well off big time: we eat fantastic rice salad every day, we have two or three mobile phones, social networks, a bathroom in the house, we have a hand in every war without being at war . . ."

"Sergio, people don't bother to vote any longer!"

Striggio looked at Leo, then wiped his mouth on a paper napkin. "Fuck those who don't vote, those shits can go screw themselves. In a democracy, they don't count. It's simple. How can they matter if they can't be bothered to exercise their democratic right? They deserve to lose it!" He was getting carried away.

"Yes, alright, but if everyone went to elect those they ought to elect . . . how long is it that you have had to hold your nose inside the voting booth?"

"A long time," Sergio admitted. "A long time."

"And so?"

"And so we deserve to have a civil war: to go back to fighting in the mountains, to find out what it's like to be hungry, to lose the right to education and free health care. To end up in the hands of abstainers and nutcases who plant bombs at Pompei and in the Colosseum . . ."

"Apocalyptic," Leo reflected.

"I was being provocative. These are ideas developed, encouraged and promoted by people who go electing others but make sure they look after themselves. Because democracy comes at a price: it has to be exercised strenuously day by day. Otherwise what's left is dictatorship, which is totally gratis." He gave a sigh at the end of his outburst.

"Not bad, eh?" Leo asked, referring to the rice salad. "I got it from downstairs, they've opened some kind of health food place . . ."

"It's greasy, doesn't taste like olive oil."

* * *

Nicolò Ludovisi took a last drag, the deepest one, on his cigarette. He was in the driver's seat of his SUV with his left arm out of the window. The car park at the apartment block was almost empty and badly lit. The wisp of smoke expanded as it rose straight from the filter wedged between his index and middle finger. He had only to spread his fingers to let go of the small fibrous cylinder and let it fall onto the cement. From there a still fainter trail of smoke continued to rise, seemingly intent on absorbing every ray of the misty, invasive light. Gaia's face appeared like the soft close-up of a silent movie star through the window frame. "You're not coming up?" she asked her husband.

Nicolò looked straight ahead. It worried him that there were no signs of life from the building opposite. "No movement," he said after a while. Gaia looked at him without answering. "There." He pointed ahead. "For an hour and a half, no movement. How many floors are there?" he said, and began counting with his index finger. "Eight. And no movement . . ."

"The police came today," Gaia said.

"What did they want?"

"Let's talk about it upstairs," she said, moving from the frame of the window towards the door that led from the car park to the lift. She wore a light cardigan over a velour tracksuit and trainers. She must have been feeling cold.

Halfway along the cement corridor lit by a series of neon tubes, Gaia realised Nicolò was following her. She reached the wide landing before the lift without looking back, and Nicolò joined her as she was waiting for the lift doors to open. He stayed behind her as though he wanted to stay close without venturing to touch her and they entered the lift more or less in that position. Gaia pressed the button for the third floor, theirs. "They wanted to see Michelangelo's room," she said as she walked into the house.

"Ah," was all he said. "And what were they looking for exactly?" he asked, without seeming to have much interest in the reply.

They passed through the living room into the kitchen.

"Something to help them find him. Have you eaten?" Nicolò shook his head. "There's some meatloaf. They think it was us, I reckon."

"Who thinks that?" Nicolò said as he sat down. He took a bottle of red wine that was on the table and poured a generous amount into a glass that Gaia had used a little earlier for water.

"The police," Gaia said, her voice beginning to lose control. "There are lots of things that would make me think the same, if I were one of them."

"You in the police?" Nicolò scoffed before emptying his glass. "I'm not hungry," he added when he saw his wife had brought him a plate with a slice of meatloaf.

"You look exhausted," she said, showing unexpected warmth. "Nicolò, what's happened?"

Ludovisi poured more wine, as though he wouldn't be satisfied until he had finished the bottle. "I don't know. I don't know," he repeated.

"You were horrible that evening at the Olimpo. What got into you?"

"Let's not talk about it anymore. It's not important any longer."

"But it is."

"I'm tired, really tired." His voice began to dry up. "It's better like that," he murmured. "Let's leave things as they are."

Gaia Ludovisi moved halfway round the table and, lifting her leg, stood directly in front of him, like a stripper who wants to settle into the lap of a customer in the front row. "We shouldn't be feeling any of what we're feeling right now," she said, blowing those words onto his lips.

"You've been really bad, really bad," he said. She could smell alcohol lightly on his breath. Without leaning forward he stuck out his tongue. It was Gaia who had to move closer to take his tongue as if it were a fruit. Nicolò grasped her by the hips and pulled her against him so that she could feel his erection. Gaia looked at him in the way that turned him on, with a mixture of surprise and fear. And he shook his head as if to say: you'll feel no pain, only pleasure.

He helped her slip down her pants without needing to take them fully off. And likewise she opened his zip, so that their genitals were freed and exposed. So that she could easily take him and he could penetrate her. In a single thrust. They came at the same time with an intensity that would very soon make them feel guilty. It was a long time since they had fucked like that. In the kitchen with no worry that Michelangelo might hear them, or see them.

"We shouldn't be feeling like this," Gaia murmured, feeling his penis turn limp inside her vagina.

"I'm feeling hungry. I'll have that slice of meatloaf," he said.

* * *

It just wasn't right for him to feel as good as he felt at that moment. It was this thought that always put things in their place and allowed Sergio to soften the sense of guilt that struck him, against all reason, after sex. This time there had been some horseplay and a few bites too many, which made his ritual, reactionary thought absolutely necessary.

"What are you thinking?" Leo asked.

"Nothing," he lied, knowing that it wasn't a real lie but only the affirmation of his need for consolation. He had been bad, and it was right that he should feel the weight of happiness that this badness had provoked. "Really, nothing," he repeated, leaning over to kiss him so that he wouldn't continue with his questioning. This was something that Leo stubbornly refused to accept about him. Not that they had ever spoken about it, but Sergio was convinced that when couples get along together, time sanctifies their silences as much as their words. Right now he wanted to lie there in peace enjoying the complete relaxation that follows orgasm; and he also wanted to enjoy with the same calm indifference that subtle sense of anxiety that gripped him when he had to come to terms with what, as a child, he had always heard described as "the mortal sin of sodomy". That formula now even seemed an integral part of pleasure. For what sense would sin have as a word if it didn't relate to something so fucking pleasurable? He realised that Leo was staring at him. "What are you looking at?" he asked.

"A big handsome man."

"I ought to take up running again," Striggio said, hoping that Leo would contradict him.

"Let's go together," he replied instead.

"You mean I've put on weight?"

"No, I mean I'd like it if we went running together, me and you. How did it go with your old man?" he asked just to change the subject.

"I could do with a cigarette."

"Don't even suggest it!" Leo's voice had turned dramatic.

"Don't worry. I said I could do with one, not that I'm going to smoke it."

Leo slipped his arm behind his back to hug him, resting his head on his chest. He could hear his heartbeat. "The point is that when you say something, nine times out of ten you're going to do it, remember?"

Sergio began to laugh. With one hand he stroked the back of Leo's neck. "My father's in a bad way. Things couldn't be worse, there's no point pretending otherwise."

"Sergio, I'm sorry." Leo hugged him even tighter.

"It's that bloody C-word," Sergio said, gazing up. He began to laugh.

"What?" Leo asked.

"Nothing: it's just that my father said he knew all about me."

"Meaning . . .?"

"Meaning that, being a good policeman, he hacked my computer."

"No!"

"Yes."

"He opened the gates of knowledge to the parallel world of Sergio Striggio?"

"Clever, you can joke if you want. I'm going for a piss," he said, disentangling himself to get up.

Leo watched him as he walked. He moved in a way that might be described as cocky, even arrogant, like those aristocrats who are taught from the earliest age to express dignity in their demeanour, their gestures and the way they walk. "You move like an Arab prince, has anyone ever told you that?" he called out from behind.

"More like a fucking model, I thought," the other replied while he pissed.

"I was wondering what Daddy Striggio found on his son's computer." They were skilled at keeping conversation going, regardless of distance.

Sergio returned to the bedroom, looked for his scattered clothes so that he could get dressed. "The highlight was a photomontage of Freddie Mercury with his cock out." And he laughed.

They both laughed.

"Photomontage? You mean fake?"

"No, I meant actual photomontage. Any problem?" Sergio asked as he put his trousers on.

"Are you leaving?" Leo said, suddenly turning sad.

"We're busy on this case of the little boy who's gone missing."

"How is you can never bring yourself to use the word 'child'?" Leo asked him point-blank.

"Maybe because at eleven years old you aren't one any longer, Dr Freud?"

"You know, I was thinking . . ." Leo said after a moment. "Why have you taken it for granted that the priest just happened to be there by chance? I mean, the evening the child disappeared."

Sergio, dressed now in his socks, pants and trousers, stopped searching for his shirt. "I don't know," he said, as if Leo really had pushed open the gates of a parallel world.

* * *

Nicolò Ludovisi arched himself slightly so that his wife could feel him better. She, on top of him, took his hands to make him grip her bare breasts.

"Tighter!" she urged. Then, seeing he wasn't going far enough, "Tighter!" she yelled, increasing the pressure of his hands to make him see how she wanted it done.

He gladly did what she told him, surprised by the level of pain she seemed to bear. At that very instant it occurred to him that this happiness of theirs was none other than a compensation, and that this pain that she seemed to be enjoying so much was the recognition of just how much time they had spent deceiving each other. He thrust still harder, tightening his buttocks and lifting his knees. He thrust until he felt the ache of his gland beating against her cervix. The loss of control became a kind of dance, with no rhythm at first and then gradually more and more harmonious. Now indeed every beat, every contact, every spasm reverberated deep down. Now indeed every tiny particle of their bodies was responding to a more extensive appeal. She began to yell, like a prisoner whose gag they had carelessly allowed to come loose. She gripped her husband's chest with an uncontrolled fury until her nails were digging into his flesh, ripping at his hairs, so that he too could discover what unimagined level of pain could be endured.

"Wait!" she ordered, feeling him too close to orgasm.

And he had to grit his teeth and contract his groin to try to hold back. "Aah!" he moaned. As if the sound of his voice would help him imagine he was somewhere else, outside of himself. "Oh! Please!" he begged.

But wrapped in a wordless discourse that included no-one else, Gaia wasn't listening. She began to hit him across the face as if he were an enemy to be brought down. Bending towards him she bit his lower lip in fury, cutting it, stopping him from any reaction.

His mouth began to bleed, his eyes clamped shut with the effort to hold back. "I'm coming," she said. "I'm coming!"

A kind of compact silence followed, similar to that of wild beasts who interrupt every vital function to feign death. Nicolò's mouth was smeared with blood, his chest grazed with scratches. There was a sudden deep breath, almost as if the two had escaped from drowning. She let go and slipped to his side. She didn't dare touch him. He smiled at the ceiling, then turned to her.

It was not right to feel so good at that moment. Yet that was how it was. Nicolò understood just how unhappy he had felt before and just how much he felt he had been watched and judged over the past eleven years. From the first day. He wouldn't have dared to express that thought, but the truth was that in that moment he felt the enthusiasm of an adolescent who had found his independence and had confused it with freedom.

Gaia seemed to have re-emerged from the shadows, exactly as Michelangelo had described, a few evenings before, as they were sitting at the Olimpo. Beside her she could hear Nicolò's breathing become more regular. She brushed a finger against his lip. "I've hurt you," she said.

"It's nothing," he said, passing his tongue over the wound.

Gaia sighed and shook her head; she couldn't explain what she had done, but felt no regret. "You're bleeding," she said.

"Yes," he said, tasting it with the tip of his tongue. "But it's nothing."

In the silence, broken only by their alternating breath, they had to come to terms with Michelangelo's absence. And to do so without even needing to mention it.

"I hated you so much," she said after a pause.

"I know," Nicolò said without turning to look at her. "And to tell the truth I had thought about leaving." Gaia realised only at that moment just how close they had been to the edge of an abyss. "When there was that business of being called into school, for example," he explained.

* * *

They had been called in by a teacher who had asked them to consider sending Michelangelo to a special school for children who are "super-endowed". That was exactly what she had said. Then, seeing the smirk on Nicolò's face, had added, "Intellectually . . . super-endowed intellectually." But these words were no use. Nicolò couldn't get out of his head the picture of a brain with an erection. "He's a child like all the others," he had retorted.

The teacher looked at him as if he didn't understand, then turned to Gaia: "A more adequate support . . ."

"You mean you don't know how to handle a boy who's smarter than average?" he asked aggressively.

Gaia looked at him. "It's for Michelangelo's good, I think," she said. The teacher nodded and Nicolò noted just how much his wife was frightened, indeed terrified, by the opinion of others. "We ought to be on his side," she added.

"Meaning?" Nicolò asked provocatively.

"Meaning giving him adequate support when it comes to his educational needs," the teacher answered for her.

"In other words, shutting him up in some place for 'special' children." He uttered the word "special" with distaste, as though he for one did not believe in it. "My view is that he ought to join a local soccer team instead," he replied, as if sport were the exact opposite of what the teacher was proposing. "It seems to me that you just want to rid yourself of a problem."

Gaia and the teacher were speechless. "I can see there's no shared view here," the teacher had declared. And by this she meant *them*: Gaia and Nicolò.

"I thought there was," he said, looking at his wife.

* * *

"We ought to have been on his side," she insisted.

"No, you wanted him to think you were the only one on his side. You knew it all and pretended to be surprised."

"Someone had to look after our son."

"And you had decided that that someone would be you," Nicolò said, but almost kindly, not as someone trying to point blame. How long had it been since they had talked to each other in this way? In that way, lying naked, free from everyone and everything? "But Michelangelo certainly can't bear any responsibility," he added, condensing a much more complex thought. It was now clear to him that, different from what he had always previously thought, it was she, in that argument over the special school, who had wanted to be rid of the problem of that incomprehensible son. He had been naive, while Gaia had obtained exactly what she wanted: not to forgo her own needs. He would have liked to say: you said you wanted the best for him, but you wanted only to be rid of him. He would have liked to say everything: how distant he felt from his son from the very first time he saw him, how little he felt he was his. He would have liked to tell her just how much, deep down, he held her responsible for the weak man he had become. But these were thoughts so instantaneous and dark that they were impossible to put into words.

"I left my family for you," he murmured so quietly that she wouldn't understand. And she didn't.

"What was that?" she asked.

"I hated you for the business over Baffo," he said. The fact that she had taken their cat to be treated by her friend who was a vet and not asked him, a vet as well, had shown just how far they had grown apart, and were fighting to the death. Now everything seemed at an end.

"The cat," she said.

They looked at each other. And for the first time they realised that the animal had gone.

* * *

"The priest, you say?" Sergio stopped thinking about his shirt and sat on the bed.

Leo, instead of replying, went to the kitchen, opened the fridge and took out a yoghurt, looked for a teaspoon in the drawer under the hob and returned to the bedroom. "The priest, yes. You said he was the one who telephoned the Questura, no?"

"Yes."

"You said your first instinct was to check the car belonging to the child's father ... You're someone who knows all about instinct." He smiled and dipped the teaspoon into the yoghurt.

"But?" Sergio asked.

"But with your father around right now, I wouldn't regard that instinct as very reliable . . ."

Sergio gave a slight smile. "You're saying it's best to forget about fathers?"

"I'm saying that maybe the person who caused the child to disappear is the one who made the call."

"You're one hell of an fundamentalist atheist. Which, I warn you, is a religion like any other."

"You're only saying that because I've caught you out. Do you want some?" he asked, offering him a spoonful of pink yoghurt.

"Is it strawberry?" The other nodded and Sergio opened his mouth. "Fuck," he said after he had swallowed. "If I've really been caught out like this . . ."

"Why do you always have to take it personally?"

"Because it *is* personal."

"As usual, you're putting the cart before the horse: it was only an idea, that's all."

"Don't get me wrong . . ."

"You sound annoyed."

"Of course I am, but not with you . . ."

Leo put the empty pot on the bedside cabinet. "It was only a thought," he repeated. "Stay here tonight – I promise I'll leave you in peace." He smiled.

"In that case I'm going," Sergio returned the smile. "And I've no change of clothes," he said, turning serious.

"We can find a clean shirt," Leo said. "I've made you feel bad."

"No, not you. It's just that what you've said about the priest was so elementary . . ."

"He never said it," Leo interrupted.

"Said what?"

"Elementary, my dear Watson. Sherlock Holmes never said it."

"Really?"

"Honest, I read Conan Doyle as if there were no tomorrow."

"An evening of revelations."

"And anyway, if I can give you a bit of advice, I'd say you weren't the only one not to think the priest might be involved. In the same situation and in the heat of the moment, I probably wouldn't have thought of it either." Leo was showing why he was the most popular teacher among the mothers of his school. In any event, the "we all make mistakes" argument had had its effect. Sergio slipped off his trousers and socks and climbed back into bed.

Arriving in the office charged with new energy, Sergio Striggio looked stern. He bumped into Menetti finishing her cup of tea from the drinks machine, and Fanti attempting, as usual, to start up his computer. "Into my office!" he announced as he had seen in TV movies. "Any news of Stelzer?" Stelzer emerged from round the corner of the corridor. "My office!" the Commissario repeated, walking ahead of them towards his workspace. Once inside he sat at his desk looking like Captain Kirk on the bridge of the *Enterprise*. "Sit down, we've a lot to do," he announced to the three already standing at the entrance.

"What's the news?" Menetti asked, taking particular note of the Commissario's shirt, a little too tight.

The news is that we have to review everything. Rethink everything," he announced with seriousness. Menetti narrowed her eyes to indicate she was at her boss' complete disposition; Fanti settled himself in the chair as if to signal that he had understood the message loud and clear; while Stelzer, a new recruit, raised his hand. Striggio nodded to him to speak.

"About that inquiry into the footballs stolen from the sports centre," he said. "There are some developments."

Striggio pursed his lips and widened them as if trying to imitate the mouth of a frog. Menetti tapped her chin with her finger in the way she did each time she tried to avoid laughing. Fanti tried to catch Stelzer's eye as if to express solidarity. "Not now!" the Commissario interrupted. "That's not what we're here to talk about."

"I thought we were here for a confab on current inquiries," Stelzer explained.

"No, Steltzer," said Striggio. "Not about the *many and complex* current inquiries, but one in particular! And if you use the word 'confab' inside here once more I'll send you off to count cattle for the local agricultural census!" Steltzer went quiet. "What exactly did we fail to consider on the night we were called to the place where an eleven-year-old – he hesitated slightly – "boy had gone missing?"

"That there was no boy?" suggested Fanti, but as though he already knew this was to be excluded.

Striggio shook his head vigorously. "Who's going to report something that hasn't happened?" he asked.

"Nutcases?" Stelzer suggested.

This time Striggio gave him no look of reproach. "An option that we can rule out, the . . ."

"Ludovisis," said Menetti helpfully.

"The Ludovisis aren't nutcases."

"But perhaps they're murderers," Menetti added.

"Or perhaps not," Striggio replied. "What exactly did we rule out that night?"

"The guy who reported it." Stelzer had beaten them to it.

Striggio pointed to Stelzer as if to say: exactly. Menetti sat up in her chair: "Oh shit!" she said.

Fanti gave a look of surprise, as if he'd taken it for granted they had already thought of that.

"The one who reported it, the priest," said Striggio, giving an emphasis that veered towards the impersonal and avoided giving the impression of any foregone conclusion. "So let's recap." The others moved closer to the Commissario like petals that close around the pistil at night. "We arrived on the scene at what time?"

Menetti fiddled with the screen of her tablet: "23.40," she answered.

"The call was made, let's say, half an hour earlier?"

"22.20," Menetti read. "According to his statement, don Giuseppe comes across the Ludovisis outside their vehicle looking for their son, who has only just disappeared. He offers to give them a hand and, a few minutes later, suggests calling the police. Which he does, in fact, at 22.20."

"Good. We arrive, we said, at 23.40. What do we do? We question the boy's parents as far as we can, and check the father's vehicle. And then?"

"And then?" Fanti asked, as though hearing the story for the first time.

Menetti's face darkened as she realised where the Commissario was aiming.

"Then we tell the person who reported it that he can go, asking him to remain available. All quite normal, no?"

"Makes perfect sense," Fanti agreed.

"No it doesn't," Menetti remarked, with the tone of someone telling herself she'd been a fool.

"Meaning?" asked Stelzer, who was proving brighter than either his tender years or his dramatically provincial, folksy appearance might have suggested.

"Exactly what you're thinking," Striggio anticipated. "Who checked the priest's car? No-one. Who checked his version of the facts? No-one."

"How do we proceed?" asked Menetti, who was starting to feel the heat of the chair beneath her.

"We start all over again," Striggio said. "I have to see Susini this afternoon and I don't want to take another bollocking. Stelzer, you check out the surveillance cameras, they're all over the place, from the parish church in via . . .?"

"Barletta, corner of via Bari," Menetti said.

"Excellent, from via Barletta as far as the Olimpo. If you see don Giuseppe's red Fiat Panda, note down where and when. Understood?" Steltzer nodded. "Go on, you can get started," the Commissario said, seeing that he hadn't made a move. Fanti went to get up as though he had been spoken to as well. "You stay," Striggio ordered, and he sat down again. "I want to know what stage we're at with the Communications unit and Nicolò . . . Ludovisi's phone." He always had some difficulty remembering the surname.

"I'm waiting for an answer, I've been asking, but still nothing."

"Well asking isn't enough: go and occupy their office and don't leave until they've told you what's inside that phone. You'll see, they'll hurry up just to get rid of you."

Striggio gestured to indicate that Fanti could now get up and give some meaning to his day. "Good fellow," he muttered to Menetti as soon as he had gone. "Such dedication to his job . . . Let's leave that and move on to us."

"Nice shirt," she cut in.

"Forget the shirt too," the Commissario said. "We've a lot to do. First, talk to the priest."

"Shall we go straight away?" Menetti asked.

"Yes, I think so, but first we need to agree a plan: I want to check the vehicle. If Michelangelo Ludovisi was inside it, he'll have left some trace . . . We have to persuade him to let us examine it, but without him knowing what we're looking for."

"We could say we have to match up the tyre marks?" Menetti suggested.

* * *

Outside that muddy aquarium of the Questura building they were greeted by a wonderful rarefaction. It had stopped snowing in the middle of the night, and everything now reverberated with a soft patina, like a glaze over the fragrant crust of a homemade sponge. The warmth and the movement of the city had cancelled every trace of snow, and the traffic had churned up the earlier pristine layer, reducing it to a brown slush along the kerb. Parts of the car park had remained intact, however, with a dazzling white. A pure white. Sergio felt hypnotised by it and a relentless chain of associations came to mind. As a child, sheets hanging on the washing line seemed to him like large teeth with no lips, forced by the wind into a laugh. And then there was his father's obsession with white shirts: one per day, always perfect and with that slight transparency that allowed a glimpse of the mortal body beneath the purity. He had long associated the arrogance of that man with the cleanness of his shirts and the perfect way in which his mother busily ironed them each morning just before he put them on. Life is never short of signals for those who know how to read them. And he would have preferred not to have known how.

On the afternoon that the results of his mother's medical tests arrived, the first thing he noted was a minute speck, perhaps of coffee, just below the collar of his father's shirt. And there seemed no doubt from this that he needed to prepare for the worst. It was August, and his mother wouldn't make it to December. On 21 November, there was a heavy snowfall over Bologna. From the fourteenth floor of the hospital, the hills could be seen covered in snow and San Luca dusted with icing sugar, like a *pandoro*. That night it snowed so much that they let him sleep in the hospital on one of the chairs they used for pushing patients from the consulting rooms to their beds. On the morning of 22 November, a thick layer of snow had obliterated everything, rounding every angle and absorbing every object, with the obstinate violence with which Pompei had been buried in ash and pumice. When he opened his eyes he saw his mother was already awake and watching him. The end of everything was nothing more than a body reduced to its last flicker by the complete apocalypse of its organs. What remained of her life was quietly moving beneath those pure white sheets, creating peaks and hollows that were the exact reproduction of the world outside the window. Except it seemed that the world outside had no interest at all in that particular apocalypse. His father arrived two hours after her last breath. He was wearing a spotless pure white shirt, perfectly ironed. Which, for those able to interpret it, was the clearest presage.

* * *

"What's the matter?" Menetti asked, waiting for him at the open door.

"Nothing," he murmured. "I don't like snow," he felt he needed to add as he fastened his seat belt.

"You don't like snow?" she said, surprised. "Who doesn't like snow?" she asked blankly.

"I don't," Striggio insisted. "Shall we get going?" he asked peremptorily, since she hadn't yet started the engine.

Her only response was to stroke the nape of his neck.

He looked at her, not quite believing what she had done.

"What are you doing?" he asked, though making it clear the question was purely rhetorical.

"I have the impression sometimes that there's someone there inside looking for help," Menetti said, then switched on the engine.

He remained staring at her until they were out of the car park. He was searching for something to say but, hard as he tried, could put nothing into words. "Stop the car," he managed to say. "Stop!" he repeated, since she didn't seem to have understood. At last she stopped.

"I don't know at what point in our . . . relationship," he began some seconds after she had switched off the engine, " . . . I gave you the impression that this could happen."

"A stroke of the neck?" she interrupted, making it clear she had perfectly understood what he was referring to.

"There's to be no stroking," he cut in.

Striggio went quiet, taking time to find the right words, and Menetti took advantage of the silence. "Very well, message received. Can we go now?" she asked, restarting the engine.

Sergio was aware of the movement of the car only because the countryside had once again begun to glide past. "It's not about stroking my neck," he said after a while as though he were talking to himself. Menetti pressed down on the accelerator so that the back of the Commissario's neck pressed against the headrest and his seat belt tightened against his collarbone.

* * *

He was ready to swear that the snow, on that wild night of agony, had made a tremendous noise as it hit the ground. What came down from the sky was glass dust, with nothing like the imagined gentleness of cream or cotton. Nothing that looked remotely like a nativity scene or an Alpine landscape or a miniature inside a dome, one of those you shake and it turns into a poetry of snowflakes. The air inside the room had become oily, and there was only death. Only the icy albino atmosphere of refrigerator boxes or mortuary chambers. His mother's brow was furrowed, and each time he went near to nurse or caress her, her eyes – the only part of her body over which she still had full control – glared at him. Everything else had been drained away by the illness. No caresses, therefore. Nothing at all. Just waiting and powerlessness. That is what that snowy night had been, a night in which he had realised just how banal death was. And he'd had to resign himself to the fact that literature, in such a situation, bore little relationship to reality. Nothing he had read about death had described its fundamental stupidity. It was like the supply of air coming to an end. Not *like*, but precisely that: the supply of air coming to an end. Death means having to look, right to the end, at all those others who carry on living around you. In his mother there was anger but – seemingly – no envy. It was impossible to say what remained of all that had made them a single item, mother and son, but to see them in that hospital room – she committed to not dying and he equally committed in begging her to die – one would have said that all that was left was the stubborn roar of the minuscule splinters of sky that gracelessly ground the railings and scratched at the panes of the windows. No caress, not even there outside. The wait was terrible.

Suddenly his mother had gestured that she wanted to go to the bathroom. To the very end she insisted on not using the bedpan: a nurse had to be called to take her. But on that night, which she didn't yet know would be her last, the nurse did not come. So he decided to take her himself. He went to his mother's bed and uncovered her with a single gesture, like a typhoon sweeping away the landscape of those pure white hills of sheet and bedcover. What he had laid bare was a body returned to infancy. He had bent over and taken her in his arms, ignoring her silent protests. She was so light, so fragile. It was impossible to imagine that a woman nearing sixty could weigh so little. And this showed him just how effective that return journey had become, which went back to the beginning in everything. Almost as if the last breath and the first whimper had, at the end, coincided. Once in the bathroom his mother had felt a sudden shame and had tried in every way possible to show she would have preferred anything, any agony, to that humiliation of being carried, deposited and washed by her own son. For her nature required her to be the giver of all she was now receiving. And in the eyes of that boy who had so suddenly become a man, it was possible to glean a substantial degree of failure. Or maybe not. Maybe all of this had happened precisely to prove she hadn't failed at all with that creature of hers. He had attempted to wash her as he would have washed a baby, but she had kept her legs tightly closed – in anger – not wanting him to see the place from which he had come. At least not with that exact intimacy. But he had gestured to her to relax and, without forcing her, allowed her to protect herself. He had then straightened her nightdress, now far too large for her, and had taken her once again in his arms, like a *Pietà* in reverse, like a Christ who holds the Madonna in his arms, and had deposited her gently on her bed. She lay there on the mattress, leaving no discernible imprint, as snow should, that snow of happier times: crumbling, weightless and deeply fragile.

* * *

There was little traffic, but even so it was moving with difficulty. Menetti was looking straight ahead with the embarrassed concentration of someone searching for something to say. Striggio seemed locked in an anxious silence and he too was looking obstinately ahead, yet without seeing anything.

"Shall we remain as agreed?" the Chief Inspector asked after a while. And her voice, for Striggio, came from the depths of time.

He looked round in surprise as if, for a moment, Menetti herself had been there in the room at the Ospedale Maggiore in Bologna where his mother had lain dying fifteen years before. Then he realised it was Bolzano, that he was in a police car in the midst of an investigation and that it had snowed heavily. "Park before the yard in front of the church, I don't want them to hear us arrive," he said.

"That's what I was going to do."

"Yes," Striggio said. "Seems it might stop snowing," he observed with a certain relief. He felt numb, as if having been suddenly woken.

Menetti watched him from the corner of her eye. She said nothing, even though it should have been quite normal to ask how a stroke of the neck, such a simple and chaste gesture of affection, had put him in such a bad mood. They'd had sex not so long before and had gone much further than a caress. She turned more sharply than necessary into via Resia, though Striggio didn't seem to notice or even register her tenseness at the wheel. "I'd say the weather's taking a turn for the worse," she said.

* * *

He was ready to swear he had learned all there was to learn, to make a promise without keeping it and to keep what he had promised and to love without receiving anything in return, even if the very fact of loving already meant receiving something in return. He was ready to forgo something extremely important, something yet to be determined, if only that headstrong mother of his would decide to give in sooner. Before him was an endless night, the incessant gurgling of the respirator, the hum of the life-support machine and the sound of the intravenous drip. Added to which, outside, was a roar of snow as solid as grains of wheat tipped onto the millstone or handfuls of rice thrown over newly-weds. And still that terrible stare that went to demonstrate without a shadow of doubt that in that room he was merely a distraction. In fact she, his mother – he realised later – had spent the final hours of her life deciding what was to be the last thing she would look at before she died. And it must have been a very hard decision, for in that room there was nothing warm or intimate to cling to in order to die with an image worthy of such a name. There was him, just him. Whom she said she loved above everything. The meaning, according to her, of her whole existence. So that her husband had often accused her of having eyes only for her son. Him and her. Shared looks, smiles, thoughts. All, everything.

* * *

Menetti parked just before the entrance to the yard behind don Giuseppe's church. From there they could reach the presbytery and the priest's apartment. Menetti got out first, not noticing that Striggio was still sitting there with an unbuckled seat belt. The notes of a piece of classical music could be heard. "The 'Valse Triste'," Striggio said to himself, then turned and realised his Chief Inspector was waiting. He joined her and they crossed the small yard in silence to the side door of the presbytery. The priest's red Panda was parked a few paces away. Striggio went up to it and peered through the rear window. Don Giuseppe was not a tidy man, that was clear. He was one of those who used the car simply as a means for getting about or as an extension of his cellar or attic. Menetti cupped her hands to screen her eyes as she looked inside the car from the driver's side: nothing particularly unusual, all describable as a perfectly ordinary disorder. Striggio turned his attention to the rear seat. There too, nothing of interest: a few sheets of paper, some till receipts, a woollen hat and a rainproof jacket of the kind petrol stations give out as free gifts. The Chief Inspector and the Commissario looked at each other, then approached the door of the presbytery. The "Valse Triste" began again for the third time. The sound came from a slightly open window on the first floor.

* * *

In that briefest moment of remembrance of what they had been he felt his mother was trying to speak. He moved his left ear close to her mouth and tried to decipher what she was straining to mumble. And he seemed to think she was saying "Goodbye".

* * *

They rang the doorbell and waited. The music could now be heard more clearly. "Sibelius," Striggio said. Menetti made a gesture as if to say: Heavens! But before she had time to make some barbed remark about the Commissario's musical prowess, the door opened. A woman of a certain age appeared, looking at them suspiciously.

"Let them in, Elda," came a voice from the top of the steps leading up to the first floor.

The entrance hall was modest and so ordinary that time seemed to have stood still. Scant sign of progress: brown and ochre patterned tiles, a mass-produced wrought-iron umbrella stand, a wood-veneered coat rack on the wall, steps of ugly champagne-coloured marble, a rickety banister with large metallic whorls and a crucifix too small for the expanse of bare wall. The "Valse Triste" started up again, in a rather brassy version, as they tackled the first steps. The priest's housekeeper led the way, not having spoken a word. Sibelius fell silent as soon as they entered the room where the priest was standing. Striggio leaned towards the record sleeve to make sure the piece wasn't actually one of those strange arrangements. No, it was an orchestra he had never heard of, conducted by a man he had never heard of. "Commissario Striggio," he announced abruptly to the priest. "Chief Inspector Menetti," he added, indicating his colleague.

The priest looked at them with a hint of anxiety, as if to say that the introduction was entirely unnecessary: they had met, they had already seen each other on the night the child went missing, when he had telephoned them.

"Fine." Striggio hesitated, as he did each time he felt he'd been wrong-footed. But he was still trying to satisfy his need for consolation, and outside, as Menetti had predicted, it had started to snow again. "Was it the 'Valse Triste'?" he asked, in a question that appeared in every respect more like a statement.

Don Giuseppe regained his composure. "Yes, of course," he said in the manner of a teacher who finds it hard to give a satisfactory answer to a pupil who has discovered hot water.

"I've not heard this version before," the Commissario observed.

"It isn't Karajan. Perhaps it's not the best, but I'm fond of it."

Menetti watched them as she might have watched two young boys competing to find out who could piss further.

"Well, of course, the Karajan version is something else: solemn, imperial . . ."

"Yes, though I'm not sure that *solemn* and *imperial* is exactly the right approach for this piece . . . Sibelius wrote it for an opera called 'Kuolema', which in Finnish means Death," the priest observed. "The 'Valse' in particular was supposed to tell the story of a boy of nineteen who watches his mother die." He was now clearly intent on overdoing it.

Striggio looked directly at his interlocutor, then turned to Menetti. The shadow of the housekeeper slid past the door of the room. "I could spend hours discussing music with you, but at the moment . . . it's not why we're here." That plural which included Menetti must have made the visit seem much more formal.

"Of course," the other agreed.

Now that Striggio had a better view of him, he looked younger than he had seemed on the night Michelangelo had disappeared. "Let's start with some personal details," he said, looking once again at Menetti, who began fiddling with her tablet. "Is Giuseppe your real name?" he asked. "I've never quite understood this thing about religious names."

"Giuseppe is my name in Christ," he replied. "I was baptised Emilio."

"Good," Striggio remarked. "Good," he repeated to buy time. "So, correct me if I'm wrong: you have stated that you happened to be at the scene of Michelangelo Ludovisi's disappearance by chance: correct? Is that so?"

Don Giuseppe hesitated. "Yes," he murmured after a while, but with little conviction.

"Yes?" Striggio insisted. The priest nodded. Striggio stood watching him in silence. The priest was sweating. "You're hot?" he asked

"I'm not used to dealing with such matters," the other said.

"What matters?"

"All of this." The priest grew nervous, pointing randomly around him.

"It's a routine check, there's nothing to worry about."

"I'm not worried, I'm petrified," don Giuseppe explained.

"About what?" Striggio asked.

"I'm not used to dealing with the police," he repeated.

"Then let's sit down and have a quiet chat, alright? Let's say that I'm here to ask for your help: you may have seen or heard something while you were there at the scene of the disappearance, something not yet taken into consideration." At this the priest seemed to relax. Menetti looked at Striggio with a mixture of surprise and admiration. "Shall we begin?" he asked with the encouragement of a modern father who wants to be his adolescent son's companion and confidant.

"Yes," said don Giuseppe, seating himself in an armchair.

"We have established that you were there by chance . . ."

"Well . . ." the priest stammered. "That's a point on which . . ."

"On which?"

"On which, perhaps . . ."

But he didn't manage to finish the sentence. A plume of black smoke rose from the yard outside. Menetti, who was nearer the window, ran to see what was happening. Striggio joined her a few seconds later. "What is it?" don Giuseppe asked a moment before seeing his car engulfed in tall flames.

"Keep back! Back from the window!" Striggio shouted, only just in time. They hurled themselves to the floor.

The car exploded with a blast. The impact shattered the windows of the house. Striggio looked around: Menetti had pulled don Giuseppe to safety behind an armchair. Thousands of glass splinters and icy flakes were snowing inside the room.

Water

So this author, reasoning upon the air that is found between the moist vapours – with which the cloud masses, above, are formed – and the seas that spread out below, wished to demonstrate that heaven is situated between water and water.

SAINT AUGUSTINE,
On the Literal Meaning of Genesis, II, 4.7

This is what he wished to demonstrate: that the world above sea level could be understood, and even interpreted, through marine creatures. If oceans, before being entities, were distances between one land and another, then it could be said that water, before being an entity, was a distance between one place and another. If humans, before being bipeds, had been fish, then it could be said that every fish was a potential human. If fish scales would become feathers, then feathers had been scales. This, and only this, was what he was interested in demonstrating. Every human who tried to go back to the water had to admit defeat. Or perhaps they went back for the very reason that they had been defeated. Take Ophelia, take Icarus. They didn't know they were going back to their point of departure. Time, History, had so distanced them from their primordial element that they could not survive there, but yet a clear awareness of such inability had not dissuaded them from trying.

Striggio had understood many things about himself from the state of immersion he felt after the blast, and this because, perhaps for the first time, he thought he was going to die: a liquid death, a drowning, like those he had faked as a child, an interruption of breathing so deep and instantaneous that in every respect it resembled a prolonged suffocation. Of the kind, they say, that forces you to look back over your whole life in just a few seconds. In his case it was instantaneous. He imagined himself trying to describe what had happened, and therefore assumed he had survived. And yet, he thought, it was precisely because he could imagine such a thing, even for just an infinitesimal moment of time, that he had died. Contrary to what he had thought until then, dying was more like wonder – not bewilderment; and no magnetic tape on fast rewind to prenatal darkness, but only a vague state of vacancy in which the only consideration is: can this be it?

As a child he had often thought of Professor Aronnax's confusion when, having resigned himself to dying in the waters of Japan and with his strength and his lungs about to give out, he hears Ned Land calling him, standing among the waves like a kind of modern-day Christ and beckoning him to go with him to the *Nautilus*. And he, the professor, summons all his remaining energy to encourage his faithful servant Conseil and to carry him with him to safety where, at last, they can both breathe. Before travelling the first of the twenty thousand leagues under the sea, there had been the certainty of dying on the surface. It was all a question of the air to be found between water and water. Survival depended on breaking this logic. On reasoning through compromise.

That sudden explosion, that sense of drowning, that instant surprise, such that he hadn't had time even to realise that he could actually have died, had left him in a state of frozen euphoria. He heard Menetti calling him, of course, and could clearly see the space around him invaded by tiny splinters of glass and snow, but it was as though he was under water. And although he wanted to reply that everything was fine, that everything was under control, he couldn't speak a word, almost as though he had become one of those hybrid creatures that have assumed one temporary state so as not to lose another, like the mermaid in the film who needs to bathe in order to revive.

He remembered being crouched against the wall below the window, hearing the explosion and the cascade of glass just in front of him first, then the blast and, only at the end, that weird sense of drowning. Until, just like Professor Aronnax, he had seen someone standing in front of him, signalling for him to join him . . .

And at that moment he wished he could have explained how the sense of drowning that had gripped him was only the symptom of a shipwreck long before this momentary fear of losing his life.

He had always thought of himself as an amphibious being, one of those who resolve their problems by altering their breathing: gills under water, lungs on the surface. He saw himself as a kind of Triton, a creature halfway between two distinct worlds: he was too hairy to aspire to the role of merman. "A bridge," as Leo used to say. An individual with no set form, thought Sergio, like a child who flounders in the swimming pool while his father, lounging comfortably in the sun by the pool, watched him from the corner of his eye while reading a newspaper and drinking an ice-cold beer. As he thought more about it, he realised that it wasn't a metaphor but an exact memory of himself when he was seven, perhaps eight. His level of communication was limited, even then, to the capacity to connect things that seemed mutually very distant. In that children's swimming pool there was no possibility of imagining an ocean, a ship-wreck, a rescue. It was most improbable that Neptune might intervene to straighten the hulls bent by the furious waves, or point out safe coves to the fleets; or to send sudden tsunamis to punish ungrateful peoples or wily princes too haughty to acknowledge his authority as a strap-ping, weather-beaten, ill-tempered god. For however much young Sergio floundered in that swimming pool less than a metre and a half deep, imagining who knows what Argonautic adventure, no-one would have come to save him, least of all his father, who did no more than shake his head as if to say he had brought a perfect cretin into the world.

"Sometimes I think, despite everything, you still don't really know me!"
Leo shouted, to make it clear there was nothing that Sergio could hide
from him. He had the tone of one of those mothers on the beach who
leave the shade of their umbrella to call back their teenage children who
have strayed too far out to sea. And Sergio resented this criticism unduly,
as he did whenever Leo was completely right. Yet Leo's impression wasn't
quite correct, since Sergio knew him as well as he knew himself. And
perhaps better. But in cases like this – when he felt himself exposed,
vulnerable – he had learned that it was better to acknowledge defeat.
And so, rather than answering back and objecting, he withdrew into a
silence that had the appearance of surrender but with an underlay of
resistance. And, to contradict him, he made a mental list of every secret
that he knew about the man he loved – the only living being he had ever
truly loved.

* * *

("Shake the Disease", also in the DMK version . . . The recordings of
Depeche Mode's live performances in general . . . *Pride and Prejudice* . . .
The twenty-two-year-old homeless Korean who sings Bocelli at the talent
show . . . *As I Lay Dying* . . . The publicity for Air France, with Mozart's
Piano Concerto no. 23, K.488, choreographed by Angelin Preljocaj for
Benjamin Millepied and Virginie Caussin . . . A town called Aggius in
Sardinia where he had ended up by chance a million summers before . . .

A painting by Antonio Donghi of a hunter sitting, legs splayed, in the kitchen of a house, with a cartridge belt and gun, and a hound between his knees . . . A small waterproof jacket bought at a department store in Stuttgart on a day of continual rain . . . The torn jeans he wore the day they had first spoken to each other, having remarked how risky it was to talk about things that then actually came to be . . . A photo of his mother when she was very young wearing a long camel overcoat, a cameo at her neck and leather gloves . . . The diary he kept at junior school . . . A filigree rosary with a gold crucifix that had belonged to his grandmother . . . Cacti in general, and regret that he couldn't manage to look after even them . . . Cookery programmes, even the tackiest . . . National Geographic documentaries, particularly those on the savannah or, rather, on the Serengeti . . . Bergen . . . The Tizio desk lamp and Alessi kettle . . . Pretending to have a certain suspicion of Pasolini . . . The sadness of trains . . . Being convinced he had understood the ending of Michelangelo Antonioni's "Eclipse" . . . His general passion for 1960s art films . . . Bergman's "Persona", for example: "The hopeless dream of being. Not seeming, but being. In every waking moment aware, alert. The tug of war . . . what you are with others and who you really are. A feeling of vertigo and a constant hunger to be finally exposed, seen through, cut down . . . even obliterated. Every tone of voice a lie. Every gesture false. Every smile a grimace." Blue, as far as the conclusion that blue is endless . . . Claiming, falsely, never to have read Whitman . . . Crying easily, in fact very easily, as happens to men who are self-aware, whatever that self-awareness might be . . . Being unable at first to get certain TV commercials . . . A passion for the lives of medieval saints, like the monk who rid a cornfield of weeds, or the saint who smiled even when being stoned, whipped and roasted over a slow flame . . .)

* * *

But this particular argument had arisen because, despite feeling dazed, Sergio had rejected medical help and had absolutely refused to get into the ambulance, letting himself be treated only for a few scratches to the neck and hands from the splinters of glass that had showered over him from the window above. About which Leo was beside himself, since that irrational idiot was denying what was obvious: that he was partially dazed and his hearing still impaired. So that each time he said something, Sergio replied: "What?"

"But look at you," said Leo. "Can't you at least go for a check-up?"

"I'm fine," Sergio muttered. "I just need a moment to recover," he insisted, but his insistence merely increased Leo's anxiety.

That was how they talked to each other, as though they could take anything for granted, like someone talking to himself, knowing full well what he chooses to say or not to say and knowing perfectly well how to fool himself even if just a little.

"I'll have a shower and soon be back on form," Sergio said.

Leo looked at him with that particular look which meant: you obviously haven't heard a single word I've just said. "I sometimes think, despite it all, that you still don't really know me!" he observed.

* * *

(The scene in which Umberto D. tries to get rid of the dog before attempting suicide ... Larkin's "High Windows" ... Eliot's *Four Quartets* ... Renzo Piano's Jean-Marie Tjibaou Cultural Centre ... Elsa Morante's *The World Saved by Kids* ... Memphis design ... Brazilian flip-flops ... The concern about white turning yellow, about black turning grey, about blue fading ... Longing for winter during the summer, and for summer during the winter ... The joke about 10 per cent of humans being conceived on an IKEA bed and the remaining 90 per cent on the floor because they couldn't put the bloody thing together ... And the episode of "The X-Files" when Mulder is reincarnated as a soldier who had died at Gettysburg ... And the exact moment when Federigo degli Alberighi has to tell Monna Giovanna that she has just eaten what she had gone to ask him for ... The wings, beak and claws of the hawk at the end of "The Hawks and the Sparrows" ... And that particular window through which you can see a canal still open and Bologna once again a city of water ... And those particular smells, wherever you smell them, in whatever city, that make you think you're in Venice ... Or that fixation about seeing Tonga ... The idea, always postponed, about getting a tattoo: a koi carp, or more accurately a *nishikigoi*, on the right arm, or a peacock tail at the base of the spine, or two bat wings on the shoulders ... Stocks of white or blue Monoprix underpants in Paris ... Anything from a Muji store ... The moment when the aircraft takes off in the words of Daniele Del Giudice ... And the city of Delft as seen by Vermeer ... And the absolute certainty that Hitler had never read *War and Peace* ... And the certainty that William Faulkner, even today, hates having to share the shelves of bookshops or libraries with Ken Follett ... Or the certainty that all swimming pools are a breeding ground for bacteria ... Oh, and when Hamlet understands that feigning madness is already in itself a form of madness ... And all Freud would have had to say about Renzo Tramaglino who rouses the chickens ... The supreme pleasure of being frightened to death over and over again on watching and rewatching "The House with Laughing Windows" or "Deep Red" ... The old cliché that there's nothing better than lying on a sofa in the warmth holding a hot drink when it's raining outside, or snuggling under a quilt when it's snowing ... The pleasure of absolute normality ... And Susan Sontag photographed on her deathbed by Annie Leibovitz ... *Memento mori* ...)

* * *

He knew everything. Of course he knew him! Sergio tightened his lips.

Leo averted his gaze by simply closing his eyelids, a gesture that required no more than minimum effort for maximum effect. So he closed his eyes, and by doing so shut out that irrational dolt. "As you wish," he said, and headed towards the kitchen, giving him "a moment to recover" alone.

* * *

(When he kissed him on the side of his neck between his ear and his shoulder . . . When he stroked him sliding down from his armpits to his hips and could distinctly feel the goose pimples beneath his palms . . . When he made him feel the pressure of his fingernails on his spine . . . When, with no warning, he got out of bed for a drink or a piss, and returned to find him waiting with a slight look of anxiety as if he had been away for so long . . . When he could ask "What's going on?" and he didn't even know how to reply, so perfect was the moment . . . Or when a second before kissing him he thought he was about to be kissed . . . When he had to quicken his pace for fear of not finding him where they had agreed to meet . . . When the anxiety of the evening compelled him to reconsider the solidity of their love . . . And when he found himself discovering in his body those lines, those proportions, which he said were so beautiful . . . When he realised that love can mean looking at oneself through the eyes of the other, but so also with hatred: all a matter of perspective . . . When on that rainy afternoon in Bologna he had led him to understand that he would let himself be loved . . . When, in other words, one understands that love is not stolen but given . . . When, in other words, one realises that if love is given, then such love can produce suffering but cannot do harm . . .)

* * *

He knew it all.

Everything.

Despite having escaped from that drowning, onto dry land. And so he stirred himself, joined Leo in the kitchen and, without him being able or willing to prevent it, hugged him, burying his whole face in the curve of his neck, which he loved to tears. And he held him so tightly that Leo could only reciprocate, holding him tightly as though they were entwined together.

They knew it all.

At the offices of the Communications Unit, Fanti felt even less at his ease than in the Commissariato. A prefabricated booth at the entrance contained a bewildered-looking young policeman. "Ceccaroli?" Fanti asked abruptly.

The young officer looked at his computer screen, which reflected a green light over his clean-shaven face, and frowned. "Ceccaroli," he said to himself in a thick German accent.

"Yes," Fanti confirmed, with a certain brusqueness that flustered the young officer. "Superintendent Ceccaroli. He's waiting for me."

The youth stopped staring at the screen and looked at him. "Office nine on the right, just at the end of the corridor," he said with a surprising lack of inflection.

Fanti nodded, then turned and headed off in the direction indicated, though what the youth had called a corridor was no more than the space between two long walls dotted with doors. Each door led to an office. Each office was marked with a number. Fanti walked as far as number eight before turning right as he had been told. Around the corner, the corridor narrowed. In five paces he reached number nine and knocked.

Ceccaroli was a scruffy, pot-bellied forty-year-old. His shirt was dangerously tight across his stomach. "Ah, Carlo," he said without looking up from the computer screen.

"Has someone been smoking?" Fanti asked.

"Stop being a prick," the other replied, unruffled.

"What's been going on in here?" Fanti looked for the corner of a desk on which to put himself.

"Leave it out," Ceccaroli grumbled. "First they're going to have it open plan, then they change their minds and coop us up in these cages with flexi-panels."

Fanti nodded solemnly. "It gives you a bit of privacy, but never enough air or light," he noted. "What do we have on the mobile phone I sent down to you?"

Ceccaroli motioned for him to come closer and look at the computer screen. Fanti moved forward with theatrical hesitation. "Well? Come on then," Ceccaroli said.

Fanti put on an expression of explicit caution. "I'll keep my distance. I'm worried I might get hit by one of your shirt buttons."

Ceccaroli shook his head. "Here we have a case of what you might call a fuck phone," he announced, ignoring his colleague's quip. Fanti smiled. His suspicions had been confirmed. "Raunchy stuff," Ceccaroli said emphatically.

Several fairly explicit images appeared on the screen, showing what personal equipment Nicolò Ludovisi had to offer a prospective partner, whoever that might be. "Hmm, the lad's in pretty good shape," Fanti had to admit, reluctantly.

"Yep," Ceccaroli confirmed.

With a certain envy, they gazed around the wonderful world of Ludovisi the stud, who, if that were not enough, had sculpted abdominal muscles and not an inch of flab on his hips.

"Who are they addressed to?" Fanti asked, patting his slight paunch with the palm of his right hand.

"Mostly to a single number, if you mean the photos. This fuck phone has just messages and appointments with two or three local women."

"He keeps himself busy."

"Except for this one here," Ceccaroli added. "It's the number of a clinic in Rovereto."

"A clinic," Fanti repeated, as though the word had some particularly evocative power. "A clinic," he said again, for the term was completely out of place if he had to imagine some link between the vet and the pictures that portrayed him in all his stately, athletic manliness.

"What are you actually looking for?" Ceccaroli asked, taking advantage of his colleague's pause for reflection. "You think it's got something to do with his son's disappearance?"

"We don't think anything at the moment," Fanti interrupted. "We have a few leads, but until there's something to link them together we don't really have a plausible theory."

"Well, I'd say we have a few more leads now. You reckon I need to do more shagging to get my stomach muscles like that?" Ceccaroli asked.

"More shagging and less eating. Never the other way round."

"Why don't you just take your stuff and get the fuck out," Ceccaroli said playfully.

Instead of answering his colleague, Fanti answered his mobile, which had begun ringing. "Yes, yes, Chief Inspector . . . No, I'm at the Communications Unit . . . Well, some fairly interesting material . . . What? Where? . . . I'll come straight away . . . But the Commissario's alright? . . . OK, I'll call Steltzer now . . . Yes, yes . . . fine . . ."

"Problems?" Ceccaroli asked, seeing his colleague's face darken.

"An explosion, vehicle in flames," Fanti said, summarily.

Ceccaroli made a strange gesture with his mouth, suggesting that the news really had surprised him. Generally, he tended not to be surprised by anything. Not there, at least. Not in Bolzano, where nothing worthy of surprise ever happened.

So the ambulance for the Commissario went back empty since there was no way of persuading him aboard. Menetti was still trying to coax him as he began to walk away. As for don Giuseppe, he looked bewildered, staring at what was left of his car and wondering why . . .

That grim snow-laden morning had been unexpectedly transformed into a radiant transparency in which every possible light was pouring directly from objects, houses, trees, mountains and from people themselves. For others, that simple change would have been reason enough to brave the road ahead with a smile on their face, but not Commissario Striggio, who, with his hearing still dulled and his sight wavering, had decided to return home on foot. He left Menetti and the paramedics behind, saying that he was prepared to sign whatever had to be signed, stressed that the responsibility would be his but that they had to let him go – an attitude wholly in keeping with his stubborn refusal to admit he was suffering any ill-effects. More than anything else, he hated to admit any personal weakness. All his life he had stuck firmly to the principle that people are weak only if they want to be, and are sick only if they want to be sick. This did much to explain the bitter taste that lingered in his mouth each time he thought of his mother's illness, and the feeling of resentment that had gripped him at the news of his father's.

Death was a form of carelessness: a failure to control oneself and one's surroundings. Just like all that was going on today, not just around him but affecting him directly, a day that had started awkwardly, murky and tremulous and which now, with no warning, had turned into an apotheosis of clarity and brilliance.

And so there was no choice but to set off walking, ignoring weakness, carrying on until his body came to believe that nothing had happened and that everything was back under control. To the age of nineteen he had slept with his eyes half-open.

* * *

"I just want to lie down for a moment," Sergio said after a while.

(When you said you knew an alternative way of stopping the process of memory erasure in "Eternal Sunshine of the Spotless Mind"; and when you bought two tickets for Prague to see the Bubeníček twins;)

"Oh no!" Leo exclaimed, without holding back.

Sergio stopped and looked at him. "No?" he asked with the consternation of someone who detects a certain alarm.

"No," Leo repeated. "It's not the best thing to do in cases such as this."

Sergio shook his head. "I'm not in shock."

"Oh no?" Leo insisted.

"Of course not!"

"Just do it for me, OK?"

"Leo, come on . . ." Striggio continued, as if unable to understand the reason for his worry. "So what do you reckon I ought to do?" he asked, waiting for Leo's permission to lie down and close his eyes. Now all he wanted to do was slip off his shoes, loosen his belt, take off his tie and undo the top buttons of his shirt. Just performing those gestures alone, he thought, would help him feel better. Yet for some unknown reason he could do nothing. Nothing at all.

Leo grasped at once the look of supplication written across Sergio's tired face. Opening his arms he went over to him as if to show that he himself was a home in which he would find refuge, a safe haven. He held the knot of Sergio's tie and slowly began to loosen it. Then he undid the first three buttons of his shirt, from his Adam's apple to the groove of his chest.

Sergio's lips parted. "I'm drowning, I'm drowning," he murmured, while a list of things he knew about himself echoed through his mind.

* * *

(When, as a child, he was afraid of seeing blood seep from the consecrated host; when Friar Lawrence whispers to Juliet: "A greater power than we can contradict / Hath thwarted our intents" just before the Prince proclaims, as an anathema: "All are punished"; when he searched Volume IV of his encyclopaedia (Bes–Calif) for the expression "neoplastic cachexia"; when he had an uncontrollable fit of giggles at the funeral of the grandfather of one his classmates; when, for a moment, it seemed that resuming his own life was like coming up for breath; and when he had transformed that breathing into his decision to face his father on his own ground and applied to join the police force without telling him;)

* * *

Leo knew how to recognise Sergio's floundering even before he put it into words: "No-one's forcing you to do what you do," he said, trying to find a tone of voice that didn't sound like a reproach.

But it was an entirely pointless effort. "Exactly, considering that I do what I do."

"So don't do it then. Sergio, that's enough!" Striggio gave Leo a look of astonishment. He couldn't understand how he had failed to see the extent of the difficulty he was now in. "And don't look at me like that!" Leo added.

"Why, how am I looking at you?" In Sergio's question there was a kind of plea, as though he needed to allow Leo more time and to understand.

Leo tried to work out what strange reason had driven Sergio to risk seeming pathetic. "You're looking at me as if to say I don't understand you," he said. And he said it stressing each individual syllable so that there could be no doubt.

Sergio gave a smile. "If you understand me it's worse."

Leo shook his head. Then he took the back of a chair as though he had decided to sit down, but instead moved it another few centimetres under the table. He went to the front door, picked up his house keys and his quilted jacket. "I have work to do," he said, and shut the door behind him, being careful not to slam it.

* * *

(When he used to watch "Gilmore Girls" in secret; when before asking him the right question he tried asking a thousand wrong ones; how irritated he looked each time he insisted on wearing check flannel shirts for work; when he was cross with himself every time he missed a call on his mobile; when, therefore, that missed call was the physical expression of their distance; when he felt so weak and so vulnerable that he was frightened of his own shadow; when he had a fit of hiccups at the dinner table or on the sofa for no apparent reason; when he was so emotionally fragile that he couldn't even look at adverts for Save the Children, or the one about the father who works on the oil rig and sends greetings to his family by Skype; when, ah yes, he felt himself drifting like in Millais' "Ophelia", pallid, with flowers floating around him; and when in the film "Les Cowboys" the man says: "I don't want you to doubt my loyalty," and the woman answers: "Is this how you say goodbye?" ;)

* * *

As if he didn't know him. Alone in the house, he felt the day turning to the yellowish pallor of a drowned man's skin. The sky was a dangerous mass of water held back by a thin wall of glass where clouds floated, some like slender jellyfish, others plump and heavy and the colour of sharks. Sergio opened his mouth wide as though he needed to fill his lungs before submerging once again.

"Is this how you say goodbye?" he could have asked Leo just a moment before he shut the door behind him, but that question hadn't come to mind. Because the right questions and answers have a terrible habit of always coming to mind when it's too late. And so Leo would perhaps have understood just how much Sergio needed to be reassured; and how even a small amount of certainty could help the glass that was preventing the sky from falling on him stay strong and intact.

IS THAT HOW YOU SAY GOODBYE? he texted, hoping it wasn't too late for some shred of consolation. He waited for an answer that didn't come. He waited half an hour, barely moving.

Frau Steltzer finished clearing the table. Her house contained some vestige of every significant event in her life: the photos of her marriage in true mountain valley style, with plumes, sledges and bells, and their honeymoon in Venice when you could still feed the pigeons and get them to flock around the newlyweds with St Mark's in the background. But finer still than that vast and magnificent background was the young, slender figure of Herr Steltzer at her side, lean and upright as though he had an everlasting future ahead of him. But no, Edmund Steltzer had died very young. Of leukaemia. So young that he wouldn't get to see his son Hermann. Here he is in another photo, already ill – yet not much thinner and lankier than he had always been and standing, in his smoke-grey junker jacket piped in red.

"I'm going . . . *ich gehe*," Hermann Steltzer said, switching back to German.

"*Du warst nur eine halbe Stunde zu Hause,*" his mother complained.

Hermann Steltzer made a rapid calculation in his head. "*Keine halbe Stunde, Mama, ich war schon um halb zwölf da.*"

She pressed him, saying that however pedantically precise he was trying to be, the fact remained that his lunch break that day was much shorter than usual. So Hermann had to admit that, yes, from that point of view his mother was right, but he had been given a task that involved much care and responsibility. And this was the reason he'd been late.

Frau Steltzer looked at her beloved son with a hint of suspicion.

That he was working, as she said, for an Italian made her feel he was in constant danger.

"*Die Verantwortung? Was für eine Verantwortung?*" she asked suspiciously.

Hermann cut her short, explaining that the very word "responsibility" prevented him for talking to strangers – to be defined in this case as anyone not involved in the current investigation.

Frau Steltzer gave a start. "*Mit Fremden? Bin ich eine Fremde?*" she snapped.

Hermann lost his patience. His mother clearly wanted to be right at all costs and pretended not to understand what she had understood perfectly well. "I didn't say you're a stranger," he yelled. "Mamma, I've got to go." He was thinking of how many hours of video recordings he still had to watch.

"*Ist es das fehlende Kind?*" she asked as if none of the previous discussion had even taken place.

"Yes," Steltzer conceded. "It's about the missing boy." He felt that replying to his mother in Italian instead of German was almost like continuing not to answer.

"*Hast du an den Bären gedacht?*"

"Bear? What bear?" he asked.

"The Bear of San Romedio," she replied in the sharp, perfect Italian spoken by the valley people.

* * *

Gaia Ludovisi finished rinsing her hair. She stayed under the shower just long enough for her husband Nicolò to decide he ought to get dressed and maybe leave. Just like two secret lovers, with that kind of anxiety that requires them, once it is all over, to wind everything back to the moment when nothing had yet happened. Hers, though, was not regret but amazement. Yes, if she had been asked how she felt at that moment she would have replied: amazed. About herself, of course, but also about how things had worked out with her husband. About how all those words unspoken for so many years had proved eloquent. And how extraordinary that sense of freedom had been, almost an urge to lose control, which had gripped them both.

* * *

On her return home, surprisingly, she had found him in the kitchen. Too relaxed.

Nicolò had allowed her just enough time to put the shopping bags on the table. He embraced her from behind. She stretched her neck just far enough for him to bury his face between her ear and shoulder joint. And he sank his face into her, knowing that portion of her body was responsive. He gripped her breasts directly through her T-shirt and felt her nipples harden. "Did you think I'd forgotten you?" he murmured.

"What do you want to do to me?" she asked, her voice aching with excitement. And she turned to look him in the eyes.

"I want to take what is mine."

Gaia had begun to unbutton his shirt from the lowest button so that she could feel the heat of his groin.

Nicolò took hold of her buttocks so that he could sit her on the table where it was easier to free her from her tights and her pants.

He was intense, quick, perfect. Like the final result of an endless, silent preparation.

* * *

As Gaia gathered up her hair she thought that all of this can happen only through consensus and only very rarely. All the literature is based on stressing that instant: the fragment of perfection that manifests itself in an infinite series of imperfections. And it deceives us into thinking that real life can be nothing other than a sum of those instances. Nothing is as deceptive as the story we tell ourselves, she thought.

Nicolò, without even getting dressed again, had remained exactly where and how she had left him. "What is it?" she asked as she came back into the kitchen. On seeing him, she had automatically folded her bathrobe over her breasts.

"What's what?" he replied. "Nothing. Aren't you hungry?"

Gaia looked at him with a hint of a smile. Nicolò had managed to retain that dangerous teenage attitude of never properly considering the consequences of what he was saying or doing. "If the question relates to the fact that you have waited for me to finish my shower before asking me to prepare you something to eat, the answer is that I'm not hungry. Are you?"

"Why are you talking like this?" Nicolò asked with the slightly carping tone of a monarch in the mood to be gracious.

"And how am I talking to you?"

"As if you're cross with me."

"No, actually I'm cross with myself. And I'm not hungry. But it's all there, take what you want," she said, pointing to the shopping bags still on the table.

Nicolò was suddenly aware that he was half naked in the kitchen of his own home. "All in good time . . ." he exclaimed, searching around for his shirt and pulling his pants up from around his ankles. "What is it I haven't understood?" he asked, looking genuinely bewildered.

It made Gaia realise that what really annoyed her about the man was the genuine sincerity with which he didn't understand things. "It's the little things you always miss, Nicolò," she said. Instead of answering, he just looked at her. His young women friends, Gaia thought, must have convinced him that this troubled, pensive look was irresistible. "I'll go and get dressed," she said, leaving him with his expression.

"OK," he replied. "Do you want to eat out somewhere?"

"No, I want you to go," Gaia said.

"What have you done to your arm?" he asked, noticing for the first time a purplish burn above her wrist.

"Did you hear what I said?" Gaia answered, covering her arm.

Nicolò Ludovisi's expression changed without him taking his eyes off her. A painfully angelic determination had replaced his pathetic attempt of moments before. "What have you done?" he repeated.

"It's nothing!" she snapped. And went to return to the bathroom.

"You thought I wouldn't notice?"

"I said it's nothing! Nothing at all . . ."

The fading light was affecting everything, qualifying every sensation, coordinating every reaction. The light was leaving in the same way as it had arrived. This time Nicolò had to strain his eyes to focus on Gaia. "I wasn't referring to that," he explained, pointing to her arm.

"Ah," she said. Love, and even indifference, meant they understood each other without the need for too many explanations. "I don't think anybody has hidden anything from anyone," she observed.

Nicolò shook his head – this time in agreement, even though it wasn't in fact true that nothing had been hidden. "Omitted," he murmured.

Gaia frowned as she tried to work out the meaning of the word he had just murmured. One of her husband's weapons was to lower his voice, to allow things said to verge on being unsaid.

"Nothing has been hidden, but something has been omitted," he repeated, and in his voice there was a kind of passion, as if he were particularly fond of that phrase.

"Yes," she conceded. "Omitted. But isn't it the occasional omission that keeps marriages alive?" she asked. "Or ends them," she added, without giving her husband time to answer.

"This is one of those things that should to be decided together," he stated. He now seemed extraordinarily calm and lucid. The close of the day had cast a shadow over his side of the table and he had become no more than a dark silhouette.

Gaia was tempted to sit down, but didn't. "One of those things that should certainly be discussed together, I agree, but not decided: each has to make their own decision."

"Are we now at the discussion or the decision stage?" Nicolò asked, though it was clear even to him that his question was rhetorical.

She lapsed into a strange bewilderment that took the form of a kind of laboured breathing. "Do you seriously think everything can just carry on as though nothing had happened?" she asked, her voice choking as she spoke.

"You're the one who thought we could carry on even though everything had already happened!" he answered, not conceding the slightest ground.

This is how they had always fought. Like this. And they realised they now hated each other with the same passion that they had loved – not a hatred that envisaged separation but one that drew them to each other. They felt so distant from how they had been before that they seemed now, on that uncertain afternoon, to be seeing each other for the first time.

Gaia finally sat down. "You see," she began. "I was prepared to take a risk, to accept whatever happened, but I hadn't expected . . ." And she stopped, as though what she was about to say was truly unsayable. "Oh . . ." she said, searching for courage, like a child on the edge of a trampoline trying to tell her father she doesn't have the courage to jump.

"Carry on," Nicolò encouraged her. "What exactly hadn't you expected?"

"You're not helping me like this."

"Have I ever threatened you? Have I ever hit you?" Gaia shook her head. She would have liked to tell him that he wasn't one of those who needed to raise their hands in order to be violent. But she didn't. "Well," he continued, misconstruing her silence. "Well, at least I haven't done that, even if I'd now give my eye teeth to knock you senseless."

His words seriously frightened her, for they were spoken by a man whose manner was totally calm and relaxed. "It's this I wanted to talk about," she said, trying to keep her resolution with no sign of surrender.

"This what?" His voice now betrayed a certain strain.

"What I hadn't anticipated," she continued, intent on not losing the thread of the conversation. "I hadn't expected that Michelangelo would understand so soon. And I couldn't let him be frightened of you."

Certainly, as a child, he could never have understood, but now, as a man, it was clear: his passion for Alberti came from the affinity he felt for his incompleteness. That marvellous theoriser had been foolishly punished by reality, which had forced him to suffer for each of his theories and their conclusions. His ideas went beyond his abilities. He understood the effect of perspective, for example, but not perspective itself. And he? He had spent the whole of his life living other people's lives, adapting himself to them like borrowed clothes.

Alone in that house that wasn't his and far from any prospect of solace, he had to welcome once more that arid sadness that he knew all too well, to invite it to sit down beside him on Leo's pristine grey sofa and to show it the dusk outside the window, the snowy air and the glass pane that still, miraculously, managed to hold up the sky. He was so alone that there was no point holding back the tears.

Lying on the side table, where Leo had left it, was *the novel*. The exercise book in which, many years before, he had thought he could write about his personal obsession. He turned its pages cautiously, noting how much his own handwriting embarrassed him. Some pages were so packed with words and corrections that, despite all the years that had gone by, they still folded like clams. One particular page carried just the heading "Ludovico III Gonzaga". And nothing else.

What else linked him to Alberti? Memory, that's what. Alberti never forgot any wrong he had suffered, especially any contract he had lost to another architect of his own generation. He would take it badly, and meanwhile he improved, fixed, refurbished things left incomplete by others. If this wasn't an exact link ... He too had a memory that was, shall we say, somewhat diseased: he could perfectly remember whole events, whole conversations word for word. And yet he didn't really know what was so special about those events or conversations to make them worth remembering so exactly.

Four years ago, for example: he and Leo had been seeing each other for no more than a week. They had just had sex. For the first time he had begun to talk without Leo needing to encourage him. He remembered every word he had said and every single response that Leo had made. And he even remembered the dampness in the air around them: it was late afternoon, they had gone so far that he had stopped feeling anxious, so that he no longer felt the urgent need to wash or cover himself that had gripped him on the first occasions. Leo's odour suddenly seemed part of his own, something that was no longer extraneous. And in the half-light, with the sounds of traffic from the street, it occurred to him that for some while he had wanted a tattoo ...

("I want to get a tattoo."

"What tattoo?"

"Well ... a couple of words."

"Something in particular?"

"More or less."

"Go on."

"Alright: 'YOU'VE WON'."

"'You've won'?"

"Yes."

"But who ... who's won?"

"Everyone else, anyone who's not me."

"Hmm ... Are you serious? And where would you have this tattoo?"

"Don't know, on my forearm?"

"It's your idea ..."

"They say it doesn't hurt so much there."

"OK, then I'll have one done as well."

". . ."

"I'm being serious."

"OK."

"'I'VE WON'."

"Stupid!"

"What do you think?"

"On a scale of one to ten?"

"Eleven! At least.")

And he could go further back in time. He would have been four or five. It was hot and he was in the yard of his grandparents' house: they lived where the city ended and via Primo Maggio began, in a low, porticoed apartment block that had just been built. His mother was happy when she could leave him there because they were far from the busy road and there was a small fenced garden beyond the portico and plenty of children to play with. But he didn't like going to his grandparents' because the place had a terrible sadness about it, even in high summer. The house reeked of tobacco and fish and there were pictures that even a four-year-old couldn't bear to look at.

Now, with a little effort, that memory became even clearer and more complete, as though he were actually there now: his grandmother's cigarette ash in the bidet by the toilet; the fake rococo pendulum clock, with a small thermometer in the bottom right that never chimed the right hour; doors of the wall cupboard covered with blue wallpaper; a fake cabinet with a metal grille that disguised the radiators; the Garzantina dictionary that his grandfather kept to help him do the crosswords; and the television always switched on for "The Streets of San Francisco". He remembered perfectly the signature tune and Karl Malden's potato nose. He even remembered how his grandmother snorted each time he told her she smoked too much.

All of this hoard, he realised in moments of solitude such as now, was his true curse. To live with the impossibility of forgetting was equivalent to remembering nothing, so much did every experience expand inside the immense archive of his mind.

* * *

All of a sudden he realised that thinking about the nature of his memory had helped him lose that sense of incompleteness he felt when he saw that single solitary line abandoned on a white page of the exercise book in which as a child he had imagined he could write his novel.

"Ludovico III Gonzaga . . ."

When Fanti entered the office, Menetti and Steltzer seemed deep in discussion. She was giving a detailed account of the visit to the priest, and the car that had suddenly exploded in the yard. Fanti heard only the last part, where she was saying it had been impossible to persuade Striggio to see a doctor, even though the blast, which had reverberated inside the priest's house, had thrown him to the ground like a rag doll.

"Oh, Fanti," Menetti said, looking up. "We were waiting for an update from you."

Fanti looked about and realised there was a kind of close complicity in the room. He was surprised to notice that Steltzer had abandoned his usual rigidly controlled appearance for a relaxed nonchalance, while Menetti was standing in an athletic pose, her left hand resting on her hip. "Do you go jogging?" he blurted out.

Elisabetta Menetti, as though in confirmation of the strange atmosphere of intimacy, didn't seem to regard the question as odd. "Yes, I do. How did it go at Communications?" she asked, as though those two apparently discordant notes were by no means out of tune.

"Aren't we waiting for Striggio?" Fanti asked, eyeing Steltzer, who was pursing his lips.

"The Commissario has taken a break, I believe. Let's carry on." Menetti slipped her hand out of her pocket and invited Fanti to sit down.

"Let's see if by putting things together . . ." Steltzer said, encouragingly. It was strange to see him so enthusiastic.

"There's only what we were expecting to find in the phone . . ." Fanti said, then gave a sideways glance to Steltzer. "It's a backup phone . . ." And he paused. Steltzer laughed with a self-restraint that still seemed excessive.

"And so?" Menetti continued.

"Yes," Fanti continued. "For pictures and messages . . . Yes, in short . . ."

"In short for those things that you men do with backup phones . . . what do you call them?" she asked, turning directly to Steltzer, who, caught by surprise, gazed blankly and shook his head as if to say he hadn't a clue what she meant.

"For illicit purposes, we call them fuck phones," Fanti explained. "Ludovisi was well at it," he added. "But, apart from a certain quantity of pictures and messages that didn't show much imagination, however explicit, he used this phone for a series of calls to a private clinic in Rovereto."

"He's conscientious," Steltzer observed. "Has medical checks. Now we have to find out if he has them because he wants to or because he has to." Menetti and Fanti looked at each other. "Don't we?" Steltzer asked, worried he had said something stupid.

"Yes," Menetti confirmed. "But frankly the news that Ludovisi was 'well at it' doesn't seem such a great revelation."

"Let's wait and see who he's 'well at it' with," Fanti suggested.

"We're investigating someone's private life for no apparent reason, Fanti. If we want to proceed along this path we need to go through Susini," Steltzer observed.

"We need to discuss it with Striggio first," Menetti said.

"Yes, yes," Fanti agreed, with a readiness that revealed how anxious he was to involve the Commissario.

"In the meantime, let's find out what clinic it is."

"I've done a quick check on the internet: the number fits a private facility just outside Rovereto." To shorten matters, Fanti began tapping on his computer keyboard, arriving at an image that bore the name VILLA SANTA SUSANNA CLINIC. He called his colleagues over to have a look. Menetti and Steltzer stood behind him. "An exclusive-looking place," he commented as he scrolled down the page.

The web page had indeed been well put together, and it seemed a very modern and efficient place. A building set among hills, with neat lawns and state-of-the-art design, more like a health spa than a clinic. The gallery of photos was followed by enthusiastic claims and names of important professional partners: NEW PARTNERSHIP! DR ALBRECHT MANNER, PLASTIC AND RECONSTRUCTIVE SURGERY; COLLABORATION BEGUN WITH ONCOLOGY TEAM; ENDOCRINOLOGIST RUPERT HUMBOLT AT VILLA SANTA SUSANNA!; ARTIFICIAL INSEMINATION!; BUNIONS!; PERCUTANEOUS NEEDLE FASCIOTOMY!

"We've got the idea," Menetti said, turning away from the screen. She went across to her desk, took her tablet and typed something. "They do everything and charge a fortune for it. But now the question is: what problem does Ludovisi have? How many calls has he made to the clinic?" she asked.

Fanti checked a small sheet of paper on which he had jotted various notes. "Here we are. Sixteen."

Steltzer whistled. Menetti gave him a sideways glance as if to remind him they were at work and he wasn't to take too many liberties. Steltzer froze.

"Sixteen calls over what time period?" the Chief Inspector asked, overlooking Stelzer's behaviour.

Fanti took a moment to check. "Three weeks," he said finally. "According to the printouts it's three weeks." Menetti noted the information on her tablet. "In any event, I've had copies of everything made," Fanti said. "Photos and printouts."

"Do we have the addresses of the women these photos were sent to?" Menetti seemed to be following a reasoning of her own.

"We don't know whether to record this, out of respect for privacy, Inspector," Fanti explained.

"Quite right, but if it turns out there was a connection between the boy's disappearance and one of these contacts, what are we going to do then? This type of privacy is legitimate just as long as children don't go missing."

Steltzer's silence and his expression said two things: that he agreed, but also that he thought too casual an approach might not be appropriate if those contacts were only to do with sex. Menetti looked at him. "Hermann, I don't like rummaging through these kinds of secrets either." She used his first name to emphasise their new team spirit.

"I'm getting on well with the video recordings," Steltzer said. "I've a couple of hours missing at the car park of the Antica Trattoria Olimpo; and two kilometres before there's a stretch of highway covered by the camera at the Cassa di Risparmio cash dispenser."

"A cash dispenser in the middle of nowhere?" Menetti asked.

"Not exactly the middle of nowhere," Steltzer said. "It's a residential area, though you would hardly notice."

"Huh," Fanti said. "Try asking how much the houses cost around there . . ."

"Houses," Steltzer repeated. "They are some houses . . ."

"I see," Menetti interrupted.

"For the moment there's no sign of the priest's car in the restaurant car park, though one frame shows the front of a car that looks like his. Maybe he was careful to park it out of the way, but nonetheless, if he was travelling in that area, the camera at the bank machine will pick it up, won't it?"

It was the longest statement they had ever heard from Steltzer. Menetti shook her head, then started writing something on her tablet saying: "Flawless thinking, Hermann, a very good job."

Susini's unnatural face, caught in the cold light of the hand-held camera of the bilingual regional news channel, appeared even more waxy than usual. It looked suspiciously as though he plucked his eyebrows or treated himself with hyaluronic acid, for his skin was that taut and translucent.

"*Die Untersuchungen gehen in alle Richtungen. Im Augenblick lässt sich keine Hypothese aufstellen,*" he was saying to the journalist questioning him. So there were no firm hypotheses, and the office he represented was following every line of inquiry. There could be no doubt, he had to admit, furrowing his Botoxed brow, that the burning of the car in the very centre of town was arson.

"*Ist dieser Fall mit dem des fehlenden Kindes verbunden?*" insisted the journalist.

Susini waited an infinite time before answering. It seemed he needed to compose himself and make sure he was at the right angle for the camera. He raised his head like someone trying to conceal his double chin before posing for a photograph. This was the question of all questions: whether there was any link between the explosion of the vehicle and the disappearance of Michelangelo Ludovisi. Behind the hint of a smile, Susini concealed a trace of disappointment. "*Im Moment deutet nichts darauf hin, dass die beiden Fälle zusammenhängen,*" he said, since there were no grounds whatsoever for saying that the two events could be linked, but nor could it be said they were unconnected. And so, having said this in his textbook German, he waved his hand to indicate that the interview was now over. The camera framed him as he climbed the steps of the Palazzo della Procura behind the journalist who was still asking questions. "*Kurz gesagt, Sie wissen nichts!*" he called out behind Procuratore Susini. And who could disagree? The only certainty about the whole business, for the moment, was that no-one knew anything.

Switching off the television in his office, the Procuratore sighed heavily. "Can we disagree?" he asked Menetti, who was standing before him.

Menetti shook her head. But she wasn't prepared to accept those words as an admission of failure, as her boss seemed to be suggesting. "We're at the start of the investigation. Shouldn't we try to work out where it's taking us before admitting defeat?"

"Do you think I ought to lose some weight?" Susini asked, without the question having any obvious connection to what they had been saying.

"They say people look at least five kilos heavier in front of TV cameras," Menetti reassured him.

Susini was pondering, perhaps about the fact that it was too early to admit defeat, or perhaps about the five kilos that people put on in front of TV cameras. "I looked for Striggio but without success," he said at last.

"Yes, I persuaded him to take a day off," Menetti lied.

"Hmm. I have to tell you, just between us, that his absence, at this very moment . . ."

"Commissario Striggio is the right person," was Menetti's only reply.

"That does you credit, but before me, now, I see not him but you."

"With all due respect, dottor Susini, and without wishing to contradict, but Commissario Striggio has coordinated every aspect of the current investigation, apart from the fact that at the moment he's dealing with a difficult personal matter . . ."

"Really? I don't know anything about that."

"He wouldn't take it kindly if he knew we were having this conversation . . ."

"I understand," Susini said after a pause. His face now had a more human appearance. "But let's get back to us: what point have we reached?" he asked, pointing Menetti to the upholstered chair in front of his desk.

Ludovico III Gonzaga

Ludovico called me to rebuild the old Basilica of Sant'Andrea at Mantua. I smiled because it was my fate to theorise and to refurbish churches. Lords liked to enter history through buildings that endorse their greatness, and on them they wanted to feel the weight of pagan marble against Christian brick. And so for Sant'Andrea, which was a ceremonial church, I thought of a triumphal arch. The triumph of faith, of course, but also of mankind, which reaches perfection along the right path. This is what I told Ludovico upon showing him the plans. And he observed how the facade seemed "excessively pagan". And I corrected him: "Classical" I said, for divine knowledge had been dispensed also to those who did not know they had received it. In the same way as a casket containing Christ's blood, vials of which had been carried as far as Mantua by Longinus, the Basilica should constitute progress not only through mystery but also through glorification of God as manifested in the work of mankind. But Ludovico was insistent that it didn't seem like a church and that the campanile I had designed to replace the existing one looked more like a municipal tower.

"You are too learned for me, Messer Alberti, and with you I risk losing. You flatter me with marble, but I remain a rustic. And I fear that if I neglect my principles I'm at risk of being lost. So I have no choice but to instruct you: infuse your science of humanity for the Glory of God, but the campanile remains . . . If the church, as you say, represents the image by which posterity shall remember me, then the campanile must represent the image I have of myself. Therefore, the old campanile stays next to the new building. You have written that ancient and modern, both of them derived from human genius, are never in conflict."

I bowed my head: "Very well, the campanile will remain."

* * *

Striggio had time to reread it before realising that the doorbell was ringing. It had been strange to take up again, as an adult, the story and project he had abandoned as a teenager. Yet he had felt the need, as if for all those years he had been waiting only for the right moment. Sitting in front of that sheet of white paper, that lone title, he had managed to find the tone and even to recall all the circumstances that had led him to recount that specific episode. The sound of the doorbell at last seeped into his thoughts. He jumped up. It had turned dark. He looked at his watch: it was just after six. In the wide-angle frame of the peephole, Menetti looked flattened. Striggio hurriedly opened the door. "How did you know I was here?" he asked.

"What job do I do, Commissario?"

"Hmm, and how did you know I wasn't at home?"

"Because this morning you didn't look like someone who wanted to go back to his own place . . ."

"Oh no?"

"No. And anyway, your place was in the opposite direction to the way you were walking. How are you?"

"Yes, fine." Striggio was careful to keep a hold on the slight lingering petulance in his voice.

Elisabetta Menetti stood in the very middle of the room, as if to indicate she was prepared to stay but also aware he might not want her around. "What have you been doing?" she asked, noticing he was still wearing the same clothes as when he had left her.

"Nothing," he said. And he wasn't lying.

"What's going on?"

Sergio Striggio shrugged his shoulders. "I had some unfinished stuff." Menetti stared at him in silence. "From long ago," he added.

"You've sorted it?" she asked.

"Hmm, sorted, that's a big word . . ."

"You've been drinking?"

"Yes, fuck it, I've been drinking." Menetti remained impassive. "You wanted something?" The admission he'd been drinking seemed enough to sober him up. "I did some writing," he explained, without her having asked him. "Sit down," he said.

Menetti sat down. "We've had a meeting to take stock," she told him. "With Fanti and Steltzer, I mean."

"Good," he said, and fell silent.

"From Communications there's nothing in particular: Nicolò Ludovisi only used that phone for sending sexy messages to women friends. And Steltzer has got no further, gone half blind watching video after video, but no luck. We're checking a CCTV at a cash machine on the highway two kilometres from the trattoria."

"A cash machine? On the highway?"

"I asked the same question . . . It's a residential area, villas in the woods . . ." Striggio nodded. "Oh, and also," she remembered just then. "There's a video still of the car park at the trattoria. I'd like you to see it. We looked at it at the Commissariato because in one corner there's part of a car which Steltzer reckons could be the priest's." She searched her bag for her tablet to show him the picture.

Outside it was starting to snow again. Striggio closed his eyes. When he reopened them Menetti had placed in front of him an enlargement of the video still. What the Commissario could see looked ordinary, the reality lent to that picture was no more than a kind of grainy, milky outline.

"There," Menetti said, pointing to the right-hand corner, but she realised that Striggio wasn't following her at all. Instead, he looked as though he had seen a ghost. "What's the matter?" she asked. "What's the matter?" she repeated, seeing that Striggio seemed to have no intention of answering. "What have you seen?" she asked again.

"Nothing, nothing," he replied after a very long pause.

And yet his eyes remained wide open as though searching for light. "Are you sure?" she asked again.

"It's not the priest's car," Striggio said abruptly, anxious now for the Chief Inspector to go. "It's a different model," he explained, adopting a brusque detachment that ought to have indicated to Menetti that it was time she left. His mind was awhirl with things to say or do to create the space needed to work on what he had just seen.

"Are you going to offer me something to drink?" she asked.

Striggio noticeably hesitated, his gaze fixed in an entirely new manner. "Let me see that picture again," he asked.

Menetti handed him the tablet and Striggio stared at the still photo from the closed-circuit camera. The ray of light from the screen warmed his face as if he were holding a matchstick between his fingers.

"What is it?" she asked again, though careful not to make the question sound aggressive.

Striggio shook his head. He seemed to want to say something but couldn't. So he returned the tablet to its owner and stood up. "A drink," he muttered to himself. "A drink." And went to the kitchen. Menetti watched him without getting up. It was clear he hadn't invited her to follow. "There's beer and fruit juice!" the Commissario shouted from the other room after a few moments. Then, hardly waiting for an answer, he returned with a can of beer, a carton of pineapple juice and two glasses, which he put down on the small table.

Menetti took the can of beer and poured half into one of the two glasses. She took a long, sensual mouthful, as if, instead of Bolzano in wintertime, she were sitting outside a bar in full sunlight barely protected by a light awning. "I was really thirsty," she said by way of excuse.

Striggio seemed on the point of coming out with all that could be seen on his face, and therefore about to say something particularly important. But for some reason he held back, so that Menetti felt sure he still didn't really trust her.

She had guessed everything, but didn't want to press him, knowing that if she moved the level of their mutual concentration by even a millimetre then everything would have collapsed. So she kept silent but, without actually watching him, followed his every move.

Striggio stretched out to take the can of beer and poured what she had left for him. She had been generous: a good half of the contents. He had put down the tablet without taking his mind, rather than his gaze, from that vapid, pointless, blurred image . . .

* * *

That was the day when he had glimpsed a suffering to which he could give no meaning, let alone a name. He knew, although he had no idea why, that his father could never serve as a point of reference for him . . . They were out for the day, or rather they had gone to see his paternal grandparents, Argia and Vittorio, near Vado in the Apennines beyond Bologna. And now they were in the car on their way home, and in that silence which engulfed them each time they made that journey, as if their weariness at pretending to represent a united family had by then used up every word. His father, who at the time had a large handlebar moustache and a wisp of forelock over his brow, always asked the same question at the same point on the route just after Casalecchio, after the bend at Parco Talon, as they were driving through Croce . . . At that point he would turn to his wife and ask: "Do you want to stop for something to eat?" And each time his wife would say no, that all she wanted was to get back home, that she could prepare something to eat, something light, from the fridge. So his father would accelerate past trattoria pizzeria Bella Napoli, where they had been perhaps once, and which Sergio, who at that time was wearing a pair of Mickey Mouse sandals, had remembered and longed to go back to.

He knew that when his father asked the question, his mother would say no. And he also knew that by interrupting a moment earlier, perhaps showing some enthusiasm about the idea of stopping to eat out, he could change the course of the evening. But he sensed that such a change might be more negative than positive. He guessed then that his mother's pain lay in having to search for words that no longer existed and that the prospect of stopping would just prolong the agony they had to suffer along that return journey. At home there were a thousand reasons for avoiding talking to each other: she busying herself in the kitchen, TV news, supper. But there inside, a few centimetres from each other, with the Apennines that softened and melted towards the centre of Bologna, there was no way of avoiding the silence. So that, for his mother, even just the idea of stopping was unbearable. And so he buried his wish, swallowing it with his saliva and watching it slip away beyond the car window. And yet each time his mother would detect the frustration in his silence. And so, to make it up to him, she would turn round as he sat in the very middle of the back seat and, with a slight smile, almost an imitation of a smile, she would promise: "At home I'll make you some chips." More than a promise, it seemed like an admission of guilt, as if his mother had always understood just how much he wanted to stop there and yet she never allowed it. As an adult he could have given a name to the combination of anxiety and desperation which that admission provoked inside him.

Many years later, on the fourteenth floor of the Ospedale Maggiore in Bologna, just before the snow covered everything, he found himself face to face with his mother. It was a place where silence weighed very heavily, so much so that even the snowflakes made an enormous noise. He realised this was the only moment left to him to tell his mother what he had to say – that he was in no way the son she had expected and that he had for years harboured within him a clear awareness of his original sin. So he sat on the bed and bent over her almost touching her nose with his. And she, without any surprise or expectation, lay watching him, like the mother of all mothers, the alpha mother, if such a person exists. Sergio had the words ready, but once again they proved useless. "I have something to tell you . . ." he murmured.

His mother gave a slight smile and shook her head gently. "I know," she said, or he seemed to hear. Or perhaps he wanted her to have said it.

He moved even closer to her, almost as if he wanted to kiss her. And he seemed to sense she was saying "Goodbye".

And so he jerked back as though he wanted the time and space to weigh up those meaningless words she was trying to speak. He didn't give her the opportunity to try again and perhaps to become clearer. For if his mother had actually spoken the word "Goodbye" then clearly they would have to learn how to say goodbye without delay.

* * *

Elisabetta Menetti emptied her glass of beer quickly, since she could see Striggio wanted to be alone. "Let's catch up on everything tomorrow morning in the office. Anyway, don't imagine you're off the hook with Susini. It's your turn tomorrow," she said, attempting a laugh.

As she stood up to go, she heard the key turn and the front door open. Leo brought in a cold blast of air, as if he were one of those devils in reverse who generate ice instead of fire. He was still taking off his quilted jacket as he entered the living room. He looked at Menetti with a mixture of surprise and uncertainty. "Chief Inspector Menetti," she said, guessing that a professional introduction would avoid the need for explanation. She had often wondered what "that man" would be like, and now she found him surprisingly handsome and masculine. Which confused her, for she had secretly hoped "that man" would be an effeminate stereotype. And yet there was nothing at all feminine about the sturdy figure standing in front of her.

"Leo," he said, as they shook hands. Now that they were face to face, "that woman" seemed to match his worst expectations and came close to all that he had always loved in women. "I see that Sergio has been an adequate host for once," he said, then went up and kissed him on the mouth.

"I was just about to go," Menetti said, still standing there.

"I hope I wasn't interrupting anything," Leo said provocatively, with his hand resting on the back of Sergio's neck in a declaration of intimacy for which he needed no-one's permission.

And Striggio let him.

* * *

"You don't have to say goodbye to me. The point is never about saying goodbye," his mother said suddenly, with a clarity in her voice that made him tremble.

"So what is the point?" he had ventured to ask. She stared at him as if unable to recover the thread of the conversation. "You were saying that the point is never about saying goodbye."

His mother looked at him, grateful for the brief reminder. "The point is about how to say goodbye," she answered.

And he understood perfectly.

In the meantime it had begun to snow with a solemn force, as in Russian novels, Romantic paintings and Arctic poems.

It began snowing with the obstinacy of someone who wants clarity but ends up just covering everything once again in a lasting whiteness. Outside, the noise was becoming deafening, and his mother began to complain that she needed to go to the bathroom. Sergio pressed the button that connected the room with the nurses on night shift, but no-one answered . . .

The previous afternoon – when the snow still seemed a presentiment – he had done something he had been planning for some time. His mother had been taken for a short cycle of treatment. The ward sister had suggested he take a break and went down to the bar for a warm drink, but he had stayed there beside the empty bed. He felt such an overwhelming sense of exhaustion that even just the idea of making a decision seemed impossible. In that bed, his mother had left a slight but exact imprint, especially on the pillow. It was in that moment of heightened awareness that Sergio realised he could do what he felt a need to do.

Sitting carefully on the bed to take the measurements, he stretched out a little further to rest his neck exactly in the hollow she had left on the pillow. And all of this to be sure that he could see exactly the last thing that she would see before she died. And so he realised that all that could be seen from that position was one totally insignificant portion of the point where the wall and ceiling joined. That was it. An ivory-coloured corner where perhaps some space might be found for hallucinations and apparitions, but which now revealed only the immense exactness with which people die. With that act, which he would never regret, he gained an understanding of the end, a capacity for disappointment and a familiarity with the prosaic which would prove to be of great use to him.

* * *

Now, for example. In the midst of that exchange of glances between Leo and Menetti, he felt it best to apply the tactical approach life had taught him. The solution was to do absolutely nothing and to let them sort it out between themselves.

"There was no way we could persuade him to be seen by a doctor," Menetti said.

Leo spread his arms as if to say there was nothing new about that, since he knew perfectly well just how stubborn Sergio could be. Their conversation must have continued and relaxed into an informal exchange, for Striggio now heard Leo describing, with loaded nonchalance, how he had once got a cut that needed two or three stitches but had refused to go to hospital to have it treated. And Menetti nodded.

"I'm going for a rest," Sergio said after a while, standing up, and did so as if he were giving them permission to continue discussing him even in his absence.

"You're feeling ill?" Leo asked, though careful not to sound over-concerned.

"Just tired."

Menetti put her hands together before her mouth as she did each time she was about to leave. "Time for me to go. I know the way," she said, and without waiting for a response, she headed for the front door.

Sergio heard the click of the lock as he entered the bedroom; and what he had seen on Menetti's tablet a little earlier came back to mind like the thrust of a knife.

Leo remained exactly where he had left him.

* * *

And so that plan, so clearly thought out, of wanting to see exactly what his mother was looking at from her bed and what, in all likelihood, she would be looking at one moment before she died, had proved disappointing. Not that he expected anything extraordinary, but he certainly didn't expect such ordinariness. When they brought her back to the room, dazed after the treatment, he decided he would no longer leave her but would watch every second of the life she had left. For when the time came he wanted to be there, sitting on her bed, bent over her, face to face, shielding her from that wall. He told himself that he would prevent her from departing with her eyes staring at that inert void.

* * *

He had fallen onto the bed without undressing. From that position he could see as far as the top of the wall in front, just above the wardrobe. Nothing new, therefore: the living and the dying muddle along while gazing at ordinary things. He saw that a small patch of damp was appearing on that side of the wall. He had never noticed it before.

* * *

Up to the age of fifteen, getting to sleep had been an agony. He didn't know exactly when it had begun, remembering only that, from a certain moment onwards, when it grew dark, his mood began to darken too.

Then it was bedtime, and that slight gloom turned into deep darkness. His throat contracted and he felt he was going to suffocate alone in his bed, with the ceiling looming over him and his blankets and sheets gradually becoming more solid, like quick-setting cement. His mother watched over him as only she knew how, letting him know that she was working out what best to do. She was in two minds – whether to give in straight away and get into the bed with him and stay there until he had fallen asleep or whether to make one last attempt at resistance and tell him that in his lovely room, a few steps away from the bed where Papà and Mamma were sleeping, nothing horrible could happen, adding that she would leave the adjoining doors open.

And that was what she did. She left the doors open. Sometimes, as a last resort, she carried him to her bed, but she would say he was too big to sleep with Mamma, and told him she could never understand how a bright, intelligent boy like him couldn't overcome that inexplicable fear. Even then, someone was asking him to explain what he didn't know how to explain. In his mother's bed, taking his father's place when he was on night duty, he slept better – there was nothing else to explain.

When he was about fifteen, his parents decided it was time to see someone who could help. His mother sometimes lost her patience. Sometimes she shouted at him. They found a child therapist. The first appointment took place in the presence of his parents. His father was so nervous that he didn't say a word, even when questioned. The therapist, not wanting to make too much of the situation there and then, asked his parents to stay behind at the end of the first session, telling Sergio that he could sit outside in the waiting room.

"We won't be long," he had promised. And Sergio obeyed.

Over the next few years, Sergio built up a detailed picture of what had then happened. The therapist had looked at his father and told him that every effort would be pointless if Sergio picked up his father's scepticism about the treatment they were about to undertake.

For Pietro, psychologists were not much different from the hordes of quacks and healers who populated the local TV channels. Yet he pretended to understand how much this torment to which his wife had subjected him was important for his son's stability. "We won't have to keep coming back, will we?" he asked. "I mean, after all, this business ought to be something that concerns only you and Sergio, no?"

"What makes you think it's something that concerns just me and your son?" the therapist asked.

Pietro tried to catch his wife's eye, but couldn't. "Perhaps because if we'd managed to sort it out for ourselves, at home I mean, we wouldn't have needed to come to you," he said.

The therapist nodded as though he entirely agreed. "And do you think this is sufficient to show it's not a problem that has anything to do with you?"

Once again Pietro looked for some sign from his wife. "At fifteen I ran away from home to go to a concert, I'll say only this . . ." He had his own unique way of leaving sentences unfinished.

"Sergio is confused," his mother ventured.

"Of course he is," Pietro said, though he didn't sound serious, which made his wife suddenly turn to him with a look of reproach. "What have I said now?" he replied. "I've just agreed with you, haven't I?"

"As you would with an idiot," she snapped. They could no longer contain their bitterness in all they said to each other. Their words cut deep.

The therapist looked at them as though, in them, he could see the root of everything. Pietro thought he was not wrong: it was from them that this complex creature had originated; they had made him and now they were destroying him . . .

* * *

"What do you feel, exactly?"

Sergio lowered his head. "Please don't ask me to draw," he muttered. "I'm no good at drawing."

"What are you good at?"

Sergio took a while to think. "At learning things," he said.

"What things?"

"Like this," he said, raising his shoulders. The therapist waited once again. "Do you know what dendrochronology is?" Sergio asked. The therapist smiled and shook his head. "It's the study of the age of a tree through the rings of its trunk. And did you know there's only one tree that can't be dated with certainty? Just one," he said. The therapist smiled again. Sergio seemed to have to wait for that smile each time he had no ready answer.

"I don't know much about trees, I have to admit," he replied.

"It's the yew. A yew can't be dated because after about three hundred years it becomes hollow and hard and starts to regrow inside itself."

"Fascinating," the therapist commented, genuinely. "And doesn't knowing these things help you?" he asked.

"In what way?" Sergio asked in reply. It was the first time he'd thought about it and the first time he'd realised that knowing was proving to be pointless. "If anything, it makes things worse," he said.

The therapist settled further into his chair. "Makes what worse?" he asked, pretending the question was not that important.

"Knowing," he said. "Knowing."

* * *

That damp patch had begun to bother him. Why had he never noticed it? It was dark enough not to be recent, and yet he had never noticed it: "Here's another of those instances when knowing is a nuisance," he thought.

Leo came into the room. "Ah, you're here," he said, as though it wasn't obvious enough.

"There's a leak between the ceiling and the wall over the wardrobe," Sergio said.

Leo remained immobile. "Yes, it's been there a few months. I've had a word with the tenant upstairs."

"Of course." Sergio spoke as though talking to himself, his eyes shut. "The other evening, when Michelangelo Ludovisi went missing, were you at the Olimpo?" he asked point-blank. "Perhaps it's worth adding that I know the answer, unless you lent your car to someone else."

"Are you playing the policeman with me?" Leo asked back, instead of answering.

"Your car was parked there at the same time as the Ludovisis'."

"And maybe it was still there when the boy disappeared three kilometres away: I've seen the television and read the newspapers."

"We're making inquiries." Sergio's voice betrayed an infinite tiredness. "Leo, you should have told me," he said, sitting up on the bed.

"It was a dinner with colleagues, to celebrate a birthday: what did I have to tell you?"

Sergio closed his eyes again.

* * *

"And what's the biggest problem about knowing?" the therapist had asked.

"Solitude. Solitude." He had said it twice because it was something so obvious that he didn't even think he had needed to say it.

* * *

Sergio got to his feet. Leo watched him like a house cat. Incapable of articulating questions, but certain they were there in full sight.

"Where are you off to?" he asked, seeing that Sergio was going to get his jacket from the living room. There was no answer. Sergio really didn't know why he couldn't answer. He wasn't hurt, he wasn't disappointed. But there were too many things going on all at the same time.

"You said you were drowning. Drowning, you said!" Leo yelled, with immense agony. "You know what? Sometimes people drown because they want to!"

Once outside the house he had to stifle a sob. He had every intention of deceiving himself that it wasn't a fit of tears. It sometimes happened. He'd been worn down by so many sleepless nights that he couldn't pretend otherwise.

The Isarco flowed towards the Adige with a strange calm. It was a silent river. Sergio decided to walk along its bank. The air was incredibly cold, and the water moved so slowly that it seemed about to freeze up: a compact mass, more fat than fluid. "Sometimes people drown because they want to!" Leo had said. How could he disagree? Even the therapist had warned him once about the danger of growing too fond of one's own illness. Although he hadn't used the word illness. It was Sergio who used it. He could. For this was the only real power he had: he could deceive the whole world but not himself. Yet this ability didn't make him any more sincere, because the self to whom he could reveal everything was all-indulgent and only too prepared to forgive.

One day his father had asked him which of the girls in his class he fancied. It was the only time he had ever tried such a matey approach. Sergio simply shook his head and told him there wasn't anyone. And, in fact, there wasn't. His father behaved as though he was just pretending to believe him and, seen from outside, that kind of conversation seemed quite normal, like between any father and son in any part of the world. And yet the lie involved in telling the truth had made it specific, momentous. That man represented as much repugnance and charm as he, a boy, his son, could love and hate at the same time. Those shirts of his, for example, always so perfect: he hated them. And yet he would one day come to realise how much he loved them on other men.

He ought to have replied that there was Sanuti, the boy in 4B. But his father hadn't asked whether or not he was in love, but whether there was any girl he fancied. There wasn't, so he hadn't lied.

He had to remove his glove to take his phone from his jacket pocket. He fumbled about for a while but eventually succeeded, and dialled a number.

"Commissario?" Fanti answered in surprise.

"Yes," Striggio said. "Listen carefully." The silence at the other end indicated that Fanti was listening obediently. "Do we have all we need from Ludovisi's mobile?"

"Everything, sir," the other replied. "Duplication and printout of contents, but it was a backup phone . . ."

"Yes, yes," the Commissario interrupted. "You need to do something for me."

"Yes, sir." A note of concern crept into Fanti's voice.

"You have to put the phone back exactly where you found it. When Ludovisi realises he has lost it, if he hasn't already noticed, he'll go looking for it. Let's have him find it again, eh, Fanti?" And he uttered this last phrase with a certain tone of complicity designed to persuade Fanti that he was part of some diabolical plan.

"OK. I'll do it first thing tomorrow morning."

"Now, Fanti. Do it now."

Fanti didn't answer. He looked about. Everything seemed so comfortable in the warmth of his house. Then he looked down at his feet, nicely warm in their felt slippers . . .

* * *

"The Trip to Bountiful" was the film Leo watched each time he wanted to cry. It was a story he knew well: the elderly Carrie runs away from her son's house and wanders through the vast middle lands of the United States to reach Bountiful, where she had been born.

That evening Leo began crying as soon as the title sequence started to roll. Alone, on the sofa at home, in exactly the same place where he and Sergio had been sitting not an hour before. Could he imagine a world so upside down as to prevent him loving and being loved by that man? The elderly Carrie looked out at the strange landscape from the window of her room. A pusillanimous son and a mean-hearted daughter-in-law had made her into the weak creature she had become, and now she had only one option: to get to the only place where she had been happy. So she set off on her journey, at the mercy of everything, prey to a world that had changed and for which she was unprepared, fragile as a child lost in a large department store. This made Leo cry. He was alone and could do so unconstrained. His phone lay beside him inert: he wouldn't be calling.

There were tears that didn't go away, and at the end of the film Leo felt a residual grief so deep that he almost couldn't stand up. So he took his phone and rang a number, waiting for an answer. "It's me," he said, then stopped to listen. "It's about Sergio. I know I promised, but I've got to tell him . . ." Once again he concentrated on listening. "I know, I know! And you have to understand me . . . Not that I have any intention of involving you, but you've got to go to them before they do anything about it . . . If it all comes out and you've kept quiet, then it'll be worse, believe me."

* * *

Striggio's second call was to Menetti. The mist that had enveloped him was clearing, and the light breeze had stiffened. "We have to go to that boy's school," he told the Chief Inspector. "Tomorrow morning, first thing," he said, and in some way he set in motion that kind of revival of thought that was going on within. He had often told himself that this job of his, chosen perhaps out of vengeance, really wasn't right for him. But now he thought exactly the opposite. That's how it went: from extreme depression to extreme exhilaration. Menetti agreed, they should certainly pay a visit to the boy's school, not least to find out how well socially integrated he was. But Striggio pointed out that Michelangelo Ludovisi's unpopularity at school was the only certain information they had on him. He hung up. He thought of going to see his father in hospital but changed his mind and headed home.

* * *

"I've told too many lies. Out of hatred. And now the truth seems out of reach ... Nothing of the person I know is left in me: I don't recognise myself in the person I see and I don't recognise my voice. This is why I lied ... It's so strange to realise how fierce passion can turn into absolute hatred. I didn't think anyone could experience a feeling of such humiliation and destruction. This is why I lied ..."

She reread it, disconcerted by the awkwardness of her urge to explain. She had always told her pupils that clarity of expression is the secret of a good composition. So she tore up all those completely pointless justifications. She took another clean sheet, and it seemed absolutely perfect. Get to the point, Sara, she said. And so, at the exact centre of the blank page, she wrote: "I've told too many lies." Perfect. She folded it into four and put it in the pocket of her coat, which lay over an arm of the chair.

Back at the Commissariato he felt as if he were a new man. He'd had a long shower, shaved, put on a grey jacket and trousers and even a tie. And like De Morcerf's guests at the Count of Monte Cristo's first entry into society, everyone watched him as he came in.

"Susini is looking for you," Menetti warned, seeming not to have noticed the transformation.

"Yes, later," he replied, looking round for Fanti. "Have you done what I asked?" he said, singling him out. Fanti nodded. "What do we know about the fire?" he asked, glancing back at Menetti.

"Arson," she said. "A rag soaked in petrol from the tank and set alight. Quite a risk . . ."

"Thought so," Striggio agreed.

"Things are getting better," Menetti observed.

Striggio nodded. "Things have got to get better," he said, then turned to Fanti. "Can you bring the printouts of all the stuff on Ludovisi's phone?"

Fanti said it would take no time at all, and was soon back at his desk with a slim file. "A list of calls, transcripts of messages, prints of images," he said.

There were four photos, all showing anatomical details: two presumably belonging to Ludovisi, two of an unidentified woman. Not unidentified for long, Striggio thought.

"Sara Heller," Fanti said, as if reading his mind. "As to the nature of their relationship, I don't think there's much doubt."

"Playing the moralist, eh?" Striggio said coolly. "It's not a crime, as far as I know, for consenting adults to send photos of their own genitals to each other."

"Who's saying otherwise?" Fanti replied, defensively. Menetti smiled.

"What we want to know is whether Ludovisi and Heller were in a relationship or whether it was purely sexual."

"So this is what we want to know, is it?" Menetti asked. "And why should this interest us?" Her question had a clearly provocative intent.

Fanti stood watching the Commissario's reaction.

"Because the two don't always go together. It sometimes happens, Chief Inspector, that mutual relationships are interpreted in opposite ways and this can produce motives," Striggio observed.

Menetti and Fanti exchanged glances. The Striggio they had before them was certainly a far brighter and more confident version of the man they had seen the previous day.

"Motives, yes of course," Menetti agreed, though not altogether convinced.

"Sara Heller is a schoolteacher," Fanti explained, "at the junior school."

Striggio drew in his lower lip.

"We've already decided to pay a visit to the school, haven't we?"

* * *

The junior school premises were impressive. Light and reason reigned throughout: a building clearly designed for teaching but warm and informal as well – a good place to learn, and also to work. This was what Striggio had felt each time he waited for Leo, sitting in his car a few metres from the main entrance, always on the opposite side of the road. And now here he was inside, accompanied by Menetti; and he had also passed Leo and noticed he had been crying.

* * *

(Each time he pretended he had some problem with his eyes to hide that he was upset; when he burst out laughing in tears; each time he caught him sniffing on the sofa in front of some soppy scene on television; when he said that certain pieces played by Richter or Einaudi made him cry; when he listened on repeat to "Please, Please, Please Let Me Get What I Want" by the Smiths; or when he put on that terrible, pathetic film about the badly treated old woman who wanted to go back home, just so that he could sob openly; and each time he watched the short clip of Anas al-Basha on Facebook . . .)

* * *

Leo had looked at him as though imploring him. How could he be so handsome after such an awful night? How? Because nature revealed in him all its monstrous partiality, that's how. He seemed – he *was* – more handsome than ever.

They asked a caretaker where the headmaster's office was. "You mean the headmistress," he said. "Follow the orange line," he added, pointing to an orange strip that disappeared round a bend in the corridor.

They followed it, and Menetti took out her tablet just before knocking on the door labelled EDUCATIONAL DIRECTOR: DOTT. IMMA CARUSO.

The headmistress greeted them with a hint of suspicion: she had passed the selection process and landed the job, but showed not a trace of goodwill. She was approaching fifty and plump, still attractive. Wrapped in a veil of melancholy that clashed with her body, impeccable hairdo and foulard matching the trimming of her Chanel-style outfit, she invited them to sit down. A practical woman, she had been expecting such a visit, since Michelangelo Ludovisi attended her school and was officially regarded as missing. She had everything about the pupil brought into her office so that it would be easier to answer questions and she declared that the whole school, in her person, was at the complete disposal of the police authorities.

"Good," Striggio replied. "We're very grateful for your cooperation. For the moment we'd like to talk to Michelangelo's teacher." He turned to Menetti so that she could remind him of the name of the teacher concerned and she hurriedly checked her tablet.

"Sara Heller," Imma Caruso replied in anticipation, before shaking her head. "Today unfortunately she's absent." She seemed genuinely sorry to have to give such news. "She has asked for two days' sick leave. Time of the year," she added.

Striggio pursed his lips in an expression that Menetti recognised as disappointment. It was followed by a general discussion about the fact that Michelangelo Ludovisi was a pupil with extraordinary abilities, and when she said "extraordinary" she meant it in the etymological sense: extra-ordinary, understood? Menetti and Striggio had understood. Oh, it was clear this boy was gifted. So much so that at various parent–teacher meetings, they had raised the possibility of sending him to a special school better suited for children of such high intelligence. His more than excellent results supported such a move.

In short, everything they already knew. They said goodbye and left.

Outside, in the school car park, they paused to take stock. The head-mistress had supplied them with all the material she could find on the missing pupil: copies of essays, drawings, reports.

"Susini will be happy," Elisabetta Menetti observed, searching for the car keys. Leo, not far away, was also about to get into his car. Menetti looked at Striggio, who looked at her. Wisely, she made no comment.

* * *

Leo got into the car. The blue sky had spread across the windscreen and gave the interior an unstable and powdery brightness. A porous tone. He had spotted Sergio and his colleague behind him, but hadn't turned to look at them. He felt he was under surveillance and sensed their gaze like the lash of a whip. Ineluctable, terrible, worse than expected, biting into the flesh and tearing into the skin.

He placed both hands on the steering wheel, as though he needed some solid support to think things through, or perhaps just to take a deep breath, and was on the point of starting the car when he heard a tap. Sergio signalled to wind down the window and Leo did so without turning to look at him. His scent of dry leaves and new-baked wafer penetrated the interior, giving Leo a start, but still he didn't turn to look at him. And not even a cloud to help him make that clarity less clear.

"How does that piece go?" Sergio asked, to emphasise the casualness with which he was ignoring Leo's obvious embarrassment. "Eh?"

"What piece?" Leo asked.

"The one you listen to when you want to play the victim." Leo bit his lip instead of answering, then went to put the car into reverse to give himself some practical reason for turning away from him.

Sergio didn't give way. He kept his elbows resting on the edge of the window and his face just a few centimetres from Leo's. "How does it go?"

"You're such a shit," Leo said in exasperation, but without starting the engine.

"No more than I have to be," Striggio replied. "We're looking for your colleague. Today, surprise, surprise, she's off sick." Leo indicated that he knew. "We have to talk to her, Leo. Did you know she's having an affair with Nicolò Ludovisi?" Leo nodded once again. "And that didn't seem sufficiently important for my investigation?" Leo's lips were now visibly quivering.

"I gave my word," he said.

This time it was Sergio who gave some sign of understanding, though not approval. "But since I have discovered this for myself, there's no longer anything to stop you, eh?"

Leo shook his head: no, there was nothing to stop him now. "That evening she asked me to go with her to the Olimpo for dinner with colleagues. When we went in I saw Ludovisi and his family sitting at a table in the corner. Sara had told me some time ago that she was in love with a married man and so I put two and two together . . . She was hoping he would see her, and he did. The Ludovisis left soon after, and we stayed on. She'd achieved what she wanted. And that was it."

"That was it?" Striggio asked, stretching his hand out to hold Leo by the base of his neck. Leo offered no resistance and the Commissario tightened his grip slightly until Leo turned towards him, their mouths almost touching. "When you speak next, tell her we're looking for her, alright?" he asked, as though his help really was needed.

"I had promised not to say anything," Leo said once again. Then he freed himself from Sergio's grip without difficulty and turned to look through the windscreen. A large crow had perched on the electronic sign indicating the number of free spaces in the car park. "She's not answering," he added. "I've been trying to call her for hours, but her phone seems to be switched off."

Sergio's only reply was to return his gaze and then put his hand to Leo's neck, to the area of flesh he so loved. Rather than gripping it, he stroked it, as an invitation to look at him once more. Almost kissing him. So close that the hairs of Leo's beard tickled his lips.

It was his way of saying that he could never, ever, manage to break free from him.

The best thing was to follow the road back – as far as the hole. In that dying stage of the morning the landscape seemed still. There are moments, Nicolò Ludovisi thought, when the air is so rarefied as to make everything look frozen. So what he now saw around him wasn't reality but a perfect replica; and things would begin to live, to grow and to age only when that momentary rarefaction was over. As he was retracing his steps along the path to the clearing where he had buried the deer, he felt sure he was in that exact expanse of time when meadows, shrubs, trees, rock, peaks and sky savour immortality. Then, on arrival, he sensed that this feeling of intangibility, which had been so clear just a moment earlier, had finally gone. He parked the car on the side of the road facing uphill and got out. The air was unexpectedly warm.

Nicolò gazed up, the greyness increasingly dense. The further he advanced into the vegetation the surer he was that there would soon be a plentiful fall of snow. They had taught him that heavy snowfalls are heralded by a kind of deceptive and sudden spring: a spring with no excitement, with no noise; a spring with no awakening.

Having reached the burial place, he quickly checked the ground.

Fortunately his mobile was exactly where he thought he had lost it.

Fanti, a short distance away, waited for Nicolò Ludovisi to get back into the car, then took out his phone and dialled a number . . .

* * *

"Well done Fanti, just in time, how lucky, excellent job . . ." Striggio was saying on the phone. Before him stretched the long corridor on the second floor of the Procura. Elisabetta Menetti, a few steps ahead, was collecting her thoughts. "Something wrong?" Striggio asked. She shook her head. A few metres from Susini's office, the Commissario signalled her to stop. "We don't know anything about Ludovisi's phone, OK? I've told Fanti to put it back where he found it."

Elisabetta Menetti gave a look of surprise. "But in that case we've absolutely nothing: the clinic, the lovers, the schoolteacher . . ."

"We have the priest."

"The priest."

"Yes, don Giuseppe and the exploding car. We'll get to the teacher through a routine inquiry at the school of the missing boy. That's enough for Susini."

"I'm afraid it won't be so simple. Yesterday he was pretty cross."

"He thinks I'm useless, I know, but the feeling's mutual."

He knocked without further ado. They found Susini on the telephone, deep in conversation. He signalled to them to sit down and made a vague gesture of apology for the fact that he couldn't free himself from the call. Sergio and Menetti waited and after a few minutes Susini hung up. There was a moment's silence, as if some signal were needed to start that scene in which the subordinate officers had come to report to their boss on an ongoing investigation.

It was Sergio who broke the ice. "I want to apologise for my absence yesterday," he said.

This approach, heavy with a strange pretence of humility, caught Susini off-guard, forcing him to shake his head as if to say it was nothing: "I hope you've recovered."

Striggio smiled. "Perfectly," he said reassuringly, with such a convincing display of energy that Menetti felt she was witnessing the most powerful expression of bipolar disorder she had ever seen.

"Where have we reached in the investigations?" Susini asked.

"We've reached a dead end," Striggio replied.

"Ah," Susini said, taken completely by surprise.

"This is your view, I know, and I have no wish to disabuse you," Striggio explained. Menetti froze in her chair.

"It is my view that when matters reach a dead end then clearly someone hasn't being doing their job properly," Susini observed.

"I'm sure the Commissario meant to say we still have many lines of inquiry open," Menetti explained.

Striggio smiled with no hint of gratitude. They were playing a difficult game, but he had no wish to be defended by his Chief Inspector. "I meant a dead end," he repeated.

"It's unheard of," Susini exclaimed. "This behaviour is unheard of!"

Menetti looked at Striggio and found him calm as the surface of a lake on a windless day – a day without even the remotest breeze. "We're following a line of inquiry that takes us straight to the priest who phoned us on the night of the disappearance," she said.

"This we have understood," Susini retorted. "Do we want to go all the way with this priest? Is it going to help us or not?"

"Oh, it is," Striggio assured him.

Susini gave him a look of disdain, as though he wanted no further dealings with him. "Have him called to the Commissariato, I want to hear him myself," he said, addressing Menetti. "I know you've been to the school."

"A few hours ago," Menetti confirmed. "We've taken some material on Michelangelo Ludovisi, which we're evaluating."

"Go ahead, evaluate, but evaluate quickly." He was about to add something on how relations with Commissario Striggio would proceed, when Striggio's phone rang.

Striggio answered, then paused to listen before jumping to his feet. "I have to go," he announced and, without waiting for permission, opened the door and left Susini's office.

The short female doctor greeted him just as he was going into the room. From her face it was clear the news was not good. "What do you mean, gone?" Striggio said, realising that he was shouting.

The doctor motioned for him to quieten down, almost begging. "He can't be far away," she said, as though the frightened man before her was someone to be pacified with routine phrases.

"If you haven't already understood, I'm the police Commissario," he explained.

At this, the doctor became flustered, saying that she had wanted to explain that an old man in his condition couldn't go unnoticed, nor could have walked very far . . . the hospital staff were already searching for him, and it would just be a matter of time before he was found.

"That old man was once a great policeman," Sergio added. "If he doesn't want to be found, then you won't find him . . ."

* * *

For Sergio's tenth birthday his mother had organised a party at home. His father hadn't been there but at around two in the morning he heard him return, go into the kitchen and pour himself a drink. His mother got out of bed, where she had also put Sergio, and went to see him. They thought he was asleep but he wasn't, and in the inhabited silence of the house he could hear what they were saying. His mother had started in an angry tone, which then turned into one of apprehension and worry

218

as his father told her that Sanzio, a colleague, had been arrested. He had done something terrible, so terrible that Pietro was now crying in his wife's arms. She had lost all of her anger and gripped her husband tightly as though she never wanted to leave him. They had been searching for common criminals but they turned out to be policemen. Which made them even more criminal. They had then searched everywhere for Sanzio, eventually finding him in a church next door to the offices of the Bologna Forensic Unit, which was housed in what used to be a monastery . . .

* * *

It was a dreadful afternoon. There were reported sightings of Pietro Striggio in several places, but none of them was him: most were local down-and-outs. By this stage they had wasted a lot of time. Menetti even sought help from her colleagues in the private security agency. At around six o'clock they had police dogs sniff the pyjamas that Pietro had left on the hospital bed, having fully dressed himself. And the dogs discovered something truly surprising: Pietro was just two floors below in the hospital chapel, sitting silently in the multicoloured half-light of the windows.

"You hadn't checked inside the building?" Sergio asked, incredulous.

Pietro had got dressed, and this was what had fooled them. How easy, how simple even for a sophisticated mind to take something mistakenly for granted. He had dressed himself, and was therefore outside. This was what anyone would have assumed. And yet Pietro, sitting in the chapel, had given his son a perfectly logical explanation:

"Who turns up in pyjamas to talk to the good Lord?"

What Pietro Striggio had to say to God was an apparent mystery: apparently asking Him to give some meaning to what he had become; to accompany him in this particular stage of his life where choices seem to have no importance. For happiness was none other than lightness, levity, a propensity to fly. He was asking Him to free his troubled son from every unnecessary thought, every anxious duty and every danger. Asking to let his illness remove from his mind all that he had lost the ability to love. He was asking for a good death. And for these prayers he needed to present himself dressed in a tie, jacket and coat. He didn't know how long he had been in there, but he knew for certain that no-one else had entered the chapel after him. And this had led him to conclude that we live in times in which no-one feels the need to present themselves before the good Lord, for everyone expects *Him* to present *Himself* to them. Which is exactly what people said about the police: "You're never there when you're needed." Those who told God that He was never there when needed should be given the same answer the police give, that without an official complaint there's no crime to investigate. The police don't go round looking for crimes. People ought to realise that. God doesn't go round looking for sinners. He can only forgive them.

"Let's go back up to your room," Sergio said.

"Don't take me back there," his father begged, without it seeming that he was begging.

"You have to finish the treatment."

"Ah, the treatment. And why? My dear Sergio, I'm dying."

Being addressed in that way struck him deep in the stomach. "Just long enough to finish the course of chemotherapy, then I'll take you home. Two days: that's all," he promised.

Pietro nodded but didn't get up. The chapel became suffused with warmth, a buzzing sound, the scent of flowers and an indigo light spreading from the windows: like being in a field of lavender.

"Do you know how I met your mother?" Pietro asked.

He began by describing where. It was a garage transformed into a private meeting place – a club, as they used to call it in those days.

His hadn't been a particularly exciting adolescence. Yet acceptable. In human memory there's no such thing as a marvellous adolescence. But she, on the other hand, was exactly that. Everyone told him she was already involved with someone else, very much involved. But in those times it meant nothing more than "she still hasn't met me" and Pietro, though no Adonis, was a very popular young male and full of the shameless presumption that made him seem tall even though he was average, muscular even though he was on the skinny side, manly yet with only the hint of a beard. It was that absurd self-assurance that made him irresistible. He didn't excel in anything, but he was the only one people remembered. The word "involved" couldn't keep him from the girl of his life. Anyway, involved with whom? With the prototype alpha male fashionable at the time – nice curls, into politics but rich enough that he could afford to be, and one whom Pasolini would have contrasted with proletarian policemen. In short, a splendid example of a rich kid who had met the most beautiful woman in the world. For Sergio's mother was absolutely that – the most beautiful woman in the world, so she had to be his. That is what people liked about Pietro: his ability to make the impossible possible. He knew what to do because he knew how to think it. This woman gave him sleepless nights and occupied his every thought. Quite simply, there was nothing that couldn't happen in such circumstances. And any argument to the contrary was completely out of the question: there was no room for doubt or discussion.

So he began to pursue her, even to harass her. In those days the word "stalker" meant nothing. The sexes behaved as they had always done: the male was allowed to play the fool; and the female had to practise the patience of centuries. This meant that the battle between the sexes was fought on a fairly even footing and with no invasion of each other's territory. No woman at that time would have accepted a male who used more make-up than she did. So Pietro set to work. He turned up in all kinds of circumstances: he went to the parties where she went and to the same restaurants. He took the beatings he deserved when the official boyfriend got fed up of him being around. He had reckoned on that. But he also reckoned that nothing in the world would make him give up, because she was the woman of his life. Period.

Until one day she faced him. She told him in no uncertain terms to piss off. Simple, direct, magnificent. Pietro felt he had never loved her more than he did at that moment and so asked her what it was that kept her from him. A stupid question, perhaps, but one she must have thought profound. Because, surprisingly, she gave him an answer. Rather than telling him to get lost for good, she explained that he lacked various features which her boyfriend possessed: well-built, handsome, curly hair. While he was of modest build, couldn't be described as handsome and had hair as thin and straight as spaghetti. So Pietro knew what he had to do. Her reply was an invitation.

It was a period when Bologna was going mad over African fashions, and some shops – as well as selling Afro objects – had rooms at the back that styled western hair in the appropriate manner. Pietro asked for curly hair and got it. And with his new head of hair he went to see her a few days later: and she looked at him bewildered. Many years later, recounting this story, Sergio's mother had said: "It was the most horrendous thing I'd ever seen, but I fell in love with him there and then. If a man can look as ridiculous as that for me, I said to myself, he's sure to love me forever . . ."

* * *

(About when he told the story of how his father Pietro had won over his mother;)

"Too dark to walk back," Sergio's mother would say each time the night filled every corner and the two of them were out somewhere without Pietro – something which happened fairly often. Now, in that gentle suburbia around the Ospedale Lorenz Böhler in via Lorenz Böhler, the night had the elegant air of a woman in her forties in a tight black dress. Everything in those latitudes had a wholesome, upright air, and it was perhaps precisely that which made the atmosphere so dense with expectation. For forty-year-old women in tight black dresses are dangerously unpredictable.

Striggio needed to hug Leo and perhaps, yet again, to ask his forgiveness. He pressed the Pronto Taxi app on his phone and waited. A pre-recorded voice asked him to enter the address where he wanted to be collected, with that indifference pre-recorded voices have: voices with no history and no context. Taxi Tornado 56 would be arriving at the entrance to the casualty department of the Böhler, as the hospital was generally known. He only had to wait for three of the five minutes estimated before the taxi arrived. He got in quietly, wrapped up in his own thoughts, and gave the address to which he hoped he would soon be taken. The taxi-driver was one of those with an axe to grind, who was forever complaining: traffic islands, cycle lanes, pedestrian areas, those who give out too many licences ... His meter ticked over with thousands of complaints of what was wrong with this run-down part of Bolzano: foreigners, needless to say; Italians, present company excluded; identity sold off; never-ending numbers of gypsies, blacks, whores ...

Twice Sergio thought of whipping out his police badge and inventing some kind of spot fine or arrestable offence, just to make the bastard shit himself, but he was too impatient to do one thing which had slipped that bastard's mind: to play the queer. So he got out of Tornado 56 without saying a word. He paid and waited for the sixteen cents change. All of a sudden, now outside Leo's apartment block, he felt better. For he alone, the thought of him, could make him feel good – even after an afternoon searching for his father and taking him back to the only place where he didn't want to be. It was Leo who gave meaning to whatever gesture his arms, his hands, his face might make. It was he who gave a language to his inability to communicate and thought to the blankness of his mind.

He used his keys to open the entrance door and climbed to the second floor. But at the apartment he put his keys away and rang the doorbell.

Leo pulled a strange face when he saw him there in front of him, like someone who hasn't yet decided whether the perfume he is smelling is one he loves or hates. "Why didn't you use your own keys?" he asked.

"Because I don't like using your house keys if I know you're mad at me," Sergio replied, still at the doorway.

"Son of a bitch," Leo replied, stepping aside to let him pass. "Bloody son of a bitch," he repeated. "With no offence to your mother, who was a saintly woman," he added.

Sergio remained silently at the doorway. He wanted to let his eyes speak. He wanted his mouth to speak without moving. "Aren't you coming in?" Leo asked. Sergio gestured no. As he did as a child each time his mother asked him whether he'd like to try sleeping by himself. "No?" Leo asked, with a hint of assertiveness, for he knew how to deal with children. He was the most popular teacher in the whole school. Sergio gestured yes. "Come here," Leo said, inviting him into his arms. Sergio allowed himself to be hugged. Leo had the smell of laundry laid out in the sun, of newly mown grass and of an afternoon breeze in a moment of unwarranted happiness and when the temperature is perfect.

They remained there, arm in arm, not saying a word. Every so often

Leo stroked the back of his neck to reassure him. Slowly he managed to lead him to the sofa. "I'll get you something warm," he whispered.

"Later," Sergio said at last. "Stay here," he implored. Leo put himself in a more comfortable position so that he could hold Sergio tight without stopping the circulation to his arm.

"Your father?" he asked after a while.

"He's dying," Sergio said, tersely.

Leo held him even tighter. "I know what we need now," he said with the confidence of one totally able to bring an end to evenings of sadness.

"You're not thinking . . ." Sergio said. "No, please, not Take That . . ." But it was already clear from his "no" that he didn't mind.

Leo jumped to his feet and disappeared into his room. He came back holding his inseparable portable loudspeaker. Sergio began laughing. And, in anticipation, he waggled his index finger to repeat his "no" to say that nothing in the world would persuade him to shift from the sofa.

* * *

Leonardo Pallavicini had become the most famous teacher at Wolff Junior School, in his first job at Bolzano, for getting his pupils to dance to Take That. He'd been teaching that class for a month: eighteen second-year children who were silent and morose, as remote as distrustful children could be. There was Carlo on the second row who was always pouting, Samira two rows behind who sat there like a little madam, Libero who seemed ready to explode, Laura Hu who said very little because she still thought in Mandarin and Gianluca who could have done TV ads . . . It was a Tuesday, a day when they were supposed to do physical education. And so the teacher, Leonardo Pallavicini, appeared in class that morning with a small but powerful loudspeaker to attach to his iPhone. He had all the desks moved to create a space in the middle and asked his eighteen little adults to stand. They all obeyed with a look of suspicion while he connected the phone to the loudspeaker and started a track. It was "Could It Be Magic", the Take That cover version: a short introduction, then the very young Robbie Williams started to sing. The teacher, Leonardo Pallavicini, began to sing along and to dance. The children watched him, while he encouraged them to do what he was doing, turned the volume high and put the song on repeat: impossible not to follow the rhythm. The children, positioned behind, began to move in time . . . When Samira began to dance, Leonardo Pallavicini realised that he adored those children and adored his job. They all danced and smiled. The nearby classes crowded round to see what was happening in 2B and very soon everyone was dancing – teachers and children, caretakers and secretaries who had a not-so-secret passion for that teacher who looked like an actor . . .

And so Leo started playing Robbie Williams, encouraging Sergio at least to play the part of Gary Barlow, who hardly moves in the videos because he can't dance, though he's a brilliant composer. And at first Sergio simply said no: hesitant and firm at the same time. Meanwhile, as the track filled the room, Leo said he had the figure of Howard Donald but couldn't ask him to do the acrobatics he did in the videos. And Sergio said he had never seen the video and anyway in 1992 he was only nine and wasn't a bit interested in Take That. But when Leo mimed them, he said, they seemed irresistible. They shouted back and forth over the music as in a club.

Sergio began to nod his head to the rhythm of the beat. Leo knew the words by heart. He hadn't yet dared to get up from the armchair but he obviously wasn't far short. So on the third repeat of the track, Leo stretched out his hands for Sergio to take hold – like when in the films the hero is left hanging over the precipice until the very last moment, like when Harrison Ford is saved from the abyss by the magnificent Rutger Hauer a few seconds before his time has come to die.

* * *

Leo turned the volume high. One of the neighbours would very soon be complaining. The chasm opened, terrible and cruel but also inviting.

Sergio gripped Leo's outstretched hands, making it look as though he were falling, pretending to be lifted up just to make him happy. He got to his feet and began to move, slowly at first, then more rhythmically, keeping going with remarkable co-ordination until, all of a sudden, he let go with a mad frenzy, as happens when a seemingly insurmountable obstacle has been overcome. Now they both danced, swaying their hips and raising their T-shirts over their stomachs, like two members of a 1990s boy band. It was so long since he'd felt like this. They danced like there was no tomorrow, following the track, which ended and started again two, three, four, five times . . .

* * *

In the middle of it all, predictably, the doorbell rang. And, judging from its persistence, it had been ringing for some time. When he heard it, Leo hurried to turn the volume down, then went to open the door. He was ready to apologise to anyone and everyone, but not to feel a moment's regret.

Surprisingly, it was Chief Inspector Elisabetta Menetti. Leo looked at her in dismay. His face was red and sweaty, and his blue eyes must have seemed even bluer. Sergio appeared behind him, smiling, but his smile dropped instantly. "Menetti?" he asked.

"Yes," she said, addressing Sergio over Leo's shoulder. "Can we talk in private?"

Leo moved to one side.

"Of course," Sergio said, tucking his T-shirt into his trouser belt.

"I hope I haven't interrupted anything," she said, though such an eventuality clearly didn't worry her in the slightest.

Sergio signalled no and motioned for her to come in. Here was reality walking towards the sofa and asking whether they had something to drink.

"A beer?" Leo suggested.

Elisabetta Menetti replied that a beer would do fine. Leo disappeared into the kitchen.

"What is it?" Striggio asked.

Elisabetta Menetti took a while to answer, then, once she had finally decided, had to stop because Leo had returned with an ice-cold can and empty glass. "The teacher, Sara Heller," she continued when Leo had gone again. "We've found her."

"Ah, good."

"Dead. Drowned."

Air

Air becomes wind when it is disturbed by a force.

LUCRETIUS, *On the Nature of Things*, VI, 685

Of the four elements, air is most powerful by far. It is the only element which both generates movement and is unaffected by it: it fans the fire, or blows it out; it reduces rock to sand, eroding it over centuries; and it produces rough or calm seas. Of the elements, air is the only one of the four that cannot be described; and unlike the others only appears to have substance. Air is dangerous and treacherous since every phenomenon is, in some way, related to it – air masses produce water, spread fire and transform the face of the earth. The Lord of the Air possesses everything: he controls all, he transforms all. He has no fear of gravity, he does not yield to pressure and he exists without it. *Up to my neck in water, The sacred flame, Feet firmly on the ground* are nothing compared with *I cannot breathe.* Any phenomenon, to be effective, for life or death, has to reckon with air: its absence or presence. It alone can exploit lunar ice or solar heat. It alone can accelerate putrefaction or preserve things intact. In its infinite, measureless realm, billions and billions of spores breed for eternity. The body, which is mass and liquid heated by the warmth of movement, finds substance in the air – in the breath that has given it life and in the murmur that has pointed a way for it. And yet air's divinity is unassuming – more corpulent than muscular, unobtrusive, discreet and deferring to every vibration, every resonance. Once there was no earth, no fire, nor even water, but air yes. Yes.

Charmless and touchy, the Lord of the Air is viewed with suspicion on Olympus. It is said that he reacts without warning and that he moves in an instant from a smile to a sneer and a howl.

He is feared and appeased, for it is he who transforms the word "phenomenon" into "phenomenal".

And so it was very difficult to say what was dangerous about that particular morning silence. It was a sensation that Striggio could not describe, could not put into words, but he could feel it. He had spent almost the whole night in the cold, in torchlight, on the stretch of canal where Sara Heller's body had been found, though once back home he had slept well. Little, but well.

* * *

Just a few hours earlier, sometime after two in the morning, he had discovered how dry a drowned corpse could seem. Sara Heller lay gaunt on the riverbank where they had placed her before loading her into the ambulance, looking as though she had been under salt rather than water. It was a stretch of water that could still be described as urban. Up where the Isarco splits into the Talvera, or Talfer, her body had lodged against the pier of a bridge, little more than a footway, from one bank to the other of that grassy shore known as Prati . . .

She had been seen by a nocturnal cyclist, floating, caught at the pier by the hem of her red dress. If she had thrown herself into the water, she couldn't have been there for long. If the cyclist had ridden past earlier, he might perhaps have seen her on the parapet and talked her out of it, as happens in films and occasionally real life. But the cyclist had been delayed by family matters and had passed by too late. According to his statement, given there and then, the woman was still flailing about as he called for help. She was caught between the expanse of water and the pier by the hem of her dress, which prevented her from sinking, but also from clinging on and saving herself. A terrible combination of circumstances, because the bright-red loose-fitting dress would become a crucial aspect of the case: it was an ordinary dress with a fairly high neckline. It appeared from an initial investigation that this was all Sara Heller was wearing when she jumped. A coat and a small bag were found at the end of the bridge. In a pocket of the coat, a note folded into four.

("I've told too many lies.")

* * *

At first the scene of the crime had been lit by headlights, giving it a remarkably spectral appearance, something very close to the last scene of "Psycho". The temperature, too, had dropped; and an icy wind had begun to blow.

Menetti was arranging for a forensic team with floodlights and at least one diver to arrive as quickly as possible. Then, seeing there were still a good twenty minutes to wait and there was no reason to fear that the body anchored to the pier by its dress would drift away, she turned off the engine to conserve the battery.

"That'll also turn off the heating," Striggio protested.

Outside the car, the surrounding world was plunged into that perfect darkness that follows a power cut. Striggio waited patiently for his eyes to adjust to the dark until he discovered that the night was unexpectedly clear. The green of the bushes and the grass had of course become a leaden grey and the surface of the water seemed as black as ink, but otherwise a kind of general luminescence gave some certainty. The red of the victim's dress, for example, looked suddenly redder, which explained what the nocturnal cyclist had meant when he said it was the colour that had attracted his attention – it had stood out in the monochromatic mass of the night, making him stop to take a closer look. Striggio thought how lights don't always bring clarity and that certain forms of darkness sometimes reveal details hidden by the facts.

In the realm of the air, this is an established principle: too much clarity, like too much darkness, confuses. The truth exists in a middling light, not in too much darkness, which detracts, nor in too much brightness, which intensifies. Not the absence of detail in pitch darkness, nor the excess of detail in full light.

Yet the very fact that the discovery had been made in the hours of darkness had prevented the news from spreading and the local press and television stations from crowding around the area.

According to the police doctor, the circumstances of Sara Heller's death and the note found in the coat indicated a voluntary act. But she was killed by an unfortunate series of contributory factors: the impossibility of her being able to float, the temperature of the water and the fact that she couldn't change her mind because of the way she had been caught. Too perfect to be true. She had certainly intended to die, but the circumstances had then prevented any change of heart. And, according to the police doctor, 90 per cent of potential suicides are averted by a change of heart.

The wind was now blowing furiously, as if to remind Striggio that he had been born in the realm of the air. The Golden Legend recounted how the wind blew from the Balkans at the time his mother began her labour pains, so much so that the ambulance carrying her to hospital was almost swept over Ponte Mascarella. Such a wind had not been recorded in Bologna in living memory, nor the snow that followed. Some said it was as bad as 1956.

And now, in the middle of the night, on the bank of the Talvera, just where the iron bridge rose from the ground, someone was saying that a sudden, violent wind like this was rare for Bolzano. Striggio looked to his right, where the top floor of the massive Questura building could be glimpsed beyond the austere but dense winter vegetation. He thought how the whole scene that led to the death of Sara Heller, whether voluntary or accidental, could have been witnessed from any of the windows of the records office. Round him now he noticed the strange agitation typical of those who are not really used to what they are doing. For his team – forensic, divers and flying squad – didn't have the admirable nonchalance characteristic of other police forces, other investigations or other regions. Added to this there was the wind, which was becoming a real problem. So, without waiting for Susini's arrival, and as soon as the measurements and photos had been taken, they started to recover the body.

There must have been something "glorious and gracious", to quote Melville, in those gusts of wind so violent and treacherous that they prevented any car door from being kept open and would have blown any hat away. Menetti gave a theatrical gesture of despair before removing the scarf from around her neck. However much she tried to keep it inside her windcheater, its tassels kept flapping against her face, so she decided to take it off and pushed it back into the car through the part-open window. Sara Heller was hauled towards the bridge and brought to dry land, the red dress clinging to her body like bandages. It could be seen at a glance that the limbs were hardening, an indication that rigor mortis was setting in. Her thin hair was plastered to her face like algae, but only briefly, for it was only a few seconds before it was ruffled by the wind.

The body was placed on a stretcher and taken to the ambulance, while the diver was helped out by his colleagues who were waiting on the bank with a blanket. Menetti made sure that all checks had been properly carried out before giving the all-clear. Striggio noted that the wind seemed to be encouraging them to bring this chapter to an end as soon as possible. And so, as the ambulance left for the pathology lab, he signalled to Menetti to join him.

"Heller's personal effects?" he asked as soon as she was within earshot.

The wind blew away the last part of the question but Menetti understood all the same. "A bag and a coat left at the end the bridge," she replied.

Striggio half-closed his eyes. "Do you have them with you?" he asked, raising his voice to compete with the gusts of wind that hampered their conversation.

"In the car," she replied.

"Good, let's go," Striggio said, leading the way.

Once inside the car, all noise seemed suddenly to stop. In the realm of the air it was enough to be wrapped in one's own cocoon to produce some sense from all that agitation.

"We have the house keys," Striggio said, searching through Heller's bag once he had put on a pair of thin blue rubber gloves. "Let's not waste time."

"A few hours won't make any difference," Menetti said. "Why not give ourselves a chance for a shower and some sleep? We have the keys, it won't make any difference," she repeated.

"Alright, drop me at Leo's."

"Just a couple of hours," she repeated, as if to put his mind at rest. Striggio nodded.

* * *

Leo lay awake waiting for him, and had kept him a warm herbal tea. They looked at each other, as words were unnecessary. The raging wind was making the streetlamps swing like fishing lights on a rough sea. But Sergio was now home and had three whole hours to sleep. There was a bang from a window left unwisely open. Sergio gave a sudden start and Leo rushed to close it. He bore the grim look of dark days. So that Striggio, before collapsing into bed, felt he had to tell him not even to think of it . . . not even to think of saying he was to blame for what had happened to his colleague.

Yet Leo couldn't stop thinking about her voice when they had spoken on the phone: determined. Yes, that was how he would have put it: determined. But he said nothing, for he could see that Sergio was too tired to listen. So they went to bed.

Sergio closed his eyes, though you couldn't have said he fell fast asleep. His sleep always had a specific quality: neither deep nor superficial; cautious, enough to allow him to rest, but too light to lose consciousness; and too vigilant for him to work out to what extent his dreams were real or just deep thoughts. But on that particular night, probably as morning was just arriving, the wind entered his dream.

There would be a snowstorm according to the radio. The crackle of the forecast reached him from the kitchen just as he was opening his eyes. The wind had swept away all mist and all uncertainty. The sky might now be said to have vanished, and there was no other description for it than an immense milky void. Leo was sitting in the kitchen staring at a cup of milk, unsure whether he could manage to drink it.

"Haven't you slept?" Sergio asked, approaching from behind.

Leo gestured as if to say hardly at all. "I can't stop thinking I might have been able to do something . . ."

"Well stop thinking it."

It was as though there'd been no interruption. As if, after those few hours' sleep, Sergio now found himself exactly where he had left off the previous night.

"Maybe I was the last one to talk to her . . ." Leo stammered.

"Maybe," Sergio agreed. "But we're checking her phone, her movements. So maybe, in fact probably, you're torturing yourself over nothing."

Leo looked doubtful, with an expression of anxious desperation. "You know what people always say? It doesn't seem real." Sergio had gone to fetch a cup from the drying rack over the sink. "What happens now?" he asked, once Sergio had sat down in front of him.

Sergio poured himself some warm milk. "What happens?" he asked in reply. "Autopsy, investigations, witnesses," he said, trying not to sound too matter-of-fact.

Leo nodded, then looked at him as though about to say something, but kept silent.

"Enough! That's it!" Sergio announced. Leo was so taken by surprise that he almost laughed. "You've nothing to do with Sara Heller's death: she had a few skeletons in the cupboard, and it's not even certain she killed herself. So please stop thinking what you're thinking – understand?"

Leo shrugged his shoulders, which in their private language meant: alright, I'm not convinced but I'll try to convince myself all the same. Sergio was still looking at him with the cup halfway between the table and his mouth. "You didn't sleep a wink a last night," he said again.

"Not much," Leo replied, though he could have said he hadn't slept at all.

Gusts of wind whistled through the crevices of the house, like freezing air forcing its way into the throat through clenched teeth. Beyond the windows, the tops of the chestnut trees in the yard swayed unrestrained, looking like witnesses shaking their heads vigorously to deny what seemed incontrovertible. Reality was mirroring the restlessness of thought. In the realm of air there is no rest, but instead a constant remixing, rethinking, reconstructing, replaying and reconsidering from unlikely angles.

* * *

Nicolò Ludovisi battled with one of the window shutters before fastening it to the hook on the outside wall. He couldn't remember a wind like this since he was a boy, though he was well aware that every recollection of a childhood phenomenon becomes more vivid than the original event. He shuddered and felt sad, as if he were an old man who knows his winter is approaching, along with a few grey hairs and a few regrets too many. That simple thought had suddenly trapped him, as though he understood at last that the age of immortality had gone forever and this appalling wind was sweeping away all certainty. He remembered how impatient he was, as a child, to become a man at all costs, as well as the certainty – which turned out to be a delusion – that, after that phase, he would live forever, even though everyone around him, without exception, had the ugly defect of growing old.

And then there was that intense love for Gaia, who embodied his every notion of perfection. On that subject there were no doubts, uncertainties or room for discussion. Years later, he still felt excited just at the thought of her naked body. Then came the birth of Michelangelo, which was followed by everything else in a rapid sequence of investment and waste, of desire and adjustment, of lies and subterfuges and of sudden revelations. And his physical body, which seemed destined to outlast him in that uncorrupted form: intangible, perfect, shaped, toned, sculpted, groomed ... endlessly definable through being conspicuous, visible – more so than all else, more than everything.

He had spent the previous night on the sofa: Gaia had been clear that their time together was over, that their marriage was finished. Yet he had stayed awake as long as possible, hoping she would come to him. But she hadn't: so everything really was over. And – this was the real point – he felt he couldn't say she was wrong. Though he also felt that all that had happened had happened without him being able to do anything about it.

And Gaia may well have known about the sad side of his new life. Even before he knew it himself. Now, for example, after an appalling night on the sofa of what was about to become his former home, he realised what a distance had opened up between himself and the woman he said he loved. It can happen like that – a sudden and uncontrollable wind bringing both turmoil and awareness. And you find yourself fastening the shutters that the wind is banging against the walls like clothes on a washing line, as well as understanding everything with a clarity that for men like Nicolò Ludovisi is best avoided.

His fragility at Sara Heller's mere suggestion that Michelangelo might not be his son had made him realise how a suspicion, however impossible, can send down very deep roots. This was his weak point. He had lived with two parents who had shown an unconditional kindness towards children not their own. His love for Gaia had estranged him from his family once and for all, for his mother had never accepted what she described as incest. And now an unspoken, futile but nagging suspicion was distancing him from Gaia.

He ought to have learned that someone can love a child simply because he has decided to call him son. And yet no. This underlying thought worried him, just as it worried him how easy it had been for his lover to make him feel vulnerable.

* * *

"But did you really think I could leave my family for you?"

And she, genuinely mystified by the frankness of the question, had said: "Yes I did, and it was you who made me think it."

A reply with zero degree of control, undiplomatic, with no purpose other than to contradict what Nicolò had just declared about the impossibility of a future together.

"But Sara, I never ever told you anything of the kind," he insisted, realising that she had given credence to a few expressions made to impress, a few vague promises spoken during unguarded moments of intimacy. "A lot of things get said in certain situations . . . You know . . . I mean when someone gets carried away . . ." All he could do was give an answer, word by word, point by point, to each of the objections of a woman who had misunderstood the sense of their relationship. And then, having performed the task of eradicating each one of her false certainties, he had to get her out of his life forever.

But Sara made no response or objection whatsoever. Except that, instead of stripping off the last of her clothes, she started to dress again. Then, after a long pause, she cleared her throat. "Your family," she repeated with a subtle sarcasm. Nicolò nodded yes. "Michelangelo?" she asked. Once again he nodded. "You are all so different," Sara observed. Nicolò shrugged his shoulders. "So very different."

"What do you mean?" Nicolò asked. He had many shortcomings but failing to pick up on innuendo was not one of them.

"Nothing," she said. "Just that you really have nothing in common."

She clearly wanted to provoke him, and it was equally clear that her provocation had hit the mark.

"That's your personal opinion," Nicolò said, so casually that it encouraged her to carry on.

"Yes, of course, just an impression, but I've seen lots of children, and families that weren't exactly what they seemed . . ."

Sara gave a smile.

* * *

Once he had fastened the shutters and closed the window again, Nicolò Ludovisi felt the warmth of the house and with it a violent regret, like someone who discovers he has lost something on which he had placed no value until that moment. He felt a stabbing pain in the pit of his stomach and a heavy shudder, almost a spasm. The shudder went deep between his sides and his back. He felt cold and tried to get dressed. Much of his stuff was in the living room, ready to be packed into bags and suitcases. But it was all stuff that served to show just how little he had accomplished in life. He switched on the TV as he waited for the coffee machine to warm up.

* * *

Gaia Ludovisi heard her husband rummaging about in the living room. Outside it was windy. She pulled the quilt up to her forehead. As a child she loved the warm cavern it created. She could imagine being Alice as she tumbles down the hole and comes face to face with other dimensions. To stop loving Nicolò would not be easy. It wouldn't be easy, either, to stop using the word love when referring to him. It had been a torment of desire; she had seen and desired him with an obstinacy that verged on madness. It had been an unquenchable passion that overlooked, and had overlooked, every possible insult, every possible betrayal, every possible promise not kept. And all possible decency. Yes – she could certainly say she had been in love, but in the most sacrificial and irrational sense of the word.

Now the wind there outside, extraordinary by anyone's standards, was carrying away what had been granted to her with the same violence and with the same bloody, lacerating wrench. She remembered the first time she had seen him, as a child, when she had been adopted by the Ludovisis: so perfect, so exactly right in her eyes, that she couldn't believe it. And she remembered how he, who had never been a complex being but more of an animal, had immediately sensed that passion. If love at first sight exists, then this was it. She recalled what may have been a fragment of Greek text, or maybe not – something she remembered from school, but which she couldn't quite locate – something like: "I saw him and felt lost." For this was exactly how she felt: lost. And he who had never had to translate any ancient poetry must have felt equally lost. That wind now announced, proclaimed, that this simultaneity didn't necessarily imply complete connection. Even though one is lost in the same moment, it doesn't mean one is lost in the same place. And so she seemed to understand that the mistake had been to align the moment with the place, when it was now so very clear that they had been lost in opposite hemispheres. They understood each other through body language, like machines each perfectly designed for the other. This would become ever clearer as time passed. For they had perfect bodies, whose perfection becomes apparent through attraction. When he finally got to undress her he realised that wherever he had been lost before, this was now where he wanted to be. And when he finally took off his shirt she experienced the kind of giddiness one has in touching one's own vision. He was that machine that she adored him for, the exact sensation that Nature had wanted to display in its every detail. She knew that while she could hate him, she would never stop desiring him, because he was lodged in that precise part of her brain that conceived perfection.

But he was certainly not absolute perfection. She knew that Nicolò was a passion all of his own, fruit of multiple experiences. And she also knew that the absolute doesn't exist. This was the reason why she had put up with his continual infidelities, as well as knowing she could never have coped by herself. Nothing about that man naked in front of her had ever made her imagine a settled life or a stable relationship. It was just insatiable desire. Then came the birth of Michelangelo, and everything else . . .

Nicolò had embodied her transgression. She was one of those women who don't know how to choose their men. Any men, whether husband or son . . .

* * *

("I've called you in to discuss a rather sensitive matter involving Michelangelo," Sara Heller had said, showing her to a seat in the school library. Gaia sat down. "I'll come to the point," she continued. "I'm worried about Michelangelo. He's rather withdrawn and sometimes behaves aggressively towards his classmates, which makes me suspect he has problems . . ."

"Are you trying to frighten me?" Gaia had asked, without concealing her concern at the mere hint of Michelangelo having "problems".

"No, it might just be a phase, but it could indicate something more serious," the teacher replied.

"More serious?" Gaia was clutching onto words as though anxious not to fall.

"How is he at home?" Sara asked.

"Quiet. Fairly . . ." Gaia replied with a slight hesitation that didn't escape the teacher's notice.

Well aware how hurtful such a question could be for a mother, Sara was still surprised to note how effectively she had hit the mark this time. "From experience I can tell you that cases like these tend to have their beginnings in the family. Does Michelangelo have much to do with cousins or uncles – the adult males in the family?"

This was the question that Gaia dreaded. "No," she mumbled. "There's us . . . just us . . . My husband has no brothers or sisters. We have no contact with his parents. It's a complicated story."

"Let's not jump to conclusions. I just felt I ought to warn you," Sara Heller said gently. She had hooked her fish and was giving it more line before pulling it out of the water.

"What should I do?" Gaia asked.

Sara looked at her, attempting a smile.)

* * *

She knew that Nicolò would never have been capable of doing Michelangelo any harm. Despite this, everything inside her yelled caution. If it had happened, it could happen again. And so she began to worry herself sick, and continued to do so until that doubt had become ancillary to the urge to act in any event. It was her fear of the world that was returning.

Now she had the motive and reason to justify why she needed to find another house and another life. It was clear: Lilo could never have managed it. Nor could Michelangelo. Not even he.

The most logical solution of course would have been to talk about it, to tackle Nicolò and ask him straight out. But she didn't think she was capable of dealing with the answer: whatever it was.

And yet, that morning, a wind was blowing so strongly that all arrogance could be swept away. A shutter started to bang. Gaia cocooned herself under the duvet. From the living room the local news could be heard crackling over the radio.

* * *

"Angel of God, who art my guardian, to whom God's love commits me here, be at my side to light and guard, to rule and guide. Amen." Don Giuseppe nodded and Elda made the sign of the cross. Then, without a word, she went to the stove, switched the gas off under the milk pan and checked to see whether any coffee was left in the pot before making another. For some time she had preferred to use barley coffee for breakfast as don Giuseppe had a tendency to drink too much caffeine and sometimes, she was sure of it, he smoked cigarettes, though he told her he had stopped. He drank his milk without complaint, though he hated the barley coffee. The wind beat frighteningly against the sheets of plastic that were taped to the skeleton of the window overlooking the yard where the explosion had happened. The glazier had come straight away but could only do a temporary repair until the replacement glass was ready.

The blast had done much damage – above all to his LP of Scandinavian music which was unusable, scratched and chipped in several places. Elda had cleared up with extraordinary efficiency as soon as the police had left the scene, being careful to remove as many traces as possible. She had gathered up broken or damaged objects, plates, the cuckoo clock, the gramophone and the record that was always on its turntable and the framed portrait of the parish outing to the Sanctuary of San Romedio a few years before, just after don Giuseppe's arrival. The frame and the glass were broken but the photo was intact. Elda had removed it from its mount and placed it, bare, on the sideboard. Now all confusion seemed a luxury, and the wind outside authorised the use of any appropriate form of defence for self-protection. This is what don Giuseppe was thinking when, having gulped down the last mouthful of milk and barley coffee, he realised that Elda had removed her apron and was trying to say something.

"We have to go," she said.

Don Giuseppe looked at her unsurprised. "It's time to start over again," he remarked.

"I thought Filippa could replace me. You know her, she's a good worker." It was a turn of phrase that expected no answer. Don Giuseppe gave no reply. "I've left everything ready, Filippa can start tomorrow morning," Elda assured him.

The priest looked at her, trying to work out whether this was to be goodbye for now or forever. "Will you let me know when the moment's right?" he asked, since his heart had opted for the latter.

Elda shook her head: "You have to stay, for the time being," she replied.

"Yes," don Giuseppe agreed. "But will it be for long?"

"We have to go, and you must be patient," she assured him without giving an answer. Then she hung her apron on the hook behind the kitchen door. "The glazier arrives at four," she reminded him, and left the room.

Alone in the kitchen, all that don Giuseppe could do was try to give some meaning to the mass of doubts that assailed him. The wind outside increased his unease, and the frantic flapping of the sheets of clear plastic attached to the wooden window frame made every prospect seem appallingly uncertain. Along with the LP record, the gramophone itself was also unusable. It was like having only answers without a shred of a question, like losing a significant part of his personal life-support system and finding himself naked in the midst of a crowd, as was happening in his recurring dreams. A nakedness far removed from sanctity and which had nothing to do with renunciation but only his inability to renounce.

* * *

Elisabetta Menetti turned the ignition. The wind drove the light beyond the mountain tops and caused the clouds to race at a prodigious speed. As he opened the door, Sergio Striggio let a small blizzard of snow into the car. He was careful to close it immediately. The thermal fabric of his windcheater gave off a bitter coldness that mingled with the artificial warmth of the car heating.

Menetti, noting that he looked reasonably well rested, flicked on her right indicator and pulled out. The road was treacherous with a thin layer of ice beneath the snow. The wind had eased slightly but was still very strong, so that the snow outside was not still and solemn but blustery and wild, like only torrential rain can be.

"Fucking weather," Striggio remarked.

"And good morning to you too," Menetti joked.

"You know where we're going, right?" the Commissario asked, just to make it clear he wasn't in the mood for either irony or intimacy.

Menetti made no reply. She carried on driving as though her boss wasn't even there in the car and, in fact, switched on the radio knowing it would annoy him. News of Sara Heller's presumed suicide was already coursing through the airwaves and, in spite of the snowstorm, had reached every household.

"Excellent," Striggio commented sarcastically. "We should have gone last night, there'll now be a crowd of people outside."

And in fact they knew they had arrived at the teacher's apartment because four or five local journalists were waiting at the main door with cameras and tape-recorders. Two of them, on recognising Striggio and Menetti, approached before they could get out of the car. This, for the Commissario, was such an ordeal that he seriously thought about ordering a sudden about-turn. In the end he opened the car door, facing the snowstorm and questions with his head down, ignoring both. He quickened his pace and reached the main door of the building, aware that Menetti had been stopped a short distance behind. "Allow us to get on with our job!" he exclaimed, with all the authority he could muster but not enough to stop these people, armed with cameras and microphones, from yelling out senseless questions impossible to answer. Menetti eventually reached the main door with the keys. They went inside, closing it behind them.

They climbed a flight of stairs to the first-floor landing: above the doorbell, a plate with the name HELLER. The key turned out to belong to the latest generation of burglar-proof locks. Yet the door was unlatched and could be opened with a simple push.

The apartment was warm and in complete darkness. Everything seemed silent and perfectly in order. Striggio and Menetti walked inside, entered a living room furnished in a nondescript style of the kind often seen when people try to imitate what they can't afford. Everything was of modest appearance and spotless – the home of a single woman who had reached a certain professional position and had organised her surround-ings with exactitude and a strangely arid sobriety. The pictures on the walls were abstract mass-produced prints chosen to tone in with the sage-coloured suede of the sofas, a fabric that used to be called nubuck, and which was on Striggio's blacklist from the time when he spent his school holidays at his grandparents' in the Apennines. He realised that the strange depression he felt in surroundings like this was because they took him back to his childhood home at a moment when he felt certain he had finally left it. As he was thinking this, he realised Menetti was waiting for some signal and was holding out a pair of thin rubber gloves. "I've brought these too," she said, producing some plastic overshoes of the kind that the parents of young swimmers have to wear in swimming pools. "Otherwise the forensic people will play hell."

"You reckon Susini will want to trouble forensics over a suicide?" Striggio said.

"You never know," Menetti replied, lifting her foot to cover her shoe.

Striggio did the same and they began to wander around the room like two aliens looking at the earth for the first time.

For Menetti, all this refinement seemed pointless. Home, for her, was a place to eat, sleep and – with the right and not always necessarily the same person – fuck. She was ready to bet any amount that here, in Heller's house, even the odds-and-ends drawer was in perfect order.

Striggio meanwhile was forming the view that this teacher's reading material left much to be desired. "All modern trash," he commented aloud.

"Sorry?" Menetti asked, distracted by an odd 1970s missile-shaped lamp, filled with liquid and coloured blobs.

"Her reading, it's crap," Striggio observed, bluntly.

Menetti shook her head. "I didn't know they were still making this kind of lamp."

The apartment gave out a non-odour typical of constant cleaning. As though every line of the surroundings was marked with restraint. It was that sober mediocrity that lingered and nestled among the tobacco colour of the pelmets, the beige curtains, the sage sofas, the mustard cushions and that bright red of the twin lampshades on the seven-drawer Swedish-pine chest.

Three doors opened onto the living room: the first, as they discovered, went to a passageway that led to a live-in kitchen and a bathroom; the second went straight to the bedroom. Through the third they heard a sudden muffled noise. It wasn't the wind rattling the windows, nor something that either of them had dropped. No, it was a muffled sound, like something heavy that had fallen straight to the floor. The unnatural silence that followed convinced them that somebody was inside. Menetti and Striggio pulled out their firearms. "Police!" the Chief Inspector shouted, pointing her pistol. "Come out with your hands up!"

Striggio, from a position further back but with his weapon in the same direction, noted a slight tremble in Menetti's voice and hands.

"Don't shoot, I'm coming out," said the voice of a man on the other side of the door.

"Move back one step. I'm opening the door now, keep your hands up!" Menetti shouted, in a tone gradually more confident.

From inside the room they could hear a slight movement of feet. Menetti stretched her arm out and felt the handle of the door, carefully keeping to one side. She heard it click, then gave a sudden push to let it swing back on its hinge. The door opened less than a metre, so that a shadow could be seen inside the room. "Hands up!" Menetti shouted again.

However hard it tried, it was clear it wouldn't make it. There was nothing the wind could do to get as far as Pietro Striggio's bed. He had monitored its action and had personified it, as far as giving it an actual face – the face of every "decent type" whom, over his forty-year career, he had had to accuse of the most atrocious crimes. Yes – this was the face of that persistent wind. The meek face of an adolescent so aware of his rights that he imagines he has no duties. He had seen quite a few of them over the years. They were a category that never changed, despite the changing times. Every generation produces its own sixteen-year-old monster who wants everything and who, one day, decides to kill parents who had worked hard all their lives for what they had. That decision is a gust of wind, and it comes without warning: at Vercelli, Montecchia di Crosara, Novi Ligure, Parma and at Pontelangorino . . .

The short black doctor appeared, accompanied by a male nurse who was pushing a trolley full of medicines. "It's treatment time," she said with her smoker's voice.

Pietro couldn't take his eyes away from the window. "What's happening outside?" he asked. The doctor stared at him, trying to understand exactly what he was referring to. "It's windy," he answered for her.

The doctor nodded in agreement. "It certainly is. Never seen anything like it. It has also started to snow. And this time it's settling."

Pietro laughed. "Something like that once happened in Bologna when I was a boy. First wind, then snow. My sister was no taller than you and had to go to school, but it was blowing so hard that she couldn't stand upright. So my father pulled her leg by saying he'd lend her his diving weights." He laughed out loud, but his laughter turned instantly into anxiety. "Is it the illness?" he asked.

The doctor, taken by surprise, reacted with a tentative smile. "It's absolutely normal to feel a little anxious," she said. "But we can do something for that as well."

Pietro shook his head. "If it weren't for these damned memories, there would be no problem. It's the wind, you see." He paused long enough to see whether the doctor had understood, but she hadn't. "It tries to get in everywhere. Even here. Even now," he tried to explain, still staring at the restless world beyond the window.

The doctor took a few steps towards the curtain and drew it across to cover the view. The room was plunged into that kind of semi-darkness redolent of sunny afternoons during endless childhood summers when parents think it right and healthy to close the shutters and send their children off unwillingly for a rest. "Let's leave the world outside to its own devices," she murmured reassuringly. "The most important thing now is for you to get better." She approached him as if to give him a goodnight kiss. But didn't. "You have a slight fever," she observed instead. "Do you feel shivery?"

Pietro shook his head. "In forty years' service I've never had a day off work for fever. I never even knew what fever was," he announced with a certain touch of pride.

"That's not necessarily a good thing," the doctor answered softly. "Organisms become healthier if they have some illness to deal with: it's a question of experience."

Pietro looked down as if he needed a moment to absorb what had just been said. "Does that mean that having been too healthy is confusing my body?"

"Something like that," she was forced to admit with a new smile that revealed a certain admiration. "Are we ready?" she asked.

Pietro tensed his arm. "Ready," he said, and he could feel the flow running through his vein from the butterfly needle taped just below the fold of his arm. Fortunately it hadn't taken long to find the vein. He had always had strong arms and thick blue veins that ran just below his pure white skin. For a brief moment he thought the wind had stopped. He closed his eyes. "I want you to make me a promise," he said after a while, before losing control. The doctor waited for him to finish. "I want you to promise that I won't die here in hospital."

"This I can promise you . . ."

"I know you think I'm selfish and that people who die at home nowadays cause nothing but trouble for those left behind. My wife died in hospital . . ."

"Alone?" the doctor asked, trying to get to the nub of Pietro's question.

"No," he said, but as though he had only just realised it. "Sergio was there with her. I wasn't." He suddenly began to cry, but without it seeming that he was crying. Just two large teardrops ran from the outer corners of his eyes and trickled down his face along his sideburns.

Nicolò Ludovisi came out with his hands up. "I'm not armed," he said.

On seeing him, Menetti lowered her gun and automatically flicked on the safety catch. Striggio took rather longer to do the same.

"I'm not armed," the man repeated, as if to persuade Striggio to lower his gun too.

Menetti took hold of him, pushing his legs astride and telling him to keep both hands on the back of his neck.

Nicolò Ludovisi did as he was told. "The door was open," he said.

Menetti began to give him a full body search.

"Did you know Sara Heller?" Striggio asked abruptly.

Ludovisi didn't even hesitate. "She taught my son."

"So you knew her, shall we say, in a professional capacity?" Striggio continued.

"Can I put my arms down?" Ludovisi asked, turning to Menetti, who nodded, adding curtly: "The Commissario asked a question."

Before Ludovisi had time to answer, a phone rang in his pocket. He gave a look of surprise when he realised the call was coming from the Commissario standing in front of him. He pulled out what Fanti had called his fuck phone. "How did you manage to get this number?" he asked, genuinely amazed.

"We're the police," Striggio replied with a certain weight. "And so I'll ask you again: between you and Sara Heller, were relations merely, shall we say, professional?" He seemed keen to keep to exactly the same tone as before.

Nicolò Ludovisi shook his head. "Can I sit down?" he asked.

Menetti moved aside and he went across to one of the four matching chairs around the plain oval table in the sitting room.

A silence followed, as though to let the wind speak from beyond the closed shutters. In that moment, those three strangers in someone else's home had understood the need to reorder every notion, every thought and every possible confession circulating in that room.

"I heard from her yesterday afternoon," Ludovisi explained, though seemingly without knowing why he had decided to commence from that point.

"You mean Sara Heller?" Striggio asked, just to make it clear he had no intention of giving him an easy time. The lingering attraction he felt for this man unsettled him.

Ludovisi nodded. "Can I have some water?" he asked.

Without a further word, Menetti went to the kitchen and searched through the wall units for a glass, found one, filled it with water, returned to the living room and handed it to Ludovisi. He drank it in one breath, his Adam's apple going up and down. Striggio fixed his eyes on an off-the-shelf picture: a solarised photograph of what must have been a New York alleyway. This type of cheap, ugly mass production managed to distract him from any inappropriate thoughts.

"She was tense. She was always tense," Ludovisi continued. Then he paused. He looked Striggio in the eye until he realised it was impossible to keep silent. "She wanted me to talk to my wife. She made threats."

Menetti pulled a chair from under the table and sat near him. "Threats?" she repeated.

"The usual things ..." Ludovisi tried to play it down, as though afraid he had already gone too far.

"Well," Striggio said, catching him out. "'Threats' and 'usual things' at the same time ... I reckon that's rather difficult ... Unless you were used to that kind of business?"

"Perhaps you can help us understand," Menetti butted in, having realised exactly how she ought to be helping out the Commissario.

"I didn't mean ..." Ludovisi stammered. "I didn't mean that it was normal, but you come across these things every day, don't you? Lovers . . . misunderstandings," In his attempt at choosing finely balanced words, he was tying himself in knots.

"Ah, misunderstandings" – Striggio seemed more enthusiastic. "If I said that Sara Heller was expecting something from you that you had no intention of giving her, would I be on the right track?"

"She wanted me to leave my wife," Ludovisi announced. He had obviously opted for the direct approach.

"And you had no intention of doing so?" Menetti added.

"Of course not. There had never been any discussion like that." Ludovisi kept his eyes fixed firmly on Striggio as he answered. His animal instinct seemed to have picked up a trail, a specific, direct, hormonal scent.

Sergio Striggio had understood the sort of person he was dealing with. "You used to meet here?"

"I have the keys," Ludovisi admitted at last.

"And so you lied just now," Menetti said.

Ludovisi agreed, without even feeling the need to explain.

"You see, it's always curious to notice at what stage people decide to start lying." Striggio said. "Have you noticed too how the real significance of the lie is to be found at its very start?"

Ludovisi gave a look of surprise and disapproval, as if to reproach the Commissario for introducing an intellectual distance between them. "I'm not sure I understand what you mean," he replied.

"You don't?" Striggio answered provocatively. "Of all the stupid remarks you could have made, you chose the most unlikely, namely that the door was open. And this even before anyone had asked you anything. Which makes me think it was crucial to you that we didn't know you had the keys to this apartment."

"I didn't know about the phone," Ludovisi admitted.

"Exactly. The power of information. You understand, don't you, that our job generally involves knowing how to use information? Information used at the wrong moment is worthless," Striggio said, though he had his eye fixed on Menetti.

"And now you know about the phone. And you know we know what's on it," the Chief Inspector added, as if to inform the Commissario that his message regarding the value of information had reached her loud and clear.

Ludovisi gave a heavy sigh: "I'm not sure, but perhaps I need a lawyer at this point."

"I'm afraid so," Striggio agreed, since he had no wish to reduce the tension that had tightened and contracted Ludovisi's body. He had to concentrate once again upon the horrible solarised picture on the wall in front of him.

"There's something in the other room that I'd like to retrieve," Ludovisi said. "I don't think it has anything to do with the death of . . . Sara . . . And I don't know why it's here. Michelangelo must have given it to her . . . Michelangelo used to give his things away . . ." he stammered. "So I'd like to have it back."

Striggio looked at Menetti, who shook her head. "What is it?" he asked.

"Oh," Ludovisi replied lightly. "It's just a picture book we used to read to Michelangelo when he was small: the story of a curious little fox who loses himself in the forest." Without waiting for permission, Ludovisi went to the room where he had found it and came out holding a small hardback book. He handed it to Striggio. "I don't really know why it's here," he repeated.

* * *

(The little fox Messy, where is he going, where is he going, alone in the wood?

Curious, he left the burrow while his parents were still fast asleep.

"The world is there outside!" he thought. "Isn't all this sleeping a waste of time?"

And so he pretended to make several large yawns and snuggled between Mummy and Daddy.

Then, when he started to feel sleepy, he kept his eyes open.

Mistress Doe had been clear on the matter: "The world awaits its heroes," she had said.

And Messy the little fox felt a hero.

"Don't listen to the Doe," said Owl. "She thinks everyone sleeps as little as she does."

And now what is Messy the little fox doing alone in the wood?

The little ant had told him that if nothing is ventured then nothing is gained.

Mummy Fox had told him that the outside world has four elements: sunshine to bring warmth, water to drink, earth to tread on and air to breathe.

Daddy Fox had told him that what matters is curiosity.

"And how do you learn to be curious?" Messy had asked.

"By making mistakes, my little one," Mummy Fox had replied.

"Then perhaps this is a mistake," Messy the little fox said to himself, alone, outside the burrow, while everyone was asleep.

The sun sleeps, the stream sleeps, the earth sleeps, and even the wind too.

The sun is so shrouded that it always seems night.

The water is so frozen that it cannot even be drunk.

The earth is hidden beneath the snow and it is hard to walk.

The air is so icy that it is hard to breathe.

And Nature carries on its course, regardless.

Messy the little fox looks at his prints in the snow, counts how many steps it has taken from the burrow.

His heavy eyelids fall shut.)

* * *

The book cover was so ingenuous that the Commissario winced. It showed a little red fox roaming among tall trees of which only the trunks and lower branches could be seen . . . The illustration might have been described as realistic, but it seemed in fact to be designed for a child of a bygone time.

"It was mine," Nicolò Ludovisi explained, as though he had read his thoughts.

"Why are you here?" Striggio asked, closing the book though holding it firmly as though he intended to keep it hostage until Ludovisi had replied.

Ludovisi took his time. He needed to find the right words. "My wife has left me," he said eventually, deciding to start on a painful note. "I have all my stuff in the car," he explained to reinforce what he had just said.

Elisabetta Menetti looked at the Commissario as if to say: this one is totally crazy.

"I heard the news on the radio, that Sara had been found. I was looking for a hotel," he continued, stringing disjointed sentences together to give his story some coherence.

Menetti shook her head. "And so you thought Sara Heller didn't need her apartment any longer . . ."

"Is that what you were thinking?" Ludovisi was so upset that these words came out in falsetto. "I wanted only . . ."

" . . . to cancel any material of a more or less compromising nature," Striggio said, completing the sentence. "Does that mean there's no point us checking her computer?"

"I deleted a few emails, that's all," Ludovisi said lightly.

Menetti was about to say something when her phone rang. She went into the other room to answer.

Left alone, Ludovisi and Striggio could study each other face to face. In silence. The Commissario had a supreme ability to remain silent. For Ludovisi, however, it was an anxious silence, anything but calm.

"She was a difficult woman," he said after a while. Striggio gave him a look that encouraged him to continue. "She had misinterpreted our relationship. And she said things about me to Michelangelo that weren't true."

"Such as?"

258

"Such as that he and I didn't resemble each other at all."

"Huh, well, many children don't look like their fathers."

"That wasn't the point, you didn't know her ... Over the past month she'd been threatening me, following me, putting around strange rumours ..."

"That Michelangelo wasn't your son, for example?"

Nicolò Ludovisi gazed at him. "Yes, that's right ..." he said, surprised.

"And did that make any difference from your point of view? I mean, having brought him up for eleven years?"

Ludovisi nodded, though not overly convinced. "I can tell you, it's a gnawing doubt all the same ..."

"And that's why you contacted Villa Santa Susanna clinic ..." Striggio couldn't finish the sentence: Menetti had reappeared, gesturing for him to follow her out.

"Susini," she said. "He wants an end to the Heller case, he says the forensic lab have confirmed that it's suicide. He wants us to interview witnesses to the facts and prepare a report so that we can close the inquiry. We're dealing with Ludovisi now, then we'll call him into the Commissariato together with the headmistress of the school and ..."

"... and Leo," Striggio said, finishing her sentence.

"Well, yes. I didn't think it necessary to say anything to Susini but I'm afraid we will have to explain we can't conduct that interview ourselves."

"That's right," Striggio agreed. "I'll tell him."

"Good." Menetti fixed the Commissario in the eye. In that particular light he seemed extraordinarily handsome. You bloody shit, she thought, I could have loved you.

"And you had better mention it to our colleagues," Striggio pondered aloud.

Having said this, they returned to the room. Nicolò Ludovisi's face, in the meantime, had turned ashen grey. "You can go," Menetti announced. "But make sure you're available to give a voluntary statement. You might even be called in this afternoon."

Ludovisi left in a hurry.

"Susini can say what he wants," Striggio said, after he had heard the front door close. "But even if it's suicide, this business can't be cleared up quite so easily. She was the teacher of a child who has gone missing, and was having an affair with the child's father . . ."

"You know what Susini's like. He wants to keep the local crime rate close to zero."

Striggio smiled. "He wants to show that we're not worth a fuck, in every sense."

At the centre of the desk under the window lay two tidy piles of exercise books, all identical. Striggio leafed through three or four at random. They were composition books from Heller's class. He stared at the touching simplicity of the handwriting. One of the children pressed so hard on the page that the paper curled.

"What's going on?" Menetti asked, seeing that Striggio had stopped to read some short compositions.

The Commissario gave no answer but handed her the exercise book, open at the page he was reading. Menetti took it and read:

* * *

". . . today the teacher played a lovely piece of music to us called 'Valse Triste', which means Sad Waltz, and it really is sad . . ."

* * *

Striggio swore to himself, without saying it aloud, while Menetti, immediately grasping the significance of the reference, handed the exercise book back to him. "Welcome to the realm of coincidences," he exclaimed, and headed for the entrance.

"Where are we going?" Menetti said pointlessly.

Meanwhile the snow had intensified, and had deterred some of the local journalists at the front door. There was such a look of concentration on Striggio's face that the few who had remained didn't dare to question him. Reaching the car, he clicked open the automatic lock and sat in the driver's seat in silence. Menetti, who had some understanding of the world, took the passenger's seat without comment.

* * *

As they drove towards don Giuseppe's presbytery, with heavy snowflakes lashing against the windscreen, he was following a train of thought all of his own. He recalled his last visit to the therapist. It was six days before his eighteenth birthday. He had kissed three girls in his class and had a burning desire for the twin brother of one of them. When it came to the question of desire, there was always a double standard to be applied: either not to go down the path of wrong or to dress it up as harmless. Going out with Martina, or even kissing her, for example, meant that he could carry on seeing and lusting after Ettore. Easy. During the three years of his sessions with the therapist, things had radically changed: his sleeplessness had been replaced by a drowsiness closer to stupor rather than to actual rest, which to him had seemed like remarkable progress, though it might have looked incapacitating or frightening to others. Thinking about this had made him accelerate, so that the car skidded on the ice. Menetti gripped the handle of the door and turned to look at him.

"I always miss the right opportunity to say things," Striggio thought aloud.

Elisabetta Menetti softened her expression as an encouragement to him to continue. But his comment was clearly no more than a fragment of a longer thought. "It happens," she commented, so as not to let the conversation hang in suspense. "You're simply concerned about what to tell your colleagues. Look, you needn't say anything."

"Of course not, but I want to tell them. I can't bear the idea of them having to ask themselves why another person has to stand in for me, even if only temporarily, to perform a simple task like interviewing somebody – somebody who's not even an actual witness, and in a case as clear-cut as suicide. They'd think something worse lay beneath it, and I don't like that, I don't like that at all." He realised then that he had overshot the junction that led to the presbytery. He braked, reversed a few metres, and turned. The snow had cleaned everything in the yard, and the shell of don Giuseppe's burned-out car had been taken away.

"Does Leo know about us?" Menetti asked abruptly.

"What is there to know?" Striggio asked in reply, yanking the key from the ignition.

Menetti closed her eyes and remained in her seat even though Striggio had opened the door to leave. "It looks as though you're stuck in the dead end of repression," she observed.

Striggio climbed straight back into the car. "I'd like to know exactly what we're talking about," he asked, annoyed.

Menetti opened the door on her side and shook her head. "About nothing, about nothing," she said, and got out.

Striggio went ahead to the door of the presbytery and rang the bell.

* * *

(How many tears did he shed, alone in the forest!
Messy thought he was strong, and now he's frightened:
there's no fire to warm him,
there's no water to drink,
there's no earth on which to walk,
only a nasty growling wind:
"What choice have you made? What choice have you made?")

* * *

Don Giuseppe himself came to open the door. "Something must have happened to the electrics," he said as he let them in. The house seemed very tidy. Much of that appearance was due perhaps to the fact that several more damaged pieces of furniture had been removed.

"Let's not beat about the bush, father!" Striggio announced in a sudden aggressive tone that surprised even Menetti.

The priest looked at him, but not sufficiently surprised to seem unaware of what he was talking about. "I don't understand ..." he ventured nonetheless.

Striggio's voice rose an octave. "You don't understand?" He looked around for some logical pretext and found it in the sheet of transparent plastic attached to the skeleton of the window and providing protection from the wind that still howled outside. He pointed to it. "You don't understand?" he repeated with a force so great that he didn't need to shout.

The priest sank into his chair and held his head in his hands. "Did you know Sara Heller?" The good thing about Elisabetta Menetti was that her questions went straight to the point.

Striggio straightened himself and stood waiting for the answer.

"Yes," don Giuseppe said, first with a nod and then in words. Then he fell silent. At that precise moment the only noise in the room was the strange flapping of the wind against the patched-up plastic that kept the window closed. The snow was now heavy and continuous, as though, after a certain period of hesitation, it was determined to fall in abundance. "She was a member of the parish group, several years ago," he explained, for he was afraid that if he hadn't broken the silence it might have ended badly. "But we hadn't seen her for some time. She had moved away from the group and to some extent, I believe, also from the ... faith."

He had said "faith" as only priests can say it, as though it were an approachable word. An easily used, uncomplicated word. Striggio remembered how much that word had been behind his childhood insomnia.

* * *

"But if I ask you whether you believe in God, what would you reply?" The therapist had asked the question not expecting a firm answer.

"I'd reply that I'm frightened about not believing," Sergio replied.

The therapist sniffed, as he did each time he had to deal with an unexpected answer, and jotted something down in his notebook.

* * *

"For some time? How long?" Menetti asked. The priest seemed to be making a quick calculation. Striggio meanwhile wandered round the room. "Days, months, years?" she asked, seeing that he hadn't yet decided how to answer.

"Months," the priest replied at last.

"Months," Menetti repeated, following Striggio from the corner of her eye. "How many months?"

Don Giuseppe shook his head. "A few months," he answered. "But I already know where these questions are leading and I cannot . . ." He stopped.

Menetti was about to reply but was interrupted by Striggio, who approached the priest with a photograph in his hand. It was the one Elda had placed on the cupboard after she had taken it from what was left of the frame. "When was this taken?" he asked. "You can answer that at least," he said sarcastically.

The priest looked at the photo as if he were seeing it for the first time: unframed, out of its usual mount, not on display and therefore visible at last, it seemed quite new to him. "A few years ago. I had just arrived in this parish. It was an outing to San Romedio."

"And who is this?" Striggio asked, pointing to the face of a young woman.

Don Giuseppe looked down. "Gaia," he replied.

Menetti froze. "Gaia Ludovisi?" she asked.

He nodded.

"And this one?" Striggio continued, pointing to the face of another woman.

"Elda," the priest answered. "My housekeeper."

"Fine, and this one?" Striggio continued, pointing again.

Don Giuseppe sighed. "Oh, you know who it is!" he protested.

"And this one?" Striggio repeated, ignoring the silent entreaties Menetti was making with her eyes.

"It's Sara Heller!" the priest shouted.

"Don't shout at me!" Striggio replied. "I'm very tired!" He seemed to be pleading but was only indicating that he had reached an impossible limit.

"I cannot," don Giuseppe moaned. He had begun to shake.

"And this one?" Striggio continued, unperturbed. Menetti took a step forward and the Commissario raised his finger to stop her.

Don Giuseppe watched both of them and understood he had no possible allies in that room. "Nicolò Ludovisi," he said with the clear voice of the martyr.

"Everything goes back to you. And should I not be annoyed?" Striggio asked.

"I understand," the priest agreed, crushed.

* * *

Sergio had a particularly clear memory of each time, when cornered, he had been forced to yield to someone who was clearly superior in physical strength, but also, above all, through their own self-certainty. He had always been afraid of people who were overly sure of themselves, and of children in general. When he was a little boy he had once even confessed to a theft he hadn't committed. He had been suspended for a week and, at home, had been given a good thrashing. He had been punished, according to his father, not because he had stolen – his father certainly didn't think he was a thief – but because he hadn't managed to get out of it. According to Pietro, those who failed to prove their innocence were guilty just the same. For in wasting other people's time they often enabled the real culprits to get away with it.

* * *

"Father, Sara Heller is dead," Striggio said with a calmness that was truly worrying.

The priest nodded his chin: "I heard the news," he said, then fell silent, though he realised just how much that silence might seem like guilt.

Striggio felt a sudden anger. He screwed up his eyes so tightly that he feared he was going to topple over and fall. When he saw the priest's face for the first time, that night as he waited for their arrival, Sergio had realised from the look in his eyes that he would make a useless witness. "However much I try to understand you, father, I have the feeling that you have no intention of letting yourself be understood," he said.

Menetti searched for a chair and sat down. A strange silence followed filled with long and tortured sighs. Striggio remained standing with his hands in his pockets.

Don Giuseppe kept his eyes fixed on the ground. "Sara was a very unhappy girl. She let herself think there was someone who loved her. She had been warned . . ."

"By whom?" Menetti asked.

"I have to stop here. It's the seal of confession, I really cannot," he said desperately.

"But if I ask you to help us as far as you can, what would you do?" Striggio's manner now suddenly seemed conciliatory. Don Giuseppe looked as though he were about to say something, but kept quiet.

The silence had grown heavy with expectancy, an immense Procrustean bed. "And if I asked you whether you truly believe in mercy? How would you reply?"

"It's not as you think," the priest continued without looking up. "I would reply that in the case of Michelangelo Ludovisi it really was a question of mercy."

"Prepare yourself and be available for further questioning," Striggio cautioned. "You will have to tell us much more than this."

The atmosphere in the Commissariato building was tense, as it was whenever Susini came to visit.

"I enjoy appearing on television," he admitted as he settled himself in Striggio's office. "But just for once I'd like to be the bearer of good news. Have you assembled everybody?" Menetti nodded. "And dottor Striggio?" he asked.

"He's in another meeting."

"Very well, call Pallavicini," Susini ordered.

Elisabetta Menetti called Leo in and left the room.

"You'll be wondering why dottor Susini is in my office dealing with the Sara Heller case." Fanti and Steltzer waited silently for Striggio to continue. "This is because one of those who might have some relevant information, Leonardo Pallavicini, is the man with whom I am currently living." Those words, in their brevity, were clearly not immediately comprehensible either to Fanti or to Steltzer, who looked at each other before turning back in unison to the Commissario. "I'm gay," he explained before either of the two felt obliged to ask for further clarification.

Menetti, who had watched the scene from behind, tried to catch Striggio's eye to offer encouragement, like a maiden aunt at her favourite nephew's Christmas concert.

Fanti had a sudden strange fit of coughing.

Steltzer turned bright red as far as the tips of the ears. "*Ich hätte das nie gesagt!*" he thought half out loud.

Menetti shook her head. Fanti flexed his eyes to hide his embarrassment . . .

* * *

Susini's interview methods were clear: have concrete ideas, ask direct questions and waste no time.

His discussion with Striggio, an hour before, had been extremely tiresome. That boy, in his view, was the exact opposite of what a good investigator should be – a view which their conversation a moment ago had only served to confirm.

"Truth is not to be found in ambiguity," could have been his motto and warning, if he had had anyone to voice it to – but Susini lived alone, and the matter seemed no more uncertain to him than Striggio's sexual preferences. In this regard, while having pretended to be indifferent, he was surprised, very surprised, for he would never have said that the Commissario was that way inclined. This, in his eyes, made him more of a risk. Just to find himself in that office which was not his own, to have to remedy a possible conflict of interests, put him into a state of discomfort – but also of elation: operating there, in that building, represented the zenith of the judicial system which sees its own shortcomings and corrects them. For him, calling Pallavicini to give evidence was the closure of a circle that revolved ceaselessly around the requirement for every operational system to be regulated by simple and straightforward rules. Striggio had claimed that if the rules were too simple and straightforward then reality is often forced to compromise, like a large foot being forced into a smaller shoe. Pallavicini in particular was the embodiment of the reason why it was now up to him, Susini, to remedy and to correct.

So Pallavicini came in and sat down in front of him. He was a completely normal looking man, indeed more handsome than the normal man, an indication that when men are too handsome they pay the price. Nothing about that young, slim, bearded male fitted the homosexual stereotype.

"Leonardo Pallavicini?" he asked.

This was a question that Leo could answer. "Yes," he said.

Susini thought he didn't seem overly concerned. He gave credence only to those who trembled and sweated before an Italian state prosecutor. "You know why you have been summoned here?"

Leo nodded without taking his eyes away from him. Susini thought he had an arrogant gaze. A gaze that men and women have when they know they are attractive. This annoyed him, and he would have been happy to place him in difficulty. "And you also know why I have been asked to conduct this interview, rather than the investigating officer?"

"I imagine so," Leo answered, unruffled.

"Well then: how would you describe your relations with Sara Heller?"

"Professional, with some occasional contact outside work."

"Interesting. So you were colleagues and, *occasionally*, friends? On those friendly occasions had she confided certain problems to you?"

"She told me she was in love with a man who didn't love her."

"And this she didn't like?"

Leo wanted to laugh, but held back. "Of course not," he said.

"Was it Heller who told you?"

"Told me what?"

"That she was unhappy about the relationship with this man which was not reciprocated."

"Not directly, but it was clear, also bearing in mind how it ended."

"And how did it end according to you?"

Here, Leo gave the first visible sign of hesitation, to Susini's immense pleasure. "Well . . . yes . . . you see . . ."

"Do you have any doubt about the fact that Heller had decided to end her own life?" Here was Susini's key question.

"I have more doubt than certainty, dottore. But I do know that recently she was an unhappy woman."

"I thought as much – that you would belong to the category of doubt," Susini remarked.

"Does a category of certainty exist?" Leo asked abruptly.

Susini smiled. Of course it existed. It was a world in which men love women, where queer schoolteachers and commissarios are not allowed to hold such important public posts, at least in a society that wishes to remain healthy. It existed, in a world that had the courage to express straightforward and uncomplicated views. By God, it existed. "Some might think so," he muttered.

Leo looked at the Procuratore with an entirely new expression. "Nothing frightens me more," he remarked.

"Is that what you teach our children?" Susini asked, though without making the question seem too malicious.

"Do you have children, dottore?"

"I don't think that's what we're talking about." Susini sidestepped.

Leo stared at him as though he had given quite a different answer to the one he had actually given. Here, he thought, was a man who used proceedings to deal with personal grudges. Everything in the man, he thought, was the expression of a furious adjustment to circumstances. And he realised that this had to be what anyone belonging to the category of certainty looked like.

The rest of the interview was an account of the facts: Sara had asked Leo to go with her to a restaurant where she knew her lover Nicolò Ludovisi would be with his family, but the evening had come to nothing because the above-mentioned lover had left the restaurant too soon. And Sara had had some kind of crisis. So Leo had taken her home. Then, when the news came out that Nicolò's son, Michelangelo Ludovisi, was missing, Leo had called Sara to explain that his personal situation prevented him from keeping silent about the events referred to above, and she had promised she would sort everything out. That was it.

* * *

End of interview. Statement signed. When Susini told him he could leave, Leo opened the door and emerged from the office – different from how he had gone in: no longer the witness, but the Commissario's boyfriend. Fanti watched him pass, then glanced across to Stelzer, who was pretending to be busy sorting out something on his desk. Menetti gave him a nod, which Leo answered with an appreciative smile. He had almost reached the exit when Sergio appeared. They stood there for a few moments, saying nothing. Striggio was aware of feeling finer than he had felt for a long while. In a better time, in a better world, he would have kissed him there in front of everyone. But he didn't, so as not to complicate matters further.

"Can I give you a lift back?" he murmured.

Leo was pleased he hadn't come up to ask how the interview with Susini had gone. "I'll take a walk, get some exercise," he replied.

"I have to visit my father," Sergio insisted, as though a certain degree of formality had suddenly become necessary and perhaps because he had noticed the attentive silence of those around them.

"Honestly, there's no need to go so far out of your way. You know I'm happy to walk."

"I know, but with this snow."

* * *

(When, in Xavier Dolan's film "Mommy", Steve sings Bocelli at the karaoke bar . . . And all the sequence of Diane's last wish with the music of Ludovico Einaudi in the background . . . and when the argument was about which version of Monteverdi's "Zefiro torna" was better: the authentic one by Philippe Jaroussky or the pop version by Karim Sulayman . . .)

* * *

At any rate, in the realm of the wind, reality came in heavy squalls. And there outside it was very cold. "I can take you back," Menetti said.

Striggio looked at him. "Alright," Leo said.

He knew he was running a risk by accepting that lift. Deep down, Leo distrusted Menetti.

All the same, he followed her down a dingy back staircase to the garage. She clicked open the automatic locking device of an unmarked car.

"You lock your cars?" Leo asked. "In the police garage?"

Menetti smiled. "Especially here," she joked.

Leo laughed too, and climbed into the car.

"This is mine," Menetti explained. "Anyone who touches it is dead."

"I get the idea," Leo said.

They fell silent before Menetti decided to turn the ignition.

"I know," Leo said after a while.

"I was wondering when would be the moment to talk about it," Menetti answered without turning to face him.

"This is it," Leo said, before repeating "I know."

Menetti pursed her lips. "I was thinking . . ." she began. "I mean, it wasn't something planned."

"That's not true," Leo said.

Menetti shrugged her shoulders.

"Shall we go?" Leo asked. He tried to think about the pile of essays he had to correct at home. But he couldn't.

Menetti, rather than starting the engine, went through the motions. "It wasn't something planned," she repeated.

"Yes, you've already said that."

"I wanted it to be clear."

"That means nothing. Can we go now?" Leo's voice had become terse and plaintive.

Menetti at last turned the key.

The wind was a little calmer, or perhaps it simply no longer seemed so remarkable. In the realm of the air, what counts is persistence: having overcome the initial impact, even a raging gale seems normal. They emerged into the light of the world from the belly of the underground garage. Leo screwed up his eyes. It was such an enamelled day that it hurt.

"Some things are hard to admit," Leo remarked after a while.

"Perhaps because too much importance is placed on things that are hard to admit," Menetti suggested.

"Things are things. When they have to be admitted, then they stop existing," Leo said.

"Is that how relationships work?"

"That's how relationships of love work."

"By fooling the other?" Menetti asked.

"By preventing it from happening. That's the difference."

Menetti pulled up, switched off the engine. "Is that why I'm living alone?"

Leo took his time. "I don't know. Are you?"

Menetti nodded. Then she began rummaging below the dashboard by Leo's knee. She took out a pack of cigarettes. "It's been there for three months, this packet," she explained. She pulled a cigarette straight out with her lips. Without undoing the seat belt she slightly opened the car door, which rattled with the force of the wind. Then, realising it wasn't such a good idea, she closed it and lowered the window instead. She lit the cigarette and gave a first long drag on it. "Do you mind?" she asked finally.

Leo smiled and shook his head. "It's your car," he said. "It's a question of territorial sovereignty. What exactly do you want from me?" he asked.

"When I was sixteen, you know, I won a school beauty competition. Miss Liceo Scientifico. Would you believe it?"

"Yes," Leo replied, without even giving it a thought. He had learned what type of questions from women had to be answered without giving the impression they needed time for thought.

Menetti smiled. "You're so bloody smart," she said, giving a particularly long drag on her cigarette.

"We're not in competition," Leo said. Menetti looked at him as though she hadn't understood his remark. "You say that someone's so bloody smart when you're talking to an opponent," he explained. "And we're not in competition," he repeated.

"Ah," Menetti exclaimed. "Straight to the point ... So you have nothing to fear."

"That's what I've just said. Shall we go?"

Menetti threw the rest of the cigarette out of the window, closed it and started up again. "Can I ask you a question?" she asked after they had gone a short way.

"Can I say no?"

"How do you reckon things will turn out now?"

"Now when?"

"Well, now you've both come out."

"Do you know something I don't?"

"No, that's not it . . . It's just that I'm concerned for Sergio."

"Fine."

"Fine what?"

"That you're concerned about him. I'll get out here, thanks." Menetti turned to look at him, and he looked back at her like a modern Perseus immune to the Medusa's gaze. "I'll get out here."

They were now in the city centre. The snow had blanked out every colour. Menetti pulled up once again. Leo undid his seat belt before the vehicle had come to a complete halt, then got out. He was weighed down by a turmoil he couldn't put into words. He started walking towards piazza Walther then turned back and gestured to Menetti to lower her window. "Fucking moralist," he said in a heavy voice. "You show your face in our area, you turn up once more in my street, and I'll show you just how *bloody smart* I am." And walked off before she could answer.

In the realm of the air, conscience has the same fury as gusts of wind that strike blindly, like arrows shot aimlessly. A passer-by in those parts would have seen an attractive woman, a beauty queen as a girl, yelling inside her closed car and banging her fists on the steering wheel.

The semi-darkness of the room gave a sense of peace. The vibrating and pulsating of the resuscitation machines seemed, in the end, an assisted silence. Sergio Striggio had passed along corridors cloaked by a muffled calm, where even his footsteps seemed cushioned by a general softness. It had been a long and difficult day . . .

At the Commissariato he had run the gamut of discreet glances and unsaid words. He had swallowed feigned comprehension and even certain gestures of solidarity. He told himself it was right that this should happen, for to define, and even to assert one's position in the world is like advancing head down against the blast of wind, like braving hurricanes . . .

Now, in the fibrillating silence of the ward, any hurricane that might be blowing outside seemed like the soundtrack for a dream sequence. A frosting of semi-darkness reigned in Pietro's room. Soft and reassuring. The drawn curtains allowed the light to drift in with a polite, almost timid gentleness.

Pietro seemed asleep.

Sergio tiptoed in, as he had been taught to do in church when mass had already started. He stopped in the middle of the room. Another few steps and he could reach the small uncomfortable armchair at the foot of the bed. But he didn't get that far. He remained there, neither still nor moving – at the exact centre of the eye of a storm, the only point of calm when all around is whirling.

"I'm not asleep," Pietro announced. "I have my eyes closed but I'm not asleep."

"Typical," Sergio remarked, to give a casual air of intimacy to the conversation. Pietro remained with his eyes closed. "Have you had your treatment?" Sergio asked.

"That's why I'm keeping my eyes closed. They're burning like hell."

"Shall I ask for some eye drops? Did you tell the doctor?"

"Forget the doctor, I reckon she's had enough of me. Are you going to sit down? You're in a hurry?" Sergio shook his head, and Pietro seemed to see him. "Sit down," he repeated. "There's something I want to tell you."

Sergio obeyed. A distant whistling could be heard through the barred windows beyond the curtains: the cries of lonely and disorientated creatures echoing in the realm of the air. "I'm not sure this is the right time for revelations," he murmured, though trying to seem relaxed.

"You do this when you're frightened," Pietro said.

"This what?"

"You start joking. As though you're looking for reassurance."

"If that's the case then I'm someone who has cried a lot." This time it was Pietro who laughed. "Your mother wanted to leave me," he said. "Oh, I know what you're thinking," he added. Sergio was about to say something, but stopped. "It wasn't because of me, it was for someone else."

"For someone else?"

"Give me something to drink, would you?" Sergio got up to bring him a beaker fitted with a right-angled straw from which Pietro could drink half-sitting and half-lying, and gave it to him. Pietro drank. "For someone else," he confirmed. Sergio went back to his chair. "She had decided to go off with him. She was in love. Which simply meant she wasn't in love with me." Sergio's breathing became slightly laboured. "You're old enough to understand, aren't you?"

"I don't know," Sergio replied with a sincerity that didn't for once strike Pietro as sarcastic. "So how was it you stayed together?" he asked, after an infinitesimal pause.

"Because he died. He had a terrible car crash. And so, one afternoon, I saw her packing her bags. 'Where are you going?' I asked, and she said she didn't know but that in any event, after what had happened, she didn't think it right to stay at home." Pietro gave out a sob. "And I asked her again. 'But where are you going?' And she said she didn't love me and that she would never love anyone else, apart from you ..." Pietro stopped. He stretched out his hand, freeing it from under the blankets in an urge for intimacy that might have seemed perfect or highly out of place. Sergio waited to understand what would be the outcome of that urge for contact, then decided to reciprocate. His father's hand had become soft, as if it had just emerged from its chrysalis. "We decided to stay together though there was no love between us. We'd got you. I could have had other women, of course, but neither of us would fall in love again."

* * *

(. . . Like when in *8½* the dead father tells Guido it was sad to be aware of having been so wrong . . .)

* * *

And yet, in that semi-darkness, it was becoming clear that there hadn't been so many mistakes. "I sometimes wanted to be completely free of everything," Pietro continued as though following his own strand of thought.

Then he withdrew into such a silence that Sergio was forced to fix his mind on the gusts of wind that beat against the windows and the outside walls. "It won't go away, this wind," he said, just as someone does when they have nothing else to talk about except the weather.

"I'm feeling better," Pietro suddenly announced.

"Ah," Sergio said, supporting that fairly neutral expression with a smile through closed lips, so that it would seem altogether like an expression of intimate satisfaction.

"It's not a good sign, you know."

"An effect of the treatment," Sergio suggested.

"At times I would have preferred to have no ties at all, you understand? And yet no, there was you and your mother. It would have been natural for me to have no compassion, and yet no."

"You ought to thank us, we saved you from yourself, didn't we?"

"My dear Sergio, what a child you were . . . what a child. You pretended to drown in a swimming pool with thirty centimetres of water. You kept me and your mother on tenterhooks."

"That's exactly what I wanted to do. And you wanted to make me think you didn't care anything about me."

"You were scary and pompous, my boy, a real disaster when it came to survival. Do you think I could have let you go off into the world so completely defenceless? I'd like to get up."

"I'm not sure that's a good idea."

"And when they asked you what you wanted to be when you grew up, first you looked at me to work out what answer would put me in the greatest difficulty, then said you wanted to be an art critic; and you started off with your project about the architect who rebuilt other people's churches." Pietro gave a gentle smile, since he wanted him to understand that he wasn't making fun of him but that it was a memory he treasured.

Sergio smiled back. "But it really was what I wanted to do. And perhaps I haven't given it up altogether. I've started writing again. Something on the campanile of San Giorgio . . ."

"You drove everyone away with that story. Then you stopped sleeping. Why were you always taking over my place in the bed, eh? You were the keeper of your mother's virtue, but it was pointless, my boy."

"And here's the result."

"You kept a photo of us in your pocket so that people could get in touch with us if you were lost." Sergio lowered his head. Pietro took his hand. "If I'm feeling better, it means we're coming to the end . . . you know this, don't you? You know this is how it happens?"

"No."

"Yes."

"I wouldn't have wanted to disappoint you for anything in the world.

278

I thought that all the unhappiness between the two of you was because of me." Now he was struggling not to cry.

"And yet it worked. You were lost once at the fairground, and took the photograph straight from your pocket and showed it to someone who recognised us, and he found us just as we were looking for you."

Sergio gave an exclamation of surprise, though it came from the fact that his father's story had made him automatically press his jacket pocket and realise that there was a photograph inside. It was the picture he had thrust in front of don Giuseppe's face.

"What do you have there?" Pietro asked.

"You won't believe this, but I have a photograph," Sergio replied. "It's to do with the inquiry. I forgot to put it with the papers. It hasn't been a particularly exhilarating day. I had to talk to my colleagues."

"A photograph," Pietro repeated. He held his hand out for Sergio to give it to him. Once he'd taken it, he studied it hard. "Who's this?" he asked after a while, in a somewhat agitated tone.

Sergio had to move closer until he was almost brushing his face.

"This one," Pietro asked, pointing to an older woman in the group.

"It's the priest's housekeeper," Sergio answered.

"The priest's housekeeper?" Pietro asked, sceptically. "But it's Lidia Bomoll. I interrogated her more than twenty years ago. Something to do with domestic violence. She was in front of me exactly as close as you are now."

"Bomoll?" Sergio echoed.

Pietro asked him to move. He lifted himself up and stayed there with his feet dangling from the bed, searching for his slippers. He stood up with surprising energy. He wasn't wrong when he claimed he was regaining his strength. "You've never heard of the Bomoll case?" he asked, waving the photograph towards Sergio.

"You're mistaken. It can't be," he muttered, but with the strange feeling that what his father had just revealed could be absolutely true. He slipped the photo out of his father's fingers and pointed to Gaia.

Pietro had the air of a chef who had just made the perfect Béarnaise.

"Gaia, of course, little Gaia . . . Those are her eyes. But that contraption you use as a telephone, can't it do all the rest?" he asked. "Search for Bomoll, living at Budrio, around 1994–95."

Sergio grabbed his phone and searched the Web.

Though it was turning dark, the atmosphere retained the opalescence of an aurora borealis. Old mountainfolk used to say that the north wind brought with it those perpetual lights, which, at the poles, stop the alternation of day and night. The night was greeted with lit torches. The covering of snow reflected even the slightest luminosity.

The snow at the entrance to the Commissariato had been shovelled away, at least on the level area before the ramp down to the garages. Sergio slowed down slightly so that his car would get a better grip on the slope. The dry contact of the wheels assured him that he was fully inside. He parked in his space and, as he got out, saw Steltzer a few metres away, climbing into his car.

"Hey!" he shouted. Steltzer turned, surprised to see him. "You've finished work? And Fanti?" Too many questions all together.

"I ought to have gone an hour ago, but Susini wouldn't leave," he replied. "I left Fanti upstairs with the Chief Inspector."

"Lock the car and come back inside with me," Striggio said, in a way that his subordinate must have found so peremptory as not to require even a minimum of explanation.

Striggio headed towards the staircase that led to the lifts, then waited for Steltzer to accompany him to the offices. Fanti and Menetti were putting away something to do with old investigations. Striggio surprised them in their concentrated silence, the silence of those who are finishing their last duties and looking forward, meanwhile, to the imminent prospect of slipping off their shoes in the warmth, having a shower and preparing a good supper.

Striggio and Steltzer's arrival broke the spell.

"We haven't understood a bloody thing," Sergio announced as he approached his office. Fanti and Steltzer followed him like the rats in the story of the Pied Piper.

"I've been on duty eight hours," Menetti protested.

"Here, come here," Striggio ordered with the air of someone who has no time to lose. Menetti joined them without dropping her hostile look.

"Steltzer, you get onto the computer now and search for everything you can find on Emilio Frari. Understood?" Steltzer nodded that he had understood, but didn't move. "Steltzer, now!" Striggio said in encouragement. Steltzer leapt up, went to his desk and switched on the computer. "Fanti, you go and check the database for anything to do with Lidia Bomoll. Shall I write it down for you?"

"Lidia Bomoll," Fanti repeated.

"Perfect. I want a printout of everything we have on her."

"What's going on?" Menetti asked, making sure to keep a hint of belligerence in her voice.

"What's going on with you?" Striggio asked back.

"Nothing's going on. I have to talk to you."

"We'll talk later, we have to go straight to the priest's place."

"I don't understand."

"I'll tell you on the way."

* * *

"We're at Budrio near Bologna, 1994. Two twins: the boy goes missing at the age of ten, vanishes. There's a large-scale investigation. It comes out that he suffered abuse from his father."

"Comes out from whom?"

"From his sister, Gaia."

"Gaia?"

Striggio smiled, not out of satisfaction but bitterness. And as he smiled, his smile itself annoyed him. "Yes, Gaia," he confirmed. Menetti's sternness seemed gradually to melt away. "Another prosecution witness, Lidia Bomoll, younger sister of Oreste Bomoll, the accused. He denies all allegations. The boy is never found, so it's impossible to corroborate the allegations of the girl and her aunt. Oreste Bomoll is released, the search for the child continues . . ."

"And the mother?"

"There is no mother. She died a few weeks after she gave birth, of septicaemia. The girl is fostered. Oreste Bomoll commits suicide a few days after his release."

"A terrible story."

"Terrible," Striggio agrees.

"So you think it's all repeated now, here."

"I think the child didn't disappear then, and hasn't done so now."

"You mean Michelangelo Ludovisi?"

"I mean him, and I mean Emilio Bomoll. He's been here, Elisabetta, in front of us all the time."

Menetti studied Striggio, understanding at the very moment he was parking the car in the yard of the presbytery.

They knocked on the door. No answer.

"What do we do?" Menetti asked.

Striggio's response came as he banged and kicked the door. "Open up!" he roared.

"Commissario, what's the matter?" Don Giuseppe had appeared behind them. He was wearing his thick jacket over his day clothes.

"Open up!" Striggio said, moving aside to let him pass.

The priest did what he was told. "What's the matter?" he asked again.

"He's always been here! Michelangelo Ludovisi has always been here."

Don Giuseppe opened the door. "There's no-one here," he protested. Menetti pushed him aside to pass. "How could you think . . ." he began. But it was clear that neither of them were listening.

They made a thorough search of the whole apartment: the

kitchen-living room, which they knew perfectly, then the priest's bedroom, which held no surprises. Finally they went to a room that seemed to have been unoccupied for some time.

"It's the bedroom where my housekeeper stayed if ever there were problems," don Giuseppe explained.

But the air in the room was too clean for it to have been unoccupied for long as the priest would have them believe. Menetti glanced at Striggio to see whether he had the same doubt. "Are you getting this smell too?" she asked.

The Commissario breathed more deeply, through his nose. It was bleach, no doubt about it. The priest, standing in the doorway, began to tremble. "How long has this room been unoccupied?" Striggio asked.

Don Giuseppe seemed flustered, but just for a moment: with a movement of the shoulders he straightened up. "Elda may have cleaned it before she went, she wanted to leave everything tidy," he explained with a certain assurance.

Striggio thought the priest's explanation would have stood up in court. But just as he was about to leave the room, he noticed something that gave him a start. *Two small holes* ... Symmetrical, like drawing pins pushed into the surface of the plaster ... *in each wall.* Using the torch of his mobile phone he began searching for the same holes on the other walls. He found them. "He's been here," he said. Menetti immediately joined him. Striggio showed her the exact point where they were, and shone the beam so they were clearly visible. "We found the same marks on the walls of his bedroom," he murmured. Then, standing up, he turned to don Giuseppe: "We have a few things to clarify, don't we, father?" he said.

* * *

"You let him escape?" Procuratore Susini seemed to be shouldering all the suffering of the world.

"He can't be far away," Striggio assured him. In the bedroom of the presbytery a team from the forensic unit was collecting every possible fingerprint.

"How could you?" Susini insisted.

"He opened the door and let us look round the house. We didn't imagine he was going to run off," Menetti explained.

"Yes, yes, of course!" Susini shouted, looking at her as though, by backing up Striggio's excuses, she were committing an act of betrayal.

* * *

Fanti's report on his search wasn't too complicated. The only news about a living person with the name Emilio Frari was that of an eighty-eight-year-old former director of the Santa Brigida orphanage at Faenza. The institute had closed in 2001 and the records, transferred in part to the parish church of the same name, went as far back as the 1940s. Nothing could be found online. "It's clear that even don Giuseppe's true name was false," Fanti concluded. In that moment of excitement, even his strange play on words made them all laugh.

"His real name is Emilio Bomoll, missing from Budrio since 1994," Striggio said. "What do we have on Lidia Bomoll?"

Steltzer looked at him with the apprehension of the class swot who wanted to show how much work he'd been doing. "Lidia Bomoll, alias Tina Maresca, alias Elena Conti, alias Elda Resegato, two arrests for fraud, one for possession of false documents."

"Have you circulated her ID photo?"

Steltzer nodded enthusiastically. "Ports, airports and railway stations are on alert. I've warned them she's travelling with a boy of eleven and have sent out the picture of Michelangelo Ludovisi."

Striggio looked satisfied. "Good work, lads," he said. Then he motioned for Menetti to come across to him. "We have to find him," he murmured.

* * *

Don Giuseppe stopped to catch his breath. On that night, which had turned out so badly, he realised there was nowhere to escape. What he really understood about himself was impossible to say. He knew only that he had tried to resist any attempt to find out the truth about him. But now, in the face of so much unhappiness, he also knew he couldn't start all over again.

He had hurried to the outskirts of the city, then reached the first stretch of countryside. The higher he climbed the colder he felt. But this didn't stop him from moving ahead. He walked until the snow reached his knees. Then he relaxed. He no longer felt cold. He had stopped trembling. The shady notes of the "Valse Triste" resounded in his temples and he began to hum them enthusiastically to himself. He was seized by a strange drowsiness. He saw his mother, whom he had never known. He saw his twin sister Gaia, whom he had lost and found again. He saw her sitting, frightened, trying to appear calm. He saw her as she tried to explain the unexplainable, to justify the unjustifiable. He saw a hope germinating from the icy coldness, a longing for peace that verged on euphoria.

He didn't feel the slightest pain. Just a kind of nostalgia, a timid faintness, a gentle powerlessness. He was dying, and yet rarely had he felt so alive. He was there, defenceless, in the cold, and yet rarely had he felt so safe. Now the lies would end, and with them his memories. His regrets would end, and his false hopes. His fears would end, and his hell. Everything would end, everything . . . And this even though, in a parallel life, he had been a priest. He hoped he had lied when he used to say that there was life after death, for, now, he didn't want another life.

("What have you done?
"What have you done?"
This is what Messy the little fox asks himself
now that the night draws in.
Nothing seems safe anymore,
the burrow is far away,

the earth unfriendly,
the water frozen,
the fire dead,
the air ice-cold ...)

* * *

"Is Mamma coming?" Michelangelo asked the woman.

The woman confirmed cautiously. "She knows where we are," she said.

"Can we say hello to Papà?" the boy asked again.

The woman shook her head. "No, he mustn't find us," she said in such a decisive tone that Michelangelo could find no effective response.

"I don't know what went wrong," he said after a while. "Why don't I remember anything? Why are we going away?"

"Because you're in danger," the woman said. "You're not old enough to understand, but you're in danger."

Michelangelo looked up at the sky. If he'd had sufficient opportunity to do so, he would have noticed that the wind had come to a complete standstill. A calmness now reigned, of frozen snow. "But how does Mamma know how to get to us?" he asked again.

"Oh, she knows!" the woman snapped. "Adults know what they are doing."

"But are you really my aunt as you said you are?"

Lidia Bomoll closed her eyes.

The windows of the Ludovisis' house were lit.

"I can't believe she's involved in kidnapping her son," Menetti remarked.

"None of this could have happened without her involvement," Striggio insisted.

"But why?" Menetti asked.

"She thought she was protecting her child and was even prepared to think her husband was a danger to him." Striggio was the first to be surprised by that explanation, as though he were intimately concerned.

"And so is this how it happened?" Menetti asked.

"Shall we go up?" Striggio said, cutting her short.

* * *

The apartment looked as neat and tidy as usual. Gaia Ludovisi was every bit as tidy and all the more attractive now that she appeared to have been crying. She invited them in and said she had been expecting them. Both noted the suitcases in the corridor.

"I've left my husband," she explained. "I intend to move."

"We think your son Michelangelo is alive," Striggio said.

Her reaction to the news was strange indeed. She undid her coat with its fur collar and sat down, then stared at the floor for an infinite time. "You have no idea what it's like to have the nagging feeling that your child has been abused," she said.

"Is that what happened?" Menetti asked.

"Like my brother," Gaia confirmed. "He was a delicate child and too intelligent for his age." It was now impossible to work out whether she was talking about her brother or her son. "Children have to be protected."

"But did Michelangelo tell you he had been abused?" Menetti asked. Striggio let her carry on, since it was clear that, whatever gap had opened up, his colleague had a smooth road ahead.

"They never say anything," Gaia retorted.

"And so?" the Chief Inspector continued.

"The teacher called me in. She told me things that suggested it was a case of sexual abuse. I wanted to report it to the police but she persuaded me not to. She said it would be a terrible ordeal for the child . . ."

"What did you do then?"

"I went to my aunt, who else? I told her: 'Aunt, it's happening all over again, the same as with Lilo.'" She said it with a smile of satisfaction and looked at the investigators as though she expected some sign of approval. "Do you see? I had no choice."

"But Sara Heller was your husband's lover!" Striggio interrupted. "Who's to say she wasn't lying? And now she's killed herself . . ."

Gaia Ludovisi reacted to this statement as one might react to any inevitable piece of news. "Yes, she was his lover. That's how she knew. That's why she left him."

"No," Elisabetta Menetti said, contradicting her. "It was your husband who left her. There are no doubts about that."

"He realised he'd been discovered," Gaia argued, unperturbed.

"Or he was the victim of a false accusation," Striggio suggested. "Sara Heller had been putting about rumours that your husband wasn't Michelangelo's true father."

"That's ridiculous."

"We have evidence," Menetti confirmed.

"You want to confuse me," she said. "You're trying to fool me, you and your stories about false accusations! Do you think I'm blind?" she said, looking Striggio straight in the eye.

"No, not blind. But people can also see things the wrong way. And they act accordingly. Where is Michelangelo now?"

Gaia Ludovisi shook her head. "I don't know," she said. "He's safe with my aunt."

Suddenly there was no further room for argument. "I have to ask you to come with us to the Commissariato," Striggio said.

But Gaia didn't appear to have heard. "I hope to die and I hope there is no life after death," she said and slumped to the ground.

* * *

The paramedics took Gaia Ludovisi to hospital. There had been a sudden loss of consciousness, but her state of health, once she recovered, was otherwise excellent. The doctors noted a large burn mark on her right wrist, which, as was clear to Striggio, had been caused when she set light to don Giuseppe's car.

"But why?" Fanti asked. "What was the reason for setting the car alight?"

"Because they realised we'd get the forensic team to examine it and they knew Michelangelo had been in there during the fake disappearance."

"We'd better tell the child's father now," Menetti observed.

"Yes," Striggio agreed. "I've had him called in for this afternoon."

"Here's some information on the priest's housekeeper," Steltzer announced, walking in without knocking. "The phone printouts show she called Heller three times, and the last time was twenty minutes before Heller killed herself."

Striggio curled his lip, as he did when he had to slot a piece of information into place. "Thanks," he said.

That word of thanks to Fanti and Steltzer seemed like a request to leave. In fact, they were happy to get out of the Commissario's office. But Menetti stayed behind. "I have to talk to you," she repeated, as though hardly any time had passed since she had first said it.

"Ah yes," Striggio said with an indifference that wounded her.

"I've asked for a transfer. And I wanted you to hear it from me."

Striggio at that point stopped everything he was doing. Such news, he thought, deserved every possible attention. "As a result of something I've done?" he asked.

"Maybe of something you *haven't* done." From her voice and her manner it seemed that Menetti wanted to make him laugh.

But her attitude alarmed Striggio. "Something serious, then, seeing as you won't give a straight answer."

* * *

Elisabetta Menetti now realised that the most obvious thing would have been to speak clearly and perhaps to use a few big words like "love" or some cliché like "I can't live without you". Or to get heavier with notions of the kind that he had led her to think something was possible between them – but at the risk of seeming like blackmail or, worse, weakness. She could, of course, have taken the path of pragmatism, explaining that her current state of mind prevented her from doing her job lucidly and efficiently, and everyone knew how committed she was to her work. She could even lie, saying that she had fallen in love with a colleague who had applied for a transfer and she intended to follow him. But when? And how? And who? She even had an urge to offend him, to insult him with her indifference. To make him understand he wasn't worth a toss, that he had another think coming if he imagined she was slavering over him. He was also queer. For if he had fooled himself into imagining he had found another woman to hurt, then he really had no idea who he was dealing with. And she could even turn to despair, why not? Without any of the above forcing her to admit why she was really running away.

* * *

"So you're running away," Striggio observed.

"Come off your high horse," she retorted.

"What are you doing then?"

"I'm not sure. I want a change. Don't you ever feel you've had enough of a certain situation?"

Striggio knew what she meant. "Of course," he said.

"The case is pretty well closed, and I've been considering this for some time. I'd like to make it clear it has nothing to do with you," she lied.

"I'd like to make clear I never had any intention of hurting or misleading you."

"No, of course."

"Of course."

"I was once the school beauty queen. Can you imagine that?"

"I once won the school championship for long jump. Can you imagine that?"

"I can imagine it very well," they both said in unison, and laughed.

"And anyway I can understand you wanting to leave," Striggio said. Menetti looked at him in vague bewilderment. "There's nothing to do around here."

"Apart from missing children and risking death from an exploding car," she joked.

"Apart from that. Yesterday there was another collision with a deer on via del Renon."

"Yes, I heard."

"And Steltzer's mother is so excited about the stories of her son's adventures that she's invited us all to go and taste her canederli."

"Don't tempt me."

"When?" Striggio asked, darkening suddenly.

"In two weeks," Menetti replied, turning serious.

"Well then, you'll still manage to make it for Frau Steltzer's lunch."

* * *

(. . . Is that how you say goodbye?)

Now that the wind had stopped, everything seemed confused. Plants debilitated and animals wearied. In that silence, everything seemed to hang in the balance. The snow was a hard crust that made every surface glimmer, and the stones of the moraines were heaps of rough pearls. In the realm of the air, absence counts as much as presence. First there had been conflict, now there was anticipation. First there had been hostility, now surrender. How magnificent was the silvery tone of that midday, how clear every contour. That lull, the spotless screen, had allowed space for reconsideration, invited reflection and offered a moment of absorption.

In the silence of the kitchen, Leo laid the steaming hot dish on the table. Sergio came in with hands still wet – he had never learned to wait until they were properly dry before leaving the bathroom.

"Smells good," he said. And he waited for Leo to sit down opposite him.

They ate in silence. It was nice like this: to sit there in peace, with nothing urgent to say.

"It's finished . . ." Leo uttered, wiping his plate.

Sergio smiled. "Menetti has asked for a transfer."

Leo didn't seem particularly moved. "Good," he remarked. "Do you want something else to eat?"

Sergio said no, though making it clear that his refusal was the result of having reached a peak of satisfaction.

"We've called Nicolò Ludovisi in this afternoon, I'd better not overdo it before our meeting," he explained. Then, seeing that Leo had finished, he stood up and began to clear the table. "Coffee?" he asked.

Leo said yes.

"I'll go back home this evening," Sergio announced as he put the coffee cup on the table. "I want to get everything ready."

"Are you sure?"

"I promised him . . ."

"I'll be thinking of you," Leo murmured.

Sergio made no answer, at least not in words.

The silence all around them was something they found difficult to get used to. They felt like soldiers at the edge of the world waiting for the Tartars to attack. Before dealing with the coffee, Striggio went to give him a hug, and Leo let him. They remained like this. The calmness around them whispered words of anticipation.

Elisabetta Menetti waited for Sergio Striggio to finish talking. "So what do you want to do?" she asked.

"I want Gaia to listen in to the interview with her husband, without her being seen. She knows where Michelangelo is, but we have no way of forcing her to talk. It's all circumstantial, and if she gets a lawyer then we're fucked. We've no other way of persuading her to talk."

"And if it doesn't work?"

"If it doesn't work, at least we've tried. News of the priest?"

"None."

At that point, Fanti came into the office. "He's arrived," he said.

"Is Gaia Bomoll here?"

"Not yet," Menetti said.

"Fine, let's show Nicolò Ludovisi into the interview room. And we'll do it so that Gaia can see everything. I'll deal with him, you keep an eye on her." Menetti agreed.

* * *

On the other side of the mirror she could see her husband's words without hearing them and observe his expressions as Striggio reconstructed what had happened. They were expressions which she knew, which she had seen throughout their life together, since when they were children. Of joy and despair, but also, above all, of self-pity. For at last he understood the full extent of the errors he had made. Striggio now had to proceed in such a way that it didn't so much seem like a trial of his faults but rather the result of a series of things left unsaid and of agreements not endorsed. Nicolò smiled from time to time, but Gaia had always known that smile of his was nothing more than a way of expressing disbelief. He was a practical man of almost cynical understatement, who could control every part of himself: every muscle, every expression. But now, on the other side of the mirror, he suddenly seemed incapable of any control and was crying and making no attempt to hold back the tears. Some terrible things had been said about him, and they were far more terrible precisely because they were entirely plausible. That he might not be Michelangelo's real father was a perfect lie, but it reflected on his irresponsibility; that he might have abused his son was an abominable lie, but it reflected on his promiscuity. All of which didn't make the lies any less serious, but nor did they show him in a better light. And that was worth crying about. Then there was the fact that Nicolò had always felt sure he could determine his own life. Now he knew it wasn't like this, now he knew that hovering over him was something he couldn't control, or even suspect. Striggio knew how destructive such awareness could be. Gaia saw her husband's words crashing and splintering against the surface of the mirrored screen that separated them. Menetti didn't lose her from sight for a moment and yet never intervened. She wanted her to yield, because she wanted an answer in full, as in the best books, in the best films, those that don't pretend to be life but offer some further chance in life.

From time to time she turned to look at the Chief Inspector as if to ask: why am I here? Then she would turn straight back to watch the words on the other side of the screen. Striggio now had to stop Nicolò from harming himself. He had begun to punch the table and to bite his hands, attempting to inflict a pain worse than the one he felt inside.

Gaia started to tremble. "Enough," she murmured. "Enough ... Enough!"

Steltzer came into the room at that moment and tried to attract the attention of Menetti, who gave him a look of irritation.

"I know," Gaia said, before Steltzer could say anything.

Menetti had been particularly struck by what Leo had said not so long before. A sign that love and awareness dwelt in the same house.

"They've found the priest, dead," Steltzer whispered to Menetti.

"That's enough," Gaia moaned. "That's enough . . ."

Then she asked for pen and paper to write down an address. Before leaving, she looked again through the mirrored glass and, in place of Nicolò, seemed to see someone else.

His home was nice and warm. Striggio had called the caretaker early that morning and asked him to go in with his key to turn up the central heating, which had been kept low while he was staying with Leo.

He didn't want Pietro to feel cold. What he had to do was probably the most difficult thing in the world, but he was not worried but excited about it. Leo, who knew about Sergio what Sergio didn't even know himself, had kept out of the way. He was available if needed.

He decided which room it would be: the one he had always intended to turn into a study, an office or a music room. It was perfect because the longest wall was the one with the window that looked out over the sloping spruce wood. Now, when lying down – he had checked – you could see the jagged tops of the trees against the sky. The question was whether it was possible to plan in every detail the last picture seen by a dying person. That question, he knew, had obsessed him ever since the time he had tried to shift the bed in the hospital where his mother lay, to ensure the last thing she saw would not be that squalid corner between the ceiling and the wall. He just had to make sure that Pietro looked ahead towards the trees that shimmered slightly, towards the fringes of cloud that were caught among the branches and towards the dazzling whiteness with which the long snowfall had tinged them. In that picture, there would be a place for him too.

* * *

"And your relationship with death?" his therapist had once asked him.

Sergio hadn't known how to answer, even though he knew what to say. He knew little about death but he knew about himself, about how he felt he was dying when he grew sleepy and was alone.

"I'll try to remember a song my father sings," he had suddenly said. "A simple, beautiful old song, 'Passacaglia della vita' . . . 'Oh how wrong you are / if you think our years / will never end, / we have to die.'"

They laughed, for it didn't seem a particularly cheerful song, however beautiful it was.

* * *

His father too, when he heard it, would give an appreciative smile. He himself would sing those simple words in almost a whisper. Perhaps he would sing them without even singing them. The intention was to say goodbye at the climax. Like two mountaineers who embrace each other on the summit, happy and sad at the same time. Happy that they have reached it and sad because that summit has now been reached. This is what he should have replied to the therapist, had he had a sufficient experience of life behind him. He and his father had misunderstood each other for too long, but all that misunderstanding would now be healed. His father would have a smiling son and a white woodland of spruces to carry him to the other world. As for him, when the moment arrived, he would position himself between the woodland and the bed to fill his last view. And he would smile. For the most important thing about saying goodbye is how we say it.

Acknowledgements

This novel has been written thanks to the generosity of many people who have patiently helped by answering my questions, some of which were indiscreet. I have bored and pestered friends and acquaintances so that I could interweave fragments of their experiences into this story. On being assured that no reader could possibly identify specific sources or situations, some heaved a sigh of relief while others showed a touch of disappointment.

Elisabetta Menetti really exists, but is not a police officer, though she would have made a good one.

My thanks to each and every one.

MARCELLO FOIS was born in Sardinia in 1960 and is one of a gifted group of writers known as "Group 13", who explore the cultural roots of their various regions. He writes for the theatre, television and cinema, and is the author of several novels, including *The Advocate*, *Memory of the Abyss*, and his *Sardinian Trilogy*, the first title of which, *Bloodlines*, was longlisted for the *Independent* Foreign Fiction Prize.

RICHARD DIXON is a former barrister, and a literary translator from Italian. His previous translations include works by Umberto Eco and Giacomo Leopardi, and poetry by Franco Buffoni and Eugenio De Signoribus.